CONAN — one of the greatest thrills of modern fiction!

Seven of the most exciting and fantastic adventures ever created — the unforgettable tales of the mighty Conan.

"Conan is the superman — or super-barbarian, rather — into whom the prolific Robert Erwin Howard was best able to inject his furious dreams of danger and power and unending adventure, of combative and sexual prowess ... Conan is a true hero of Valhalla, battling and suffering great wounds by day, carousing and wenching by night, and plunging into fresh adventures tomorrow."

— FRITZ LEIBER

Chronological order of the CONAN series:

CONAN
CONAN OF CIMMERIA
CONAN THE FREEBOOTER
CONAN THE WANDERER
CONAN THE ADVENTURER
CONAN THE BUCCANEER
CONAN THE WARRIOR
CONAN THE USURPER
CONAN THE CONQUEROR
CONAN THE AVENGER
CONAN OF AQUILONIA
CONAN OF THE ISLES
CONAN THE SWORDSMAN
CONAN THE LIBERATOR
CONAN THE SWORD OF SKELOS
CONAN THE ROAD OF KINGS
CONAN THE REBEL
CONAN AND THE SPIDER GOD

Illustrated CONAN novels:

CONAN AND THE SORCERER
CONAN: THE FLAME KNIFE
CONAN THE MERCENARY
THE TREASURE OF TRANICOS

Other CONAN novels:

THE BLADE OF CONAN
THE SPELL OF CONAN

CONAN

Robert E. Howard, L. Sprague de Camp
and
Lin Carter

ACE BOOKS, NEW YORK

The letter from Robert E. Howard to P. Schuyler Miller was originally published in *The Coming of Conan*, by Robert E. Howard, N.Y.: Gnome Press, Inc., 1953; copyright 1953 by Gnome Press.

The Hyborian Age, Part I, by Robert E. Howard, was originally published in *The Phantagraph* for February, August, and October-November, 1936; reprinted in the booklet, *The Hyborian Age*, by the Los Angeles-New York Cooperative Publications, 1938; in *Skull-Face and Others*, by Robert E. Howard, Sauk City, Wis.: Arkham House, 1946; in *The Coming of Conan* (revised by John D. Clark); and in *King Kull*, by Robert E. Howard and Lin Carter, N.Y.: Lancer Books, Inc., 1967.

The Tower of the Elephant, by Robert E. Howard, was originally published in *Weird Tales* for March, 1933; copyright 1933 by Popular Fiction Publishing Co.; reprinted in *Skull-Face and Others* and in *The Coming of Conan.*

The Hall of the Dead, by Robert E. Howard and L. Sprague de Camp, was originally published in *The Magazine of Fantasy and Science Fiction* for February, 1967; copyright © 1966 by Mercury Press, Inc. L. Sprague de Camp wrote the story in accordance with an outline found in 1966 by Glenn Lord among Howard's papers.

The God in the Bowl, by Robert E. Howard, was originally published in *Space Science Fiction* for September, 1952; copyright 1952 by Space Publications, Inc.: reprinted in *The Coming of Conan.*

Rogues in the House, by Robert E. Howard, was originally published in *Weird Tales* for January, 1934; copyright 1934 by Popular Fiction Publishing Co.; reprinted in *Terror by Night*, ed. by Christine Campbell Thompson, Lon.: Selwyn & Blount, Ltd., 1934; in *Skull-Face and Others;* in *The Coming of Conan;* and in *More Not at Night*, ed. by Christine Campbell Thompson, Lon.: Arrow Books, Ltd., 1961.

CONAN

An Ace Book / published by arrangement with
the Estate of Robert E. Howard

PRINTING HISTORY
Ace edition / September 1982

For information address: The Berkley Publishing Group,
200 Madison Avenue, New York, New York 10016.

ISBN: 0-441-11481-4

Ace Books are published by The Berkley Publishing Group,
200 Madison Avenue, New York, New York 10016.

PRINTED IN THE UNITED STATES OF AMERICA

30 29 28 27 26 25 24 23

Contents

Introduction (de Camp) 9
Letter from R. E. Howard to P. S. Miller 16
The Hyborian Age, Part 1 (Howard) 21
The Thing in the Crypt (Carter & de Camp) 34
The Tower of the Elephant (Howard) 51
The Hall of the Dead (Howard & de Camp) 81
The God in the Bowl (Howard) 107
Rogues in the House (Howard) 131
The Hand of Nergal (Howard & Carter) 162
The City of Skulls (Carter & de Camp) 189

Pages 6 and 7: A map of the world of Conan in the Hyborian Age, based upon notes and sketches by Robert E. Howard and upon previous maps by P. Schuyler Miller, John D. Clark, David Kyle, and L. Sprague de Camp, with a map of Europe and adjacent regions superimposed for reference.

VANAHEIM
ASGARD
CIMMERIA
WESTERN OCEAN
PICTISH WILDERNESS
BORDER KI
MARCHES
GUNDERLAND
Galparan
NEMEDIA
TAURAN
Tanasul
Black River
BOSSONIAN
Shirki R.
AQUILONIA
Belverus
Num
Tarantia
Shamar
Thunder River
Khorotas R.
Tybor R.
OPHIR
POITAIN
Alimane R.
Khorshemish
Kordava
ZINGARA
Baracha Isles
ARGOS
Messantia
Isle of the Black Ones
Asgalun
SHEM
River
Khemi
Luxur
Sukhmet
KUSH
DARF
Xuthal
Xucho
Zarkheba R.

HYPERBOREA
BRYTHUNIA
ZAMORA
Steppes
to Zamorian border
HYRKANIA
VILAYET SEA
To Khitai
TURAN
CORINTHIA
Shadizar
Arenjun
Isle of Iron Statues
KHAURAN
extended
Later
Akif
KOTH
Aghrapur
KHORAJA
Desert
Zaporoska R.
Xapur
Zamboula
Khawarizm
Styx
Ft. Ghori
Ilbars R.
Kuthchemes
STYGIA
To Vendhya
KESHAN
Alkmeenon
Keshia
PUNT
IRANISTAN
ZEMBABWEI
Black Kingdoms

COVER PAINTING BY FRANK FRAZETTA

The biographical paragraphs between the stories are based upon *A Probable Outline of Conan's Career*, by P. Schuyler Miller and Dr. John D. Clark, published in *The Hyborian Age* (1938), and on the expanded version of this essay, *An Informal Biography of Conan the Cimmerian*, by P. Schuyler Miller, John D. Clark, and L. Sprague de Camp, published in *Amra*, Vol. 2, No. 4,

Introduction

ROBERT ERVIN HOWARD (1906–36) was born in Peaster, Texas (not in Cross Plains, as has been written elsewhere), and spent most of his life in Cross Plains, in the center of Texas between Abilene and Brownwood. His father was a local physician, and both his parents came of pioneer stock. Howard received his main education in Cross Plains and completed his high-school career in Brownwood, at Brownwood High School and Howard Payne Academy. After taking a few courses at Brownwood College, he plunged into free-lance writing.

As a boy, Howard's precocious intellect made him something of a misfit, especially in Texas. For a time he suffered the bullying that is the usual lot of brilliant but puny boys. Partly as a result, he became a sport and exercise fanatic and an accomplished boxer and horseman. That soon ended the bullying, especially since in maturity he was six feet tall and weighed over 200 pounds, most of it muscle. His personality was introverted, unconventional, moody, and hot-tempered, given to emotional extremes and violent likes and dislikes. Like most young writers, he read voraciously. He was a pen pal of the fantasy writers H. P. Lovecraft and Clark Ashton Smith.

During his last ten years (1927–36), Howard turned out a huge volume of general pulp-magazine fiction: sport, detective, western, historical, oriental-adventure, weird, and ghost stories, besides his poetry and his many fantasies. In his late twenties he earned more money from his writings than any other man in Cross Plains, including the town banker—although that is not saying much, since during the Depression years magazine rates were low and payment often late.

Although moderately successful in his work and a big, powerful man like his heroes, Howard was maladjusted to the point of psychosis. For several years before his death, he talked of suicide. At thirty, learning that his aged mother—to whom he was excessively devoted—was on the point of death, he ended a promising literary career by shooting himself. His novella "Red Nails," a Conan story, and his interplanetary novel *Almuric* were published posthumously in *Weird Tales*.

Howard wrote several series of tales of heroic fantasy, most of them published in *Weird Tales*. Howard was a natural story-teller, whose narratives are unsurpassed for vivid, gripping, headlong action. His heroes—King Kull, Conan, Bran Mak Morn, Turlogh O'Brien, Solomon Kane—are larger than life: men of mighty thews, hot passions, and indomitable will, who easily dominate the stories through which they stride. Howard thus explained his preference for heroes of massive muscles but simple minds:

"They're simpler. You get them in a jam, and no one expects you to rack your brains inventing clever ways for them to extricate themselves. They are too stupid to do anything but cut, shoot, or slug themselves into the clear." (E. Hoffmann Price: "A Memory of R. E. Howard," in *Skull-Face and Others*, by Robert E. Howard, copyright © 1946 by August Derleth.)

Of all Howard's fantasies, the most popular have been the Conan stories. These are laid in Howard's imaginary Hyborian Age, about twelve thousand years ago, between the sinking of Atlantis and the beginning of recorded history. He wrote—or at least began—over two dozen Conan stories. Of these, eighteen were published during or just after his lifetime, one in a fan magazine and the rest in *Weird Tales*. Howard explained how he came to write about Conan thus:

"While I don't go so far as to believe that stories are inspired by actually existing spirits or powers (though I am rather opposed to flatly denying anything) I have sometimes wondered if it were possible that unrecognized forces of the past or present—or even the future—work through the thought and actions of living men. This occurred to me when I was writing the first stories of the Conan series especially. I know that for months I had been absolutely barren of ideas, completely unable to work up anything sellable. Then the man Conan seemed suddenly to grow up in my mind without much labor on my part and immediately a stream of stories flowed off my pen—or rather off my typewriter—almost without effort on my part. I did not seem to be creating, but rather relating events that had occurred. Episode crowded on episode so fast that I could scarcely keep up with them. For weeks I did nothing but write of the adventures of Conan. The character took complete possession of my mind and crowded out everything else in the way of story-writing. When I deliberately tried to write something else, I couldn't do it. I do not attempt to explain this by esoteric or occult means, but the facts remain. I still write of Conan more powerfully and with more understanding than any of my other characters. But the time will probably come when I will suddenly find myself unable to write convincingly of him at all. This has happened in the past with nearly all my rather numerous characters; suddenly I find myself out of contact with the conception, as if the man himself had been standing at my shoulder directing my efforts, and had suddenly turned and gone away, leaving me to search for another character." (Letter to Clark

Ashton Smith, December 14, 1933; published in *Amra*, vol. II, no. 39; copyright © 1966 by the Terminus, & Ft. Mudge Electrick Street Railway Gazette.)

"It may sound fantastic to link the term 'realism' with Conan; but as a matter of fact—his superantural adventures aside—he is the most realistic character I have ever evolved. He is simply a combination of a number of men I have known, and I think that's why he seemed to step full-grown into my consciousness when I wrote the first yarn of the series. Some mechanism in my subconsciousness took the dominant characteristics of various prize-fighters, gunmen, bootleggers, oil field bullies, gamblers, and honest workmen I had come in contact with, and combining them all, produced the amalgamation I call Conan the Cimmerian." (Letter to Clark Ashton Smith, July 23, 1935; published in *The Howard Collector*, vol. I, no. 5; copyright © 1964 by Glenn Lord; reprinted in *Amra*, vol. II, no. 39.)

During the last two decades, a large number of unpublished story manuscripts have turned up in collections of Howard's papers. These include eight Conan stories, some complete and some in the form of unfinished manuscripts, outlines, or fragments. It has been my lot to prepare most of these stories for publication, completing those that were incomplete. I have also, in collaboration with my colleagues Lin Carter and Björn Nyberg, written several pastiches, based upon hints in Howard's notes and letters, to fill gaps in the saga. Two of these are included in the present volume.

When the story "The God in the Bowl" appeared in manuscript in 1951, I revised it considerably for publication. For the present edition, however, I have gone back to the original manuscript and produced a version much closer to the original, with a bare minimum of editorial changes. The present volume is chronologically the first volume of the complete Conan saga.

"Heroic fantasy" is the name I have given to a subgenre of fiction, otherwise called the "sword-and-sorcery" story. It is a story of action and adventure laid in a more or less imaginary world, where magic works and where modern science and technology have not yet been discovered. The setting may (as in the Conan stories) be this Earth as it is conceived to have been long ago, or as it will be in the remote future, or it may be another planet or another dimension.

Such a story combines the color and dash of the historical costume romance with the atavistic supernatural thrills of the weird, occult, or ghost story. When well done, it provides the purest *fun* of fiction of any kind. It is escape fiction wherein one escapes clear out of the real world into one where all men are strong, all women beautiful, all life adventurous, and all problems simple, and nobody even mentions the income tax or the dropout problem or socialized medicine.

William Morris pioneered the heroic fantasy in Great Britain in the 1880s. In the early years of this century, Lord Dunsany and Eric R. Eddison developed the genre further. In the 1930s, the appearance of the magazines *Weird Tales* and, later, *Unknown Worlds* furnished outlets for stories of this type, and many memorable sword-and-sorcery narratives were written. These include Howard's stories of Conan, Kull, and Solomon Kane; Clark Aston Smith's macabre tales of Hyperborea, Atlantis, Averoigne, and the future continent Zothique; Henry Kuttner's Atlantean stories; C. L. Moore's narratives of Jirel of Joiry; and Fritz Leiber's Gray Mouser stories. (I might also mention Fletcher Pratt's and my tales of Harold Shea.)

After the Second World War, the magazine market for stories of this kind shrank, and it looked for a while as if fantasy had become a casualty of the machine age. Then, with the publication of J. R. R. Tolkien's trilogy, *The*

Fellowship of the Ring, and the reprinting of many earlier works in the field, the genre revived. Now it is flourishing again, and it is inevitable that one of its giants—Robert E. Howard—and his greatest imaginative effort—the Conan saga—should be made available.

L. Sprague de Camp

CONAN

Letter from R. E. Howard to P. S. Miller

Early in 1936, two fans of Howard's Conan stories—P. Schuyler Miller, the educator and science-fiction writer, and Dr. John D. Clark, the chemist—worked out, from the stories that had appeared up to then, an outline of Conan's career and a map of the world in the Hyborian Age. Miller wrote Howard about the results of this research. He received a reply, written just three months before Howard's death, which sheds light on Howard's concept of Conan and of the setting for the stories:

Lock Box 313
Cross Plains, Texas
March 10, 1936

Dear Mr. Miller:

I feel indeed honored that you and Dr. Clark should be so interested in Conan as to work out an outline of his career and a map of his environs. Both are surprizingly accurate, considering the vagueness of the data you had to work with. I have the original map—that is the one I drew up when I first started writing about Conan—around here somewhere and I'll see if I can't find it and let you have a look at it. It includes only the countries west of Vilayet and north of Kush. I've never attempted to map the southern and eastern kingdoms, though I have a fairly clear outline of their geography in my mind. However, in writing about them I feel a certain amount of license, since the inhabitants of the western Hyborian nations were about as ignorant concerning the peoples and countries of the south and east as the people of medieval Europe were ignorant of Africa and Asia. In writing about the western Hyborian nations I feel confined within the limits of known and inflexible boundaries and territories, but in fictionizing the rest of the world, I feel able to give my imagination freer play. That is, having adopted a certain conception of geography and ethnology, I feel compelled to abide by it, in the interests of consistency. My conception of the east and south is not so definite or so arbitrary.

Concerning Kush, however, it is one of the black kingdoms south of Stygia, the northern-most, in fact, and has given its name to the whole southern coast. Thus, when an Hyborian speaks of Kush, he is generally speaking of not the kingdom itself, one of many such kingdoms, but of the Black Coast in general. And he is likely to speak of any black man as a Kushite, whether he happens to be a Keshani, Darfari, Puntan, or Kushite proper. This is natural, since the Kushites were the first black men with whom the Hyborians came in contact—Barachan pirates trafficking with and raiding them.

As for Conan's eventual fate—frankly I can't predict it. In writing these yarns I've always felt less as creating them than as if I were simply chronicling his adventures as he told them to me. That's why they skip about so much, without following a regular order. The average adventurer, telling tales of a wild life at random, seldom follows any ordered plan, but narrates episodes widely separated by space and years, as they occur to him.

Your outline follows his career as I have visualized it pretty closely. The differences are minor. As you deduct, Conan was about seventeen when he was introduced to the public in "The Tower of the Elephant." While not fully matured, he was riper than the average civilized youth at that age. He was born on a battle field, during a fight between his tribe and a horde of raiding Vanir. The country claimed by and roved over by his clan lay in the northwest of Cimmerian, but Conan was of mixed blood, although a pure-bred Cimmerian. His grandfather was a member of a southern tribe who had fled from his own people because of a blood-feud and after long wanderings, eventually taken refuge with the people of the north. He had taken part in many raids into the Hyborian nations in his youth, before his flight, and perhaps it was the tales he told of those softer countries which roused in Conan, as a child, a desire to see them. There are many things concerning Conan's life of which I am not certain myself. I do not know, for instance, when he got his first sight of civilized people. It might have been at Vanarium, or he might have made a peaceable visit to some frontier town before that. At Vanarium he was already a formidable antagonist, though only fifteen. He stood six feet and weight 180 pounds, though he lacked much of having his full growth.

There was the space of about a year between Vanarium and his entrance into the thief-city of Zamora. During this time he returned to the northern territories of his tribe, and made his first journey beyond the boundaries of Cimmeria. This, strange to say, was north instead of south. Why or how, I am not certain, but he spent some months among a tribe of the AEsir, fighting with the Vanir and the Hyperboreans, and developing a hate for the latter which lasted all his life and later affected his policies as king of Aquilonia. Captured by them, he escaped southward and came into Zamora in time to make his debut in print.

I am not sure that the adventure chronicled in "Rogues in the House" occurred in Zamora. The presence of opposing factions of politics would seem to indicate otherwise, since Zamora was an absolute despotism where differing political opinions were not tolerated. I am of the opinion that the city was one of the small city-states lying just west of Zamora, and into which Conan had wandered after leaving Zamora. Shortly after this he returned for a brief period to Cimmeria, and there were other returns to his native land from time to time. The chronological order of his adventures is about as you have worked it out, except that they covered a little more time. Conan was about forty when he seized the crown of Aquilonia, and was about forty-four or forty-five at the time of "The Hour of the Dragon." He had no male heir at that time, because he had never bothered to formally make some woman his queen, and the sons of concubines, of which he had a goodly number, were not recognized as heirs to the throne.

He was, I think, king of Aquilonia for many years, in a turbulent and unquiet reign, when the Hyborian civilization had reached its most magnificent high-tide, and every king had imperial ambitions. At first he fought on the defensive, but I am of the opinion that at last he was forced into wars of aggression as a matter of self-preservation. Whether he succeeded in conquering a world-wide empire, or perished in the attempt, I do not know.

He travelled widely, not only before his kingship, but after he was king. He travelled to Khitai and Hyrkania, and to the even less known regions north of the latter and south of the former. He even visited a nameless continent in the western hemisphere, and roamed among the islands adjacent to it. How much of this roaming will get into print, I cannot foretell with any accuracy. I was much interested in your remarks concerning findings on the Yamal Peninsula, the first time I had heard anything about that. Doubtless Conan had first-hand acquaintance with the people who evolved the culture described, or their ancestors, at least.

Hope you find "The Hyborian Age" interesting. I'm enclosing a copy of the original map. Yes, Napoli's done very well with Conan, though at times he seems to give him a sort of Latin cast of the countenance which isn't according to type, as I conceive it. However, that isn't enough to kick about.

Hope the enclosed data answers your questions satisfactorily; I'd be delighted to discuss any other phases you might wish, or go into more details about any point of Conan's career or Hyborian history or geography you might desire. Thanks again for your interest, and best wishes, for yourself and Dr. Clark.

Cordially,
Robert E. Howard

P.S. You didn't mention whether you wanted the map and chronology returned, so I'm taking the liberty or retaining them to show to some friends, if you want them back, please let me know.

The Hyborian Age, Part 1

"The Hyborian Age," which Howard mentioned in the preceding letter, was an essay that he had composed some years before, when he began writing the Conan stories. In this essay, he set forth the pseudo-history of prehistoric times that he used as a background for the stories. About the time he wrote the letter to Miller, he sent a copy of the essay to H. P. Lovecraft, the weird-story writer, with a request to forward it for publication in a fan magazine, The Phantagraph, *to Donald A. Wollheim, a fan who later became a science-fiction writer and editor. Several instalments were published in this magazine before it ceased publication, and the entire essay was published in booklet form in 1938 by another fan group. Here is the part of* "The Hyborian Age" *that tells of events up to the time of Conan, together with Howard's apologetic note explaining that he did not mean the essay to be taken seriously as authentic history.*

(Nothing in this article is to be considered as an attempt to advance any theory in opposition to accepted history. It is simply a fictional background for a series of fiction stories. When I began writing the Conan stories a few years ago, I prepared this "history" of his age and the peoples of that age, in order to lend him and his sagas a greater aspect of reality. And I found that by adhering to the "facts" and spirit

of that history, in writing the stories, it was easier to visualize (and therefore to present) him as a real flesh-and-blood character rather than the ready-made product. In writing about him and his adventures in the various kingdoms of his Age, I have never violated the "facts" or spirit of the "history" here set down, but have followed the lines of that history as closely as the writer of actual historical fiction follows the lines of actual history. I have used this "history" as a guide to all the stories in this series that I have written.)

OF THAT EPOCH known by the Nemedian chroniclers as the Pre-Cataclysmic Age, little is known except the latter part, and that is veiled in the mists of legendry. Known history begins with the waning of the Pre-Cataclysmic civilization, dominated by the kingdoms of Kamelia, Valusia, Verulia, Grondar, Thule, and Commoria. These peoples spoke a similar language, arguing a common origin. There were other kingdoms, equally civilized, but inhabited by different, and apparently older races.

The barbarians of that age were the Picts, who lived on islands far out on the western ocean; the Atlanteans, who dwelt on a small continent between the Pictish Islands and the main, or Thurian Continent; and the Lemurians, who inhabited a chain of large islands in the eastern hemisphere.

There were vast regions of unexplored land. The civilized kingdoms, though enormous in extent, occupied a comparatively small portion of the whole planet. Valusia was the westernmost kingdom of the Thurian Continent; Grondar the easternmost. East of Grondar, whose people were less highly cultured than those of their kindred kingdoms, stretched a wild and barren expanse of deserts. Among the less arid stretches of desert, in the jungles, and among the mountains, lived scattered clans and tribes of primitive savages. Far to the south there was a mysterious civilization, unconnected with the Thurian culture, and apparently pre-human in its nature. On the far eastern shores of the Continent there lived another race, human, but mysterious and non-Thurian, with which the Lemurians from time to time came in contact. They apparently came from a shadowy and nameless continent lying somewhere east of the Lemurian Islands.

The Thurian civilization was crumbling; their armies were composed largely of barbarian mercenaries. Picts, Atlanteans, and Lemurians were their generals, their statesmen, often their kings. Of the bickerings of the kingdoms, and the wars between Valusia and Commoria, as well as the conquests by which the Atlanteans founded a kingdom on the mainland, there are more legends than accurate history.

Then the Cataclysm rocked the world. Atlantis and Lemuria sank, and the Pictish Islands were heaved up to form the mountain peaks of a new continent. Sections of the Thurian Continent vanished under the waves, or sinking, formed great inland lakes and seas. Volcanoes broke forth and terrific earthquakes shook down the shining cities of the empires. Whole nations were blotted out.

The barbarians fared a little better than the civilized races. The inhabitants of the Pictish Islands were destroyed, but a great colony of them, settled among the mountains of Valusia's southern frontier, to serve as a buffer against foreign invasion, was untouched. The Continental kingdom of the Atlanteans likewise escaped the common ruin, and to it came thousands of their tribesmen in ships from the sinking land. Many Lemurians escaped to the eastern coast of the Thurian Continent, which was comparatively untouched. There they were enslaved by the ancient race which already dwelt there, and their history, for thousands of years, is a history of brutal servitude.

In the western part of the Continent, changing conditions created strange forms of plant and animal life, Thick jungles covered the plains, great rivers cut their roads to the sea, wild mountains were heaved up, and lakes covered the ruins of old cities in fertile valleys. To the continental kingdom of the Atlanteans, from sunken areas, swarmed myriads of beasts and savages—ape-men and apes. Forced to battle continually for their lives, they yet managed to retain vestiges of their former state of highly-advanced barbarism. Robbed of metals and ores, they became workers in stone like their distant ancestors, and had attained a real artistic level, when their struggling culture came into contact with the powerful Pictish nation. The Picts had also reverted to flint, but had advanced more rapidly in the matter of population and war-science. They had none of the Atlanteans' artistic nature; they were a ruder, more practical, more prolific race. They left no pictures painted or carved on ivory, as did their enemies, but they left remarkably efficient flint weapons in plenty.

These stone age kingdoms clashed, and in a series of bloody wars, the outnumbered Atlanteans were hurled back into a state of savagery, and the evolution of the Picts was halted. Five hundred years after the Cataclysm the barbaric kingdoms have vanished. It is now a nation of savages—the Picts—carrying on continual warfare with tribes of savages—the Atlanteans. The Picts had the advantage of numbers and unity, whereas the Atlanteans had fallen into looselyknit clans. That was the West of that day.

In the distant East, cut off from the rest of the world by the heaving up of gigantic mountains and the forming of a chain of vast lakes, the Lemurians are toiling as slaves of their ancient masters. The far south is still veiled in mystery. Untouched by the Cataclysm, its destiny is still pre-human. Of the civilized races of the Thurian Continent, a remnant of one of the non-Valusian nations dwells among the low mountains of the southeast—the Zhemri. Here and there about the world are scattered clans of apish savages, entirely ignorant of the rise and fall of the great civilizations. But in the far north another people are slowly coming into existence.

At the time of the Cataclysm, a band of savages, whose development was not much above that of the Neanderthal, fled to the north to escape destruction. They found the snow-countries inhabited only by a species of ferocious snow-apes—huge, shaggy, white animals, apparently native to that climate. These they fought and drove beyond the Artic Circle, to perish, as the savages thought. The latter, then, adapted themselves to their hardy new environment and throve.

After the Pictish-Atlantean wars had destroyed the beginnings of what might have been a new culture, another, lesser cataclysm further altered the appearance of the original continent, left a great inland sea where the chain of lakes had been, to further separate west from east, and the attendant earthquakes, floods and volcanoes completed the ruin of the barbarians which their tribal wars had begun.

A thousand years after the lesser cataclysm, the western world is seen to be a wild country of jungles and lakes and torrential rivers. Among the forest-covered hills of the northwest exist wandering bands of ape-men, without human speech, or the knowledge of fire or the use of implements. They are the descendants of the Atlanteans, sunk back into the squalling chaos of jungle-bestiality from which ages ago their ancestors so laboriously crawled. To the southwest dwell scattered clans of degraded, cave-dwelling savages, whose speech is of the most primitive form, yet who still retain the name of Picts, which has come to mean merely a term designating men—themselves, to distinguish them from the true beasts with which they contend for life and food. It is their only link with their former stage. Neither the squalid Picts nor the apish Atlanteans have any contact with other tribes or peoples.

Far to the east, the Lemurians, levelled almost to a bestial plane themselves by the brutishness of their slavery, have risen and destroyed their masters. They are savages among the ruins of a strange civilization. The survivors of that civilization, who have escaped the fury of their slaves, have come westward. They fall upon that mysterious prehuman kingdom of the south and overthrow it, substituting their own culture, modified by contact with the older one. The newer kingdom is called Stygia, and remnants of the older nation seemed to have survived, and even been worshipped, after the race as a whole had been destroyed.

Here and there in the world small groups of savages are showing signs of an upward trend; these are scattered and unclassified. But in the north, the tribes are growing. These people are called Hyborians, or Hybori; their god was Bori—some great chief, whom legend made even more ancient as the king who led them into the north, in the days of the great Cataclysm, which the tribes remember only in distorted folklore.

They have spread over the north and are pushing southward in leisurely treks. So far they have not come in contact with any other races; their wars have been with one another. Fifteen hundred years in the north country have made them a tall, tawny-haired, grey-eyed race, vigorous and warlike, and already exhibiting a well-defined artistry and poetism of nature. They still live mostly by the hunt, but the southern tribes have been raising cattle for some centuries. There is one exception in their so far complete isolation from other races: a wanderer into the far North returned with the news that the supposedly deserted ice wastes were inhabited by an extensive tribe of apelike men, descended, he swore, from the beasts driven out of the more habitable land by the ancestors of the Hyborians. He urged that a large war-party be sent beyond the Arctic Circle to exterminate these beasts, whom he swore were evolving into true men. He was jeered at; a small band of adventurous young warriors followed him into the North, but none returned.

But tribes of the Hyborians were drifting south, and as the population increased this movement became extensive. The following age was an epoch of wandering and conquest. Across the history of the world tribes and drifts of tribes move and shift in an ever changing panorama.

Look at the world five hundred years later. Tribes of tawny-haired Hyborians have moved southward and westward, conquering and destroying many of the small unclassified clans. Absorbing the blood of conquered races, already the descendants of the older drifts have begun to show modified racial traits, and these mixed races are attacked fiercely by new, purer-blooded drifts, and swept before them, as a broom sweeps debris impartially, to become even more mixed and mingled in the tangled debris of races and tag-ends of races.

As yet the conquerors have not come in contact with the older races. To the southeast the descendants of the Zhemri, given impetus by new blood resulting from admixture with some unclassified tribe, are beginning to seek to revive some faint shadow of their ancient culture. To the west the apish Atlanteans are beginning the long climb upward. They have completed the cycle of existence; they have long forgotten their former existence as men; unaware of any other former state, they are starting the climb unhelped and unhindered by human memories. To the south of them the Picts remain savages, apparently defying the laws of Nature by neither progressing nor retrogressing. Far to the south dreams the ancient mysterious kingdom of Stygia. On its eastern borders wander clans of nomadic savages, already known as the Sons of Shem.

Next to the Picts, in the broad valley of Zingg, protected by great mountains, a nameless band of primitives, tentatively classified as akin to the Shemites, has evolved an advanced agricultural system and existence.

Another factor has added to the impetus of Hyborian drift. A tribe of that race has discovered the use of stone in building, and the first Hyborian kingdom has come into being—the rude and barbaric kingdom of Hyperborea, which had its beginning in a crude fortress of boulders heaped to repel tribal attack. The people of this tribe soon abandoned their horsehide tents for stone houses, crudely but mightily built, and thus protected, they grew strong. There are few more dramatic events in history than the rise of the rude, fierce kingdom of Hyperborea, whose people turned abruptly from their nomadic life to rear dwellings of naked stone, surrounded by cyclopean walls—a race scarcely emerged from the polished stone age, who had by a freak of chance, learned the first rude principles of architecture.

The rise of this kingdom drove forth many other tribes, for, defeated in war, or refusing to become tributary to their castle-dwelling kinsmen, many clans set forth on long treks that took them halfway around the world. And already the more northern tribes are beginning to be harried by gigantic blond savages, not much more advanced than ape-men.

[The Lemurian migration that founded the kingdom of Stygia comprised two branches. While the south-

ern branch created Stygia, the northern branch simultaneously founded the powerful empire of Acheron, with purple-towered Python as its capital, in the lands to the north and west. Five hundred years after the founding of Acheron, the first of the Hyborian wanderers reached its borders, to recoil from the priests and warriors of the South. For nearly two thousand years, Acheron warred against the invading Hyborians. At last the barbarians swept over Acheron and blotted it out, to be stopped at last by the disciplined armies of Acheron's sister empire, her southern neighbor Stygia. L.S.deC.]

The tale of the next thousand years is the tale of the rise of the Hyborians, whose warlike tribes dominate the western world. Rude kingdoms are taking shape. The tawny-haired invaders have encountered the Picts, driving them into the barren lands of the West. To the northwest, the descendants of the Atlanteans, climbing unaided from apedom into primitive savagery, have not yet met the conquerors. Far to the east the Lemurians are evolving a strange semi-civilization of their own. To the south the Hyborians have founded the kingdom of Koth, on the borders of those pastoral countries known as the Lands of Shem, and the savages of those lands, partly through contact with the Hyborians, partly through contact with the Stygians who have ravaged them for centuries, are emerging from barbarism. The blond savages of the far north have grown in power and numbers so that the northern Hyborian tribes move southward, driving their kindred clans before them. The ancient kingdom of Hyperborea is overthrown by one of those northern tribes, which, however, retains the old name. Southeast of Hyperborea a kingdom of the Zhemri has come into being, under the name of Zamora. To the southwest, a tribe of Picts have invaded the fertile valley of Zingg, conquered the agricultural people there, and settled among them. This mixed race was in turn conquered later by a roving tribe of Hybori, and from these mingled elements came the kingdom of Zingara.

Five hundred years later the kingdoms of the world are clearly defined. The kingdoms of the Hyborians Aquilonia, Nemedia, Brythunia, Hyperborea, Koth, Ophir, Argos, Corinthia, and one known as the Border Kingdom —dominate the western world. Zamora lies to the east, and Zingara to the southwest of these kingdoms—peoples alike in darkness of complexion and exotic habits, but otherwise unrelated. Far to the south sleeps Stygia, untouched by foreign invasion, but the peoples of Shem have exchanged the Stygian yoke for the less galling one of Koth. The dusky masters have been driven south of the great river Styx, Nilus, or Nile, which, flowing north from the shadowy hinterlands, turns almost at right angles and flows almost due west through the pastoral meadowlands of Shem, to empty into the great sea. North of Aquilonia, the westernmost Hyborian kingdom, are the Cimmerians, ferocious savages, untamed by the invaders, but advancing rapidly because of contact with them; they are the descendants of the Atlanteans, now progressing more steadily than their old enemies the Picts, who dwell in the wilderness west of Aquilonia.

Another five centuries and the Hybori peoples are the possessors of a civilization so virile that contact with it virtually snatched out of the wallow of savagery such tribes as it touched. The most powerful kingdom is Aquilonia, but others vie with it in strength and splendor. The Hyborians have become a considerably mixed race; the nearest to the ancient root-stock are the Gundermen of Gunderland, a northern province of Aquilonia. But this mixing has not weakened the race. They are supreme in the western world, though the barbarians of the wastelands are growing in strength.

In the north, golden-haired, blue-eyed barbarians, descendants of the blond arctic savages, have driven the remaining Hyborian tribes out of the snow countries, except the ancient kingdom of Hyperborea, which resists their onslaught. Their country is called Nordheim, and they are divided into the red-haired Vanir of Vanaheim, and the yellow-haired Æsir of Asgard.

Now the Lemurians enter history again as Hyrkanians. Through the centuries they have pushed steadily westward, and now a tribe skirts the southern end of the great inland sea—Vilayet—and establishes the kingdom of Turan on the southwestern shore. Between the inland sea and the eastern borders of the native kingdoms lie vast expanses of steppes and in the extreme north and extreme south, deserts. The non-Hyrkanian dwellers of these territories are scattered and pastoral, unclassified in the north, Shemitish in the south, aboriginal, with a thin strain of Hyborian blood from wandering conquerors. Toward the latter part of the period other Hyrkanian clans push westward, around the northern extremity of the inland sea, and clash with the eastern outposts of the Hyperboreans.

Glance briefly at the peoples of that age. The dominant Hyborians are no longer uniformly tawny-haired and grey-eyed. They have mixed with other races. There is a strong Shemitish, even a Stygian strain among the peoples of Koth, and to a lesser extent, of Argos, while in the case of the latter, admixture with the Zingarans has been more extensive than with the Shemites. The eastern Brythunians have intermarried with the dark-skinned Zamorians, and the people of southern Aquilonia have mixed with the brown Zingarans until black hair and brown eyes are the dominant type in Poitain, the southernmost province. The ancient kingdom of Hyperborea is more aloof than the others, yet there is alien blood in plenty in its veins, from the capture of foreign women—Hyrkanians, Æsir, and Zamorians. Only in the province of Gunderland, where the people keep no slaves, is the pure Hyborian stock found unblemished. But the barbarians have kept their blood-stream pure; the Cimmerians are tall and powerful, with dark hair and blue or grey eyes. The people of Nordheim are of similar build, but with white skins, blue eyes, and golden or red hair. The Picts are of the same type as they always were—short, very dark, with black eyes and hair. The Hyrkanians are dark and generally tall and slender, though a squat slant-eyed type is more and more common among them, resulting from mixture with a curious race of intelligent, though stunted, aborigines, conquered by them among the mountains east of Vilayet, on their west-ward drift. The Shemites are generally of medium height, though sometimes when mixed with Stygian blood, gi-gantic, broadly and strongly built, with hook noses, dark eyes, and blue-black hair. The Stygians are tall and well-made, dusky, straight-featured—at least the ruling classes are of that type. The lower classes are a downtrodden, mongrel horde, a mixture of Negroid, Stygian, Shemitish, even Hyborian bloods. South of Stygia are the vast black kingdoms of the Amazons, the Kushits, the Atlaians, and the hybrid empire of Zimbabwe.

Between Aquilonia and the Pictish wilderness lie the Bossonian marches, peopled by descendants of an aborigi-nal race, conquered by a tribe of Hyborians, early in the first ages of the Hyborian drift. This mixed people never attained the civilization of the purer Hyborians, and was pushed by them to the very fringe of the civilized world. The Bossonians are of medium height and complexion, their eyes brown or grey, and they are mesocephalic. They live mainly by agriculture, in large walled villages, and are part of the Aquilonian kingdom. Their marches extend from the Border Kingdom in the North to Zingara in the Southwest, forming a bulwark for Aquilonia against both the Cimmerians and the Picts. They are stubborn defensive fighters, and centuries of warfare against northern and western barbarians have caused them to evolve a type of defense almost impregnable against direct attack.

This was the world of Conan's time.

The Thing in the Crypt

The greatest hero of Hyborian times was not a Hyborian but a barbarian, Conan the Cimmerian, about whose name whole cycles of legend revolve. From the elder civilizations of Hyborian and Atlantean times, only a few fragmentary, half-legendary narratives survive. One of these, The Nemedian Chronicles, *gives most of what is known about the career of Conan. The section concerning Conan begins:*

> *Know, O Prince, that between the years when the oceans drank Atlantis and the gleaming cities, and the years of the rise of the Sons of Aryas, there was an Age undreamed of, when shining kingdoms lay spread across the world like blue mantles beneath the stars—Nemedia, Ophir, Brythunia, Hyperborea, Zamora with its dark-haired women and towers of spider-haunted mystery, Zingara with its chivalry, Koth that bordered on the pastoral lands of Shem, Stygia with its shadow-guarded tombs, Hyrkania whose riders wore steel and silk and gold. But the proudest kingdom of the world was Aquilonia, reigning supreme in the dreaming west. Hither came Conan the Cimmerian, black-haired, sullen-eyed, sword in hand, a thief, a reaver, a slayer, with gigantic melancholies and gigantic mirth, to tread the jeweled thrones of the Earth under his sandaled feet.*

In Conan's viens flowed the blood of ancient Atlantis, swallowed by the seas eight thousand years before his time. He was born into a clan that claimed an area in the northwest of Cimmeria. His grandfather was a member of a southern tribe who had fled from his own people because of a blood feud and, after long wandering, took refuge with the people of the North. Conan himself was born on a battlefield, during a fight between his tribe and a horde of raiding Vanir.

There is no record of when the young Cimmerian got his first sight of civilization, but he was known as a fighter around the council fires before he had seen fifteen snows. In that year, the Cimmerian tribesmen forgot their feuds and joined forces to repel the Gundermen, who had pushed across the Aquilonian frontier, built the frontier post of Venarium, and begun to colonize the southern marches of Cimmeria. Conan was a member of the howling, blood-mad horde that swept out of the northern hills, stormed over the stockade with sword and torch, and drove the Aquilonians back across their frontiers.

At the sack of Venarium, still short of his full growth, Conan already stood six feet tall and weighed 180 pounds. He had the alertness and stealth of the born woodsman, the iron-hardness of the mountain man, the Herculean physique of his blacksmith father, and a practical familiarity with knife, ax, and sword.

After the plunder of the Aquilonian outpost, Conan returns for a time to his tribe. Restless under the conflicting urges of his adolescence, his tradition, and his times, he spends some months with a band of the Æsir in fruitless raiding against the Vanir and the Hyperboreans. This latter campaign ends with the sixteen-year-old Cimmerian in chains. He does not, however, remain a captive long...

1. *Red Eyes*

For two days the wolves had trailed him through the woods, and now they were closing in again. Looking back over his shoulder, the boy caught glimpses of them: shaggy, hulking shapes of shadowy gray, loping amongst the black tree trunks, with eyes that burned like red coals in the gathering murk. This time, he knew, he could not fight them off as he had done before.

He could not see very far, because all around him rose, like the silent soldiers of some bewitched army, the trunks of millions of black spruces. Snow clung in dim, white patches to the northern slopes of the hills, but the gurgle of thousands of rills from melting snow and ice presaged the coming of spring. This was a dark, silent, gloomy world even in high summer; and now, as the dim light from the overcast faded with the approach of dusk, it seemed more somber than ever.

The stripling ran on, up the heavily wooded slope, as he had run for the two days since he had fought his way out of the Hyperborean slave pen. Although a purebred Cimmerian, he had been one of a band of raiding Æsir, harrying the borders of the Hyperboreans. The gaunt, blond warriors of that grim land had trapped and smashed the raiding party; and the boy Conan, for the first time in his life, had tasted the bitterness of the chains and the lash that were the normal lot of the slave.

He had not, however, long remained in slavery. Working at night while others slept, he had ground away at one link of his chain until it was weak enough for him to snap. Then, during a heavy rainstorm, he had burst loose. Whirling a four-foot length of heavy, broken chain, he had slain his overseer and a soldier who had sprung to block his way, and vanished into the downpour. The rain that hid him from sight also baffled the hounds of the search party sent after him.

Although free for the moment, the youth had found himself with half the breadth of a hostile kingdom between him and his native Cimmeria. So he had fled south into the wild, mountainous country that separated the southern marches of Hyperborea from the fertile plains of Brythunia and the Turanian steppes. Somewhere to the south, he had heard, lay the fabulous kingdom of Zamora —Zamora with its dark-haired women and towers of spider-haunted mystery. There stood famous cities: the capital, Shadizar, called the City of Wickedness; the thief-city of Arenjun; and Yezud, the city of the spider god.

The year before, Conan had had his first taste of the luxuries of civilization when, as one of the blood-mad horde of Cimmerian clansmen that had poured over the walls of Venarium, he had taken part in the sack of that Aquilonian outpost. The taste had whetted his appetite for more. He had no clear ambition or program of action; nothing but vague dreams of desperate adventures in the rich lands of the South. Visions of glittering gold and jewels, unlimited food and drink, and the hot embraces of beautiful women of noble birth, as his prizes of valor, flitted through his naïve young mind. In the South, he thought, his hulking size and strength should somehow easily bring him fame and fortune among the city-bred weaklings. So he headed south, to seek his fate with no more equipment than a tattered, threadbare tunic and a length of chain.

And then the wolves had caught his scent. Ordinarily, an active man had little to fear from wolves. But this was the end of winter; the wolves, starving after a bad season, were ready for any desperate chance.

The first time they had caught up with him, he had wielded the chain with such fury that he left one gray wolf writhing and howling in the snow with a broken back, and another dead with a smashed skull. Scarlet gore spattered the melting snow. The famished pack had slunk away from this fierce-eyed lad with the terrible whirling chain, to feast upon their own dead brethren instead, and young Conan had fled southward. But, ere long, they were again upon his track.

Yesterday, at sunset, they had caught up with him at a frozen river on the borders of Brythunia. He had fought them on the slippery ice, swinging the bloody chain like a flail, until the boldest wolf had seized the iron links between grim jaws, tearing the chain from his numb grasp. Then the fury of the battle and the hurtling weight of the pack had broken the rotten ice beneath them. Conan found himself gasping and choking in the icy flood. Several wolves had fallen in with him—he had a brief impression of a wolf, half immersed, scrabbling frantically with its forepaws at the edge of the ice—but how many had succeeded in scrambling out, and how many had been swept under the ice by the swift current, he never learned.

Teeth chattering, he hauled himself out on the ice on the farther side, leaving the howling pack behind. All night he had fled south through the wooded hills, half-naked and half-frozen, and all this day. Now they had caught up with him again.

The cold mountain air burned in his straining lungs, until every breath was like inhaling the blast from some hellish furnace. Devoid of feeling, his leaden legs moved like pistons. With each stride, his sandaled feet sank into the water-soaked earth and came out again with sucking sounds.

He knew that, bare-handed, he stood little chance against a dozen shaggy man-killers. Yet he trotted on without pausing. His grim Cimmerian heritage would not let him give up, even in the face of certain death.

Snow was falling again—big, wet flakes that struck with a faint but audible hiss and spotted the wet, black earth and the towering black spruces with a myriad dots of white. Here and there, great boulders shouldered out of the needle-carpeted earth; the land was growing ever more rocky and mountainous. And herein, thought Conan, might lie his one chance for life. He could take a stand with his back against a rock and fight the wolves off as they came at him. It was a slim chance—he well knew the steel-trap quickness of those lean, wiry, hundred-pound bodies—but better than none.

The woods thinned out as the slope grew steeper. Conan loped toward a huge mass of rocks that jutted from the hillside, like the entrance to a buried castle. As he did so, the wolves broke from the edge of the thick woods and raced after him, howling like the scarlet demons of Hell as they track and pull down a doomed soul.

2. *The Door in the Rock*

Through the white blur of whirling snow, the boy saw a yawning blackness between two mighty planes of rock and flung himself toward it. The wolves were upon his heels—he thought he could feel their hot, reeking breath upon his bare legs—when he hurled himself into the black cleft that gaped before him. He squeezed through the opening just as the foremost wolf sprang at him. Drooling jaws snapped on empty air; Conan was safe.

But for how long?

Stooping, Conan fumbled about in the dark, pawing the rough stone floor as he sought for any loose object with which to fight off the howling horde. He could hear them padding about in the fresh snow outside, their claws scraping on stone. Like himself, they breathed in quick pants. They snuffled and whined, hungry for blood. But not one came through the doorway, a dim, gray slit against the blackness. And that was strange.

Conan found himself in a narrow chamber in the rock, utterly black save for the feeble twilight that came through the cleft. The uneven floor of the cell was strewn with litter blown in by centuries of wind or carried in by birds and beasts: dead leaves, spruce needles, twigs, a few scattered bones, pebbles, and chips of rock. There was nothing in all this trash that he could use for a weapon.

Stretching to his full height—already inches over six feet—the boy began exploring the wall with outstretched hand. Soon he came upon another door. As he groped his way through this portal into pitch-blackness, his questing fingers told him that here were chisel marks on the stone, forming cryptic glyphs in some unknown writing. Unknown, at least, to the untutored boy from the barbarous northlands, who could neither read nor write and who scorned such civilized skills as effeminate.

He had to stoop double to wedge himself through the inner door, but beyond it he could once more stand erect. He paused, listening warily. Although the silence was absolute, some sense seemed to warn him that he was not alone in the chamber. It was nothing he could see, hear, or smell, but a sense of *presence*, different from any of these.

His sensitive, forest-trained ears, listening for echoes, told him that this inner chamber was much larger than the outer one. The place smelt of ancient dust and bats' droppings. His shuffling feet encountered things scattered about the floor. While he could not see these objects, they did not feel like the forest litter that carpeted the antechamber. They felt more like man-made things.

As he took a quick step along the wall, he stumbled over one such object in the dark. As he fell, the thing splintered with a crash beneath his weight. A snag of broken wood scraped his shin, adding one more scratch to those of the spruce boughs and the wolves' claws. Cursing, he recovered himself and felt in the dark for the thing he had demolished. It was a chair, the wood of which had rotted so that it easily broke beneath his weight.

He continued his explorations more cautiously. His

groping hands met another, larger object, which he presently recognized as the body of a chariot. The wheels had collapsed with the rotting of their spokes, so that the body lay on the floor amid the fragments of spokes and pieces of the rims.

Conan's questing hands came upon something cold and metallic. His sense of touch told him that this was probably a rusty iron fitting from the chariot. This gave him an idea. Turning, he groped his way back to the inner portal, which he could barely discern against the all-pervading blackness. From the floor of the antechamber he gathered a fistful of tinder and several stone chips. Back in the inner chamber, he made a pile of the tinder and tried the stones on the iron. After several failures, he found a stone that emitted a bright flash of sparks when struck against the iron.

Soon he had a small, smoky fire sputtering, which he fed with the broken rungs of the chair and the fragments of the chariot wheels. Now he could relax, rest from his terrible cross-country run, and warm his numbed limbs. The briskly burning blaze would deter the wolves, which still prowled about the outer entrance, reluctant to pursue him into the darkness of the cave but also unwilling to give up their quarry.

The fire sent a warm, yellow light dancing across the walls of roughly dressed stone. Conan gazed about him. The room was square and even larger than his first impressions had told him. The high ceiling was lost in thick shadows and clotted with cobwebs. Several other chairs were set against the walls, together with a couple of chests that had burst open to show their contents of clothing and weapons. The great stone room smelt of death—of ancient things long unburied.

And then the hair lifted from the nape of his neck, and the boy felt his skin roughen with a supernatural thrill. For there, enthroned on a great, stone chair at the further end of the chamber, sat the huge figure of a naked man, with a naked sword across his knees and a cavernous skull-face staring at him through the flickering firelight.

Almost as soon as he sighted the naked giant, Conan knew he was dead—long ages dead. The corpse's limbs were as brown and withered as dry sticks. The flesh on its huge torso had dried, shrunk, and split until it clung in tatters to naked ribs.

This knowledge, however, did not calm the youth's sudden chill of terror. Fearless beyond his years in war, willing to stand against man or brute beast in battle, the boy feared neither pain, nor death, nor mortal foes. But he was a barbarian from the northern hills of backward Cimmeria. Like all barbarians, he dreaded the supernatural terrors of the grave and the dark, with all its dreads and demons and the monstrous, shambling things of Old Night and Chaos, with which primitive folk people the darkness beyond the circle of their campfire. Much rather would Conan have faced even the hungry wolves than remain here with the dead thing glaring down at him from its rocky throne, while the wavering firelight painted life and animation into the withered skull-face and moved the shadows in its sunken sockets like dark, burning eyes.

3. *The Thing on the Throne*

Although his blood ran chill and his nape hairs prickled, the boy fiercely took hold of himself. Bidding his night-fears be damned, he strode stiff-legged across the vault for a closer look at the long-dead thing.

The throne was a square boulder of glassy, black stone, roughly hollowed into the likeness of a chair on a foot-high dais. The naked man had either died while sitting in it or had been placed upon it in a sitting position after his death. Whatever garments he had worn had long since mouldered away to fragments. Bronze buckles and scraps of leather from his harness still lay about his feet. A necklace of unshaped nuggets of gold hung about his neck; uncut gems winked from golden rings on his claw-like hands, which still clasped the arms of the throne. A horned helm of bronze, now covered with a green, waxy coating of verdegris, crowned the pate above the withered, brown horror of the face.

With iron nerve, Conan forced himself to peer into those time-eaten features. The eyes had sunken in, leaving two black pits. Skin had peeled back from dried lips, letting the yellow fangs grin in a mirthless leer.

Who had he been, this dead thing? A warrior of ancient times—some great chief, feared in life and still enthroned in death? None could say. A hundred races had roved and ruled these mountainous borderlands since Atlantis sank beneath the emerald waves of the Western Ocean, eight thousand years before. From the horned helm, the cadaver might have been a chief of the primal Vanir or Æsir, or the primitive king of some forgotten Hyborian tribe, long since vanished into the shadows of time and buried under the dust of ages.

Then Conan's gaze dropped to the great sword that lay across the corpse's bony thighs. It was a terrific weapon: a broadsword with a blade well over a yard in length. It was made of blued iron—not copper or bronze, as might have been expected from its obvious age. It might have been one of the first iron weapons borne by the hand of man; the legends of Conan's people remembered the days when men hewed and thrust with ruddy bronze, and the fabrication of iron was unknown. Many battles had this sword seen in the dim past, for its broad blade, although still keen, was notched in a score of places where, clanging, it had met other blades of sword and ax in the slash and parry of the mêlée. Stained with age and spotted with rust, it was still a weapon to be feared.

The boy felt his pulses pound. The blood of one born

to war seethed within him. Crom, what a sword! With a blade like that, he could more than hold his own against the starving wolves that padded, whined, and waited without. As he reached for the hilt with eager hand, he failed to see the warning flicker that moved within those shadowed eye sockets in the skull-head of the ancient warrior.

Conan hefted the blade. It seemed as heavy as lead—a sword of the Elder Ages. Perhaps some fabled hero-king of old had borne it—some legendary demigod like Kull of Atlantis, king of Valusia in the ages before Atlantis foundered beneath the restless sea . . .

The boy swung the sword, feeling his thews swell with power and his heart beat faster with pride of possession. Gods, what a sword! With such a blade, no destiny was too high for a warrior to aspire to! With a sword such as this, even a half-naked young barbarian from the raw Cimmerian wilderness might hack his way across the world and wade through rivers of gore to a place among the high kings of earth!

He stood back from the throne of stone, feinting and cutting the air with the blade, getting the feel of the age-worn hilt against his hard palm. The keen old sword whistled through the smoky air, and the flickering light of the fire glanced in sparkling rays from the planes of the blade to the rough stone walls, whipping along the sides of the chamber like little, golden meteors. With this mighty brand in his grasp, he could face not only the hungry wolves outside but a world of warriors as well.

The boy expanded his chest and boomed out the savage war cry of his folk. The echoes of that cry thunderously reverberated about the chamber, disturbing ancient shadows and old dust. Conan never paused to think that such a challenge, in such a place, might rouse things other than shadows and dust—things that by all rights should have slumbered without interruption through all future eons.

He stopped, frozen in mid-stride, as a sound—an indescribable, dry creaking—came from the throne side of the crypt. Wheeling, he saw . . . and felt the hair lift from his scalp and the blood turn to ice in his veins. All his superstitious terrors and primal night-fears rose howling, to fill his mind with shadows of madness and horror. For the dead thing lived.

4. *When Dead Men Walk*

Slowly, jerkily, the cadaver rose from its great stone chair and glared at him from its black pits, whence now living eyes seemed to blaze forth with a coldly malignant stare. Somehow—by what primeval necromancy the boy Conan could not guess—life still animated the withered mummy of the long-dead chief. Grinning jaws moved open and shut in a fearful pantomime of speech. But the only sound was the creaking that Conan had heard, as if the shriveled remains of muscles and tendons rubbed dryly together. To Conan, this silent imitation of speech was more terrible than the fact that the dead man lived and moved.

Creaking, the mummy stepped down from the dais of its ancient throne and swiveled its skull in Conan's direction. As its eyeless gaze fixed itself on the sword in Conan's hand, lurid witch fires burned within the hollow sockets. Stalking clumsily across the chamber, the mummy advanced upon Conan like a shape of nameless horror from the nightmares of a mad fiend. It extended its bony claws to snatch the sword from Conan's strong young hands.

Numb with superstitious terror, Conan retreated step by step. The firelight painted the mummy's black, monstrous shadow on the wall behind it. The shadow rippled over the rough stone. Save for the crackle of the flames as they bit into the pieces of ancient furniture with which Conan had fed the fire, the rustle and creak of the cadaver's leathery muscles as they propelled it step by faltering step across the crypt, and the panting breath of the youth as he struggled for air in the grip of terror—save for these sounds, the tomb was silent.

Now the dead thing had Conan backed against a wall. One brown claw stretched jerkily out. The boy's reaction was automatic; instinctively, he struck out. The blade whistled and smote the outstretched arm, which cracked like a broken stick. Still clutching at empty air, the severed hand fell with a dry clack to the floor; no blood spurted from the dry stump of the forearm.

The terrible wound, which would have stopped any living warrior, did not even slow the walking corpse. It merely withdrew the stump of the maimed arm and extended the other.

Wildly, Conan burst from the wall, swinging his blade in great, smashing strokes. One blow caught the mummy in the side. Ribs snapped like twigs under the impact, and the cadaver was hurled off its feet with a clatter. Conan stood panting in the center of the room clutching the worn hilt in a sweaty palm. With widened eyes he watched as slowly, creakily, the mummy dragged itself to its feet again and began mechanically shuffling toward him, its remaining claw extended.

5. *Duel With the Dead*

Around and around they went, circling slowly. Conan swung lustily but retreated step by step before the unstoppable advance of the dead thing that came on and on.

A blow at its remaining arm missed as the mummy

jerked the member out of the path of the sword; the impetus swung Conan half around and, before he could recover, it was almost upon him. Its claw-hand snatched at him, caught a fold of his tunic, and ripped the rotten cloth from his body, leaving him naked except for sandals and loincloth.

Conan danced back and swung at the monster's head. The mummy ducked, and again Conan had to scramble to keep out of its grip. At last he caught it a terrific blow on the side of the head, shearing off one horn of the helm. Another blow sent the helmet itself clanging into a corner. Another bit into the dry, brown skull. The blade stuck for an instant—an instant that almost undid the boy, whose skin was scraped by ancient black nails as he frantically tugged his weapon loose.

The sword caught the mummy in the ribs again, lodged for a nearly fatal second in the spine, and then was jerked loose once more. Nothing, it seemed, could stop it. Dead, it could not be hurt. Always it staggered and shuffled toward him, untiring and unfaltering, even though its body bore wounds that would have laid a dozen stout warriors moaning in the dirt.

How can you kill a thing that is already dead? The question echoed madly in Conan's brain. It went round and round until he thought he would go mad with the repetition of it. His lungs labored; his heart pounded as if it were about to burst. Slash and strike as he would, nothing could even slow the dead thing that shuffled after him.

Now he struck with greater cunning. Reasoning that if it could not walk it could not pursue him, he drove a fierce, back-handed slash against the mummy's knee. A bone cracked, and the mummy collapsed, groveling in the dust of the cavern floor. But still the unnatural life burned within the mummy's withered breast. It staggered to its feet again and lurched after the boy, dragging its crippled leg behind it.

Again Conan struck, and the dead thing's lower face was shorn away; the jawbone went rattling off into the shadows. But the cadaver never stopped. With its lower face a mere expanse of broken white bone beneath the uncanny glow in its eye sockets, it still shambled after its antagonist in tireless, mechanical pursuit. Conan began to wish he had stayed outside with the wolves rather than sought shelter in this cursed crypt, where things that should have died a thousand years ago still stalked and slew.

Then something caught his ankle. Off balance, he fell full-length to the rough stone floor, kicking wildly to free his leg from that bony grip. He stared down and felt his blood freeze when he saw the severed hand of the corpse clutching his foot. Its bony claws bit into his flesh.

Then a grisly shape of nightmare horror and lunacy loomed over him. The broken, mangled face of the corpse leered down into his, and one claw-hand darted towards his throat.

Conan reacted by instinct. With all his might, he brought both sandaled feet up against the shrunken belly of the dead thing stooping over him. Hurled into the air, it fell with a crash behind him, right in the fire.

Then Conan snatched at the severed hand, which still gripped his ankle. He tore it loose, rolled to his feet, and hurled the member into the fire after the rest of the mummy. He stopped to snatch up his sword and whirled back toward the fire—to find the battle over.

Desiccated by the passage of countless centuries, the mummy burned with the fury of dry brushwood. The unnatural life within it still flickered as it struggled erect, while flames ran up its withered form, leaping from limb to limb and converting it into a living torch. It had almost clambered out of the fire when its crippled leg gave way, and it collapsed in a mass of roaring flame. One blazing arm dropped off like a twitching stick. The skull rolled through the coals. Within minutes the mummy was utterly consumed, but for a few glowing coals of blackened bone.

6. *The Sword of Conan*

Conan let out his breath with a long sigh and breathed deeply once again. The tension drained out of him, leaving him weary in every limb. He wiped the cold sweat of terror from his face and combed back the tangle of his black hair with his fingers. The dead warrior's mummy was at last truly dead, and the great sword was his. He hefted it again, relishing its weight and power.

For an instant he thought of spending the night in the tomb. He was deathly tired. Outside, the wolves and the cold waited to bring him down, and not even his wilderness-bred sense of direction could keep him on his chosen course on a starless night in a strange land.

But then revulsion seized him. The smoke-filled chamber stank, now, not only of the dust of ages but also of the burning of long-dead human flesh—a strange odor, like nothing Conan's keen nostrils had ever detected before, and altogether revolting. The empty throne seemed to leer at him. That sense of presence that had struck him when he first entered the inner chamber still lingered in his mind. His scalp crawled and his skin prickled when he thought of sleeping in this haunted chamber.

Besides, with his new sword, he was filled with confidence. His chest expanded, and he swung the blade in whistling circles.

Moments later, wrapped in an old fur cloak from one of the chests and holding a torch in one hand and the sword in the other, he emerged from the cave. There was no sign of the wolves. A glance upward showed that the sky was clearing. Conan studied the stars that glimmered between patches of cloud, then once more set his footsteps to southward.

The Tower of the Elephant

Continuing on southward, through the wild mountains that separate the eastern Hyborian nations from the Turanian steppes, Conan eventually comes to Arenjun, the notorious Zamorian "City of Thieves." Green to civilization and wholly lawless by nature, he finds—or carves—a niche for himself as a professional thief, among a people to whom thievery is an art and an honored calling. Being still very young and more daring than adroit, his progress in his new profession at first is slow.

TORCHES FLARED murkily on the revels in the Maul, where the thieves of the East held carnival by night. In the Maul they could carouse and roar as they liked, for honest people shunned the quarters, and watchmen, well paid with stained coins, did not interfere with their sport. Along the crooked, unpaved streets with their heaps of refuse and sloppy puddles, drunken roisterers staggered, roaring. Steel glinted in the shadows where rose the shrill laughter of women, and the sounds of scufflings and strugglings. Torchlight licked luridly from broken windows and wide-thrown doors, and out of those doors, stale smells of wine and rank sweaty bodies, clamor of drinking jacks and fists hammered on rough tables, snatches of obscene songs, rushed like a blow in the face.

In one of those dens merriment thundered to the low smoke-stained roof, where rascals gathered in every stage of rags and tatters—furtive cutpurses, leering kidnappers, quick-fingered thieves, swaggering bravoes with their wenches, strident-voiced women clad in tawdry finery. Native rogues were the dominant element—dark-skinned, dark-eyed Zamorians, with daggers at their girdles and guile in their hearts. But there were wolves of half a dozen outland nations there as well. There was a giant Hyperborean renegade, taciturn, dangerous, with a broadsword strapped to his great gaunt frame—for men wore steel openly in the Maul. There was a Shemitish counterfeiter, with his hook nose and curled blue-black beard. There was a bold-eyed Brythunian wench, sitting on the knee of a tawny-haired Gunderman—a wandering mercenary soldier, a deserter from some defeated army. And the fat gross rogue whose bawdy jests were causing all the shouts of mirth was a professional kidnapper come up from distant Koth to teach woman-stealing to Zamorians who were born with more knowledge of the art than he could ever attain. This man halted in his description of an intended victim's charms and thrust his muzzle into a huge tankard of frothing ale. Then blowing the foam from his fat lips, he said, "By Bel, god of all thieves, I'll show them how to steal wenches; I'll have her over the Zamorian border before dawn, and there'll be a caravan waiting to receive her. Three hundred pieces of silver, a count of Ophir promised me for a sleek young Brythunian of the better class. It took me weeks, wandering among the border cities as a beggar, to find one I knew would suit. And is she a pretty baggage!"

He blew a slobbery kiss in the air.

"I know lords in Shem who would trade the secret of the Elephant Tower for her," he said, returning to his ale.

A touch on his tunic sleeve made him turn his head, scowling at the interruption. He saw a tall, strongly made youth standing beside him. This person was as much out of place in that den as a grey wolf among mangy rats of the gutters. His cheap tunic could not conceal the hard, rangy lines of his powerful frame, the broad heavy shoulders, the massive chest, lean waist, and heavy arms. His skin was brown from outland suns, his eyes blue and smoldering; a shock of tousled black hair crowned his broad forehead. From his girdle hung a sword in a worn leather scabbard.

The Kothian involuntarily drew back; for the man was not one of any civilized race he knew.

"You spoke of the Elephant Tower," said the stranger, speaking Zamorian with an alien accent. "I've heard much of this tower; what is its secret?"

The fellow's attitude did not seem threatening, and the Kothian's courage was bolstered up by the ale and the evident approval of his audience. He swelled with self-importance.

"The secret of the Elephant Tower?" he exclaimed. "Why, any fool knows that Yara the priest dwells there with the great jewel men call the Elephant's Heart, that is the secret of his magic."

The barbarian digested this for a space.

"I have seen this tower," he said. "It is set in a great garden above the level of the city, surrounded by high walls. I have seen no guards. The walls would be easy to climb. Why has not somebody stolen this secret gem?"

The Kothian stared wide-mouthed at the other's simplicity, then burst into a roar of derisive mirth, in which the others joined.

"Harken to this heathen!" he bellowed. "He would steal the jewel of Yara!—Harken, fellow," he said, turning portentously to the other, "I suppose you are some sort of a northern barbarian—"

"I am a Cimmerian," the outlander answered, in no friendly tone. The reply and the manner of it meant little to the Kothian; of a kingdom that lay far to the south, on the borders of Shem, he knew only vaguely of the northern races.

"Then give ear and learn wisdom, fellow," said he.

pointing his drinking jack at the discomfited youth. "Know that in Zamora, and more especially in this city, there are more bold thieves than anywhere else in the world, even Koth. If mortal man could have stolen the gem, be sure it would have been filched long ago. You speak of climbing the walls, but once having climbed, you would quickly wish yourself back again. There are no guards in the gardens at night for a very good reason—that is, no human guards. But in the watch chamber, in the lower part of the tower, are armed men, and even if you passed those who roam the gardens by night, you must still pass through the soldiers, for the gem is kept somewhere in the tower above."

"But if a man *could* pass through the gardens," argued the Cimmerian, "why could he not come at the gem through the upper part of the tower and thus avoid the soldiers?"

Again the Kothian gaped at him.

"Listen to him!" he shouted jeeringly. "The barbarian is an eagle who would fly to the jeweled rim of the tower, which is only a hundred and fifty feet above the earth, with rounded sides slicker than polished glass!"

The Cimmerian glared about, embarrassed at the roar of mocking laughter that greeted this remark. He saw no particular humor in it and was too new to civilization to understand its discourtesies. Civilized men are more discourteous than savages because they know they can be impolite without having their skulls split, as a general thing. He was bewildered and chagrined and doubtless would have slunk away, abashed, but the Kothian chose to goad him further.

"Come, come!" he shouted. "Tell these poor fellows, who have only been thieves since before you were spawned, tell them how you would steal the gem!"

"There is always a way, if the desire be coupled with courage," answered the Cimmerian shortly, nettled.

The Kothian chose to take this as a personal slur. His face grew purple with anger.

"What!" he roared. "You dare tell us our business, and intimate that we are cowards? Get along; get out of my sight!" And he pushed the Cimmerian violently.

"Will you mock me and then lay hands on me?" grated the barbarian, his quick rage leaping up; and he returned the push with an open-handed blow that knocked his tormenter back against the rude-hewn table. Ale splashed over the jack's lip, and the Kothian roared in fury, dragging at his sword.

"Heathen dog!" he bellowed. "I'll have your heart for that!"

Steel flashed and the throng surged wildly back out of the way. In their flight they knocked over the single candle and the den was plunged in darkness, broken by the crash of upset benches, drum of flying feet, shouts, oaths of people tumbling over one another, and a single strident yell of agony that cut the din like a knife. When a candle was relighted, most of the guests had gone out by doors and broken windows, and the rest huddled behind stacks of wine kegs and under tables. The barbarian was gone; the center of the room was deserted except for the gashed body of the Kothian. The Cimmerian, with the unerring instinct of the barbarian, had killed his man in the darkness and confusion.

2

The lurid lights and drunken revelry fell away behind the Cimmerian. He had discarded his torn tunic and walked through the night naked except for a loincloth and his high-strapped sandals. He moved with the supple ease of a great tiger, his steely muscles rippling under his brown skin.

He had entered the part of the city reserved for the

temples. On all sides of him they glittered white in the starlight—snowy marble pillars and golden domes and silver arches, shrines of Zamora's myriad strange gods. He did not trouble his head about them; he knew that Zamora's religion, like all things of a civilized, long-settled people, was intricate and complex and had lost most of the pristine essence in a maze of formulas and rituals. He had squatted for hours in the courtyards of the philosophers, listening to the arguments of theologians and teachers, and come away in a haze of bewilderment, sure of only one thing, and that, that they were all touched in the head.

His gods were simple and understandable; Crom was their chief, and he lived on a great mountain, whence he sent forth dooms and death. It was useless to call on Crom, because he was a gloomy, savage god, and he hated weaklings. But he gave a man courage at birth, and the will and might to kill his enemies, which, in the Cimmerian's mind, was all any god should be expected to do.

His sandalled feet made no sound on the gleaming pave. No watchmen passed, for even the thieves of the Maul shunned the temples, where strange dooms had been known to fall on violators. Ahead of him he saw, looming against the sky, the Tower of the Elephant. He mused, wondering why it was so named. No one seemed to know. He had never seen an elephant, but he vaguely understood that it was a monstrous animal, with a tail in front as well as behind. This a wandering Shemite had told him, swearing that he had seen such beasts by the thousands in the country of the Hyrkanians; but all men knew what liars were the men of Shem. At any rate, there were no elephants in Zamora.

The shimmering shaft of the tower rose frostily in the stars. In the sunlight it shone so dazzlingly that few could bear its glare, and men said it was built of silver. It was round, a slim, perfect cylinder, a hundred and fifty feet in height, and its rim glittered in the starlight with the great jewels which crusted it. The tower stood among the waving, exotic trees of a garden raised high above the general level of the city. A high wall enclosed this garden, and outside the wall was a lower level, likewise enclosed by a wall. No lights shone forth; there seemed to be no windows in the tower—at least not above the level of the inner wall. Only the gems high above sparkled frostily in the starlight.

Shrubbery grew thick outside the lower, or outer wall. The Cimmerian crept close and stood beside the barrier, measuring it with his eye. It was high, but he could leap and catch the coping with his fingers. Then it would be child's play to swing himself up and over, and he did not doubt that he could pass the inner wall in the same manner. But he hesitated at the thought of the strange perils which were said to await within. These people were strange and mysterious to him; they were not of his kind—not even of the same blood as the more westerly Brythunians, Nemedians, Kothians, and Aquilonians, he had heard of those civilized mysteries in times past. The people of Zamora were very ancient and, from what he had seen of them, very evil.

He thought of Yara, the high priest, who worked strange dooms from this jeweled tower, and the Cimmerian's hair prickled as he remembered a tale told by a drunken page of the court—how Yara had laughed in the face of a hostile prince, and held up a glowing, evil gem before him, and how rays shot blindingly from that unholy jewel, to envelop the prince, who screamed and fell down, and shrank to a withered blackened lump that changed to a black spider which scampered wildly about the chamber until Yara set his heel upon it.

Yara came not often from his tower of magic, and always to work evil on some man or some nation. The king of Zamora feared him more than he feared death, and kept himself drunk all the time because that fear was more than he could endure sober. Yara was very old—centuries old, men said, and added that he would live for ever because of the magic of his gem, which men called the Heart of the Elephant; for no better reason than this they named his hold the Elephant's Tower.

The Cimmerian, engrossed in these thoughts, shrank quickly against the wall. Within the garden someone was passing, who walked with a measured stride. The listener heard the clink of steel. So, after all, a guard did pace those gardens. The Cimmerian waited, expecting to hear him pass again on the next round; but silence rested over the mysterious gardens.

At last curiosity overcame him. Leaping lightly, he grasped the wall and swung himself up to the top with one arm. Lying flat on the broad coping, he looked down into the wide space between the walls. No shrubbery grew near him, though he saw some carefully trimmed bushes near the inner wall. The starlight fell on the even sward, and somewhere a fountain tinkled.

The Cimmerian cautiously lowered himself down on the inside and drew his sword, staring about him. He was shaken by the nervousness of the wild at standing thus unprotected in the naked starlight, and he moved lightly around the curve of the wall, hugging its shadow, until he was even with the shrubbery he had noticed. Then he ran quickly toward it, crouching low, and almost tripped over a form that lay crumpled near the edges of the bushes.

A quick look to right and left showed him no enemy, in sight at least, and he bent close to investigate. His keen eyes, even in the dim starlight, showed him a strongly-built man in the silvered armor and crested helmet of the Zamorian royal guard. A shield and a spear lay near him, and it took but an instant's examination to show that he had been strangled. The barbarian glanced about uneasily. He knew that this man must be the guard he had heard pass his hiding place by the wall. Only a short time had passed, yet in that interval nameless hands had reached out of the dark and choked out the soldier's life.

Straining his eyes in the gloom, he saw a hint of motion through the shrubs near the wall. Thither he glided, gripping his sword. He made no more noise than a panther stealing through the night, yet the man he was stalking heard. The Cimmerian had a dim glimpse of a huge bulk close to the wall, felt relief that it was at least human; then the fellow wheeled quickly with a gasp that sounded like panic, made the first motion of a forward plunge, hands clutching, then recoiled as the Cimmerian's blade caught the starlight. For a tense instant neither spoke, standing ready for anything.

"You are no soldier," hissed the stranger at last. "You are a thief like myself."

"And who are you?" asked the Cimmerian in a suspicious whisper.

"Taurus of Nemedia."

The Cimmerian lowered his sword.

"I've heard of you. Men call you a prince of thieves."

A low laugh answered him. Taurus was tall as the Cimmerian, and heavier; he was big-bellied and fat, but his every movement betokened a subtle dynamic magnetism, which was reflected in the keen eyes that glinted vitally, even in the starlight. He was barefooted and carried a coil of what looked like a thin, strong rope, knotted at regular intervals.

"Who are you?" he whispered.

"Conan, a Cimmerian," answered the other. "I came seeking a way to steal Yara's jewel, that men call the Elephant's Heart."

Conan sensed the man's great belly shaking in laughter, but it was not derisive.

"By Bel, god of thieves!" hissed Taurus. "I had thought only myself had courage to attempt *that* poaching. These Zamorians call themselves thieves—bah! Conan, I like your grit. I never shared an adventure with anyone; but, by Bel, we'll attempt this together if you're willing."

"Then you are after the gem, too?"

"What else? I've had my plans laid for months; but you, I think, have acted on a sudden impulse, my friend."

"You killed the soldier?"

"Of course. I slid over the wall when he was on the other side of the garden. I hid in the bushes; he heard me, or thought he heard something. When he came blundering over, it was no trick at all to get behind him and suddenly grip his neck and choke out his fool's life. He was like most men, half blind in the dark. A good thief should have eyes like a cat."

"You made one mistake," said Conan.

Taurus' eyes flashed angrily.

"I? I, a mistake? Impossible!"

"You should have dragged the body into the bushes."

"Said the novice to the master of the art. They will not change the guard until past midnight. Should any come searching for him now and find his body, they would flee at once to Yara, bellowing the news, and give us time to escape. Were they not to find it, they'd go beating up the bushes and catch us like rats in a trap."

"You are right," agreed Conan.

"So. Now attend. We waste time in this cursed discussion. There are no guards in the inner garden—human guards, I mean, though there are sentinels even more deadly. It was their presence which baffled me for so long, but I finally discovered a way to circumvent them."

"What of the soldiers in the lower part of the tower?"

"Old Yara dwells in the chambers above. By that route we will come—and go, I hope. Never mind asking me how. I have arranged a way. We'll steal down through the top of the tower and strangle old Yara before he can cast any of his accursed spells on us. At least we'll try; it's the chance of being turned into a spider or a toad, against the wealth and power of the world. All good thieves must know how to take risks."

"I'll go as far as any man," said Conan, slipping off his sandals.

"Then follow me." And turning, Taurus leaped up, caught the wall and drew himself up. The man's suppleness was amazing, considering his bulk; he seemed almost to glide up over the edge of the coping. Conan followed him, and lying flat on the broad top, they spoke in wary whispers.

"I see no light," Conan muttered. The lower part of the tower seemed much like that portion visible from outside the garden—a perfect, gleaming cylinder, with no apparent openings.

"There are cleverly constructed doors and windows," answered Taurus, "but they are closed. The soldiers breathe air that comes from above."

The garden was a vague pool of shadows, where feathery bushes and low, spreading trees waved darkly in the starlight. Conan's wary soul felt the aura of waiting menace that brooded over it. He felt the burning glare of unseen eyes, and he caught a subtle scent that made the short hairs on his neck instinctively bristle as a hunting dog bristles at the scent of an ancient enemy.

"Follow me," whispered Taurus; "keep behind me, as you value your life."

Taking what looked like a copper tube from his girdle, the Nemedian dropped lightly to the sward inside the wall. Conan was close behind him, sword ready, but Taurus pushed him back, close to the wall, and showed no inclination to advance, himself. His whole attitude was of tense expectancy, and his gaze, like Conan's, was fixed on the shadowy mass of shrubbery a few yards away. This shrubbery was shaken, although the breeze had died down. Then two great eyes blazed from the waving shadows, and behind them other sparks of fire glinted in the darkness.

"Lions!" muttered Conan.

"Aye. By day they are kept in subterranean caverns below the tower. That's why there are no guards in this garden."

Conan counted the eyes rapidly.

"Five in sight; maybe more back in the bushes. They'll charge in a moment—"

"Be silent!" hissed Taurus, and he moved out from the wall, cautiously as if treading on razors, lifting the slender tube. Low rumblings rose from the shadows, and the blazing eyes moved forward. Conan could sense the great slaverings jaws, the tufted tails lashing tawny sides. The air grew tense—the Cimmerian gripped his sword, expecting the charge and the irresistible hurtling of giant bodies. Then Taurus brought the mouth of the tube to his lips and blew powerfully. A long jet of yellowish powder shot from the other end of the tube and billowed out instantly in a thick green-yellow cloud that settled over the shrubbery, blotting out the glaring eyes.

Taurus ran back hastily to the wall. Conan glared without understanding. The thick cloud hid the shrubbery, and from it no sound came.

"What is that mist?" the Cimmerian asked uneasily.

"Death!" hissed the Nemedian. "If a wind springs up and blows it back upon us, we must flee over the wall. But no, the wind is still, and now it is dissipating. Wait until it vanishes entirely. To breathe it is death."

Presently only yellowish shreds hung ghostily in the air; then they were gone, and Taurus motioned his companion forward. They stole toward the bushes, and Conan gasped. Stretched out in the shadows lay five great tawny shapes, the fire of their grim eyes dimmed for ever. A sweetish, cloying scent lingered in the atmosphere.

"They died without a sound!" muttered the Cimmerian. "Taurus, what was that powder?"

"It was made from the black lotus, whose blossoms wave in the lost jungles of Khitai, where only the yellow-skulled priests of Yun dwell. Those blossoms strike dead any who smell of them."

Conan knelt beside the great forms, assuring himself that they were indeed beyond power of harm. He shook his head; the magic of the exotic lands was mysterious and terrible to the babarians of the north.

"Why can you not slay the soldiers in the tower in the same way?" he asked.

"Because that was all the powder I possessed. The obtaining of it was a feat which in itself was enough to make me famous among the thieves of the world. I stole it out of a caravan bound for Stygia, and I lifted it, in its cloth-of-gold bag, out of the coils of the great serpent which guarded it, without waking him. But come, in Bel's name! Are we to waste the night in discussion?"

They glided through the shrubbery to the gleaming foot of the tower, and there, with a motion enjoining silence, Taurus unwound his knotted cord, on one end of which was a strong steel hook. Conan saw his plan and asked no questions, as the Nemedian gripped the line a short distance below the hook and began to swing it about his head. Conan laid his ear to the smooth wall and listened, but could hear nothing. Evidently the soldiers within did not suspect the presence of intruders, who had made no more sound than the night wind blowing through the trees. But a strange nervousness was on the barbarian; perhaps it was the lion smell which was over everything.

Taurus threw the line with a smooth, rippling motion of his mighty arm. The hook curved upward and inward in a peculiar manner, hard to describe, and vanished over the jeweled rim. It apparently caught firmly, for cautious jerking and then hard pulling did not result in any slipping or giving.

"Luck the first cast," murmured Taurus. "I—"

It was Conan's savage instinct which made him wheel suddenly; for the death that was upon them made no sound. A fleeting glimpse showed the Cimmerian the giant tawny shape, rearing upright against the stars, towering over him for the death stroke. No civilized man could have moved half so quickly as the barbarian moved. His sword flashed frostily in the starlight with every ounce of desperate nerve and thew behind it, and man and beast went down together.

Cursing incoherently beneath his breath, Taurus bent above the mass and saw his companion's limbs move as he strove to drag himself from under the great weight that lay limply upon him. A glance showed the startled Nemedian that the lion was dead, its slanting skull split in half. He laid hold of the carcass and, by his aid, Conan thrust it aside and clambered up, still gripping his dripping sword.

"Are you hurt, man?" gasped Taurus, still bewildered by the stunning swiftness of that touch-and-go episode.

"No, by Crom!" answered the barbarian. "But that was as close a call as I've had in a life noways tame. Why did not the cursed beast roar as charged?"

"All things are strange in this garden," said Taurus. "The lions strike silently—and so do other deaths. But come—little sound was made in that slaying, but the soldiers might have heard, if they are not asleep or drunk. That beast was in some other part of the garden and escaped the death of the flowers, but surely there are no more. We must climb this cord—little need to ask a Cimmerian if he can."

"If it will bear my weight," grunted Conan, cleansing his sword on the grass.

"It will bear thrice my own," answered Taurus. "It was

woven from the tresses of dead women, which I took from their tombs at midnight, and steeped in the deadly wine of the upas tree, to give it strength. I will go first—then follow me closely."

The Nemedian gripped the rope and, crooking a knee about it, began the ascent; he went up like a cat, belying the apparent clumsiness of his bulk. The Cimmerian followed. The cord swayed and turned on itself, but the climbers were not hindered; both had made more difficult climbs before. The jeweled rim glittered high above them, jutting out from the perpendicular of the wall, so that the cord hung perhaps a foot from the side of the tower—a fact which added greatly to the ease of the ascent.

Up and up they went, silently, the lights of the city spreading out further and further to their sight as they climbed, the stars above them more and more dimmed by the glitter of the jewels along the rim. Now Taurus reached up a hand and gripped the rim itself, pulling himself up and over. Conan paused a moment on the very edge, fascinated by the great frosty jewels whose gleams dazzled his eyes—diamonds, rubies, emeralds, sapphires, turquoises, moonstones, set thick as stars in the shimmering silver. At a distance their different gleams had seemed to merge into a pulsing white glare; but now, at close range, they shimmered with a million rainbow tints and lights, hypnotizing him with their scintillations.

"There is a fabulous fortune here, Taurus," he whispered; but the Nemedian answered impatiently, "Come on! If we secure the Heart, these and all other things shall be ours.'

Conan climbed over the sparkling rim. The level of the tower's top was some feet below the gemmed ledge. It was flat, composed of some dark blue substance, set with gold that caught the starlight, so that the whole looked like a wide sapphire flecked with shining gold dust. Across from the point where they had entered there seemed to be a sort of chamber, built upon the roof. It was of the same silvery material as the walls of the tower, adorned with designs worked in smaller gems; its single door was of gold, its surface cut in scales and crusted with jewels that gleamed like ice.

Conan cast a glance at the pulsing ocean of lights which spread far below them, then glanced at Taurus. The Nemedian was drawing up his cord and coiling it. He showed Conan where the hook had caught—a fraction of an inch of the point had sunk under a great blazing jewel on the inner side of the rim.

"Luck was with us again," he muttered. "One would think that our combined weight would have torn that stone out. Follow me; the real risks of the venture begin now. We are in the serpent's lair, and we know not where he lies hidden."

Like stalking tigers they crept across the darkly gleaming floor and halted outside the sparkling door. With a deft and cautious hand Taurus tried it. It gave without resistance, and the companions looked in, tensed for anything. Over the Nemedian's shoulder Conan had a glimpse of a glittering chamber, the walls, ceiling, and floor of which were crusted with great, white jewels, which lighted it brightly and which seemed its only illumination. It seemed empty of life.

"Before we cut off our last retreat," hissed Taurus, "go you to the rim and look over on all sides; if you see any soldiers moving in the gardens, or anything suspicious, return and tell me. I will await you within this chamber."

Conan saw scant reason in this, and a faint suspicion of his companion touched his wary soul, but he did as Taurus requested. As he turned away, the Nemedian slipped inside the door and drew it shut behind him. Conan crept about the rim of the tower, returning to his starting point without having seen any suspicious movement in the vaguely waving sea of leaves below. He turned toward the door—suddenly from within the chamber there sounded a strangled cry.

The Cimmerian leaped forward, electrified—the gleaming door swung open, and Taurus stood framed in the cold blaze behind him. He swayed and his lips parted, but only a dry rattle burst from his throat. Catching at the golden door for support, he lurched out upon the roof, then fell headlong, clutching at his throat. The door swung to behind him.

Conan, crouching like a panther at bay, saw nothing in the room behind the stricken Nemedian, in the brief instant the door was partly open—unless it was not a trick of the light which made it seem as if a shadow darted across the gleaming floor. Nothing followed Taurus out on the roof, and Conan bent above the man.

The Nemedian stared up with dilated, glazing eyes, that somehow held a terrible bewilderment. His hands clawed at his throat, his lips slobbered and gurgled; the suddenly he stiffened, and the astounded Cimmerian knew that he was dead. And he felt that Taurus had died without knowing what manner of death had stricken him. Conan glared bewilderedly at the cryptic golden door. In that empty room, with its glittering jeweled walls, death had come to the prince of thieves as swiftly and mysteriously as he had dealt doom to the lions in the gardens below.

Gingerly the barbarian ran his hands over the man's half-naked body, seeking a wound. But the only marks of violence were between his shoulders, high up near the base of his bull neck—three small wounds, which looked as if three nails had been driven deep in the flesh and withdrawn. The edges of these wounds were black, and a faint smell as putrefaction was evident. Poisoned darts? thought Conan—but in that case the missiles should be still in the wounds.

Cautiously he stole toward the golden door, pushed it open, and looked inside. The chamber lay empty, bathed in the cold, pulsing glow of the myriad jewels. In the very center of the ceiling he idly noted a curious design—a black eight-sided pattern, in the center of which four gems glittered with a red flame unlike the white blaze of the other jewels. Across the room there was another door, like the one in which he stood, except that it was not carved in the scale pattern. Was it from that door that death had come? —and having struck down its victim, had it retreated by the same way?

Closing the door behind him, the Cimmerian advanced into the chamber. His bare feet made no sound on the crystal floor. There were no chairs or tables in the chamber, only three or four silken couches, embroidered with gold and worked in strange serpentine designs, and several silver-bound mahogany chests. Some were sealed with heavy golden locks; others lay open, their carven lids thrown back, revealing heaps of jewels in a careless riot of splendor to the Cimmerian's astounded eyes. Conan swore beneath his breath; already he had looked upon more wealth that night than he had ever dreamed existed in all the world, and he grew dizzy thinking of what must be the value of the jewel he sought.

He was in the center of the room now, going stooped forward, head thrust out warily, sword advanced, when again death struck at him soundlessly. A flying shadow that swept across the gleaming floor was his only warning, and his instinctive sidelong leap all that saved his life. He had a flashing glimpse of a hairy black horror that swung past him with a clashing of frothing fangs, and something splashed on his bare shoulder that burned like drops of liquid hell-fire. Springing back, sword high, he saw the horror strike the floor, wheel, and scuttle toward him with appalling speed—a gigantic black spider, such as men see only in nightmare dreams.

It was as large as a pig, and its eight thick hairy legs drove its ogreish body over the floor at headlong pace; its four evilly gleaming eyes shone with a horrible intelligence, and its fangs dripped venom that Conan knew, from the burning of his shoulder where only a few drops had splashed as the thing struck and missed, was laden with swift death. This was the killer that had dropped from its perch in the middle of the ceiling on a strand of web, on the neck of the Nemedian. Fools that they were, not to have suspected that the upper chambers would be guarded as well as the lower!

These thoughts flashed briefly through Conan's mind as the monster rushed. He leaped high, and it passed beneath him, wheeled, and charged back. This time he evaded its rush with a sidewise leap and struck back like a cat. His sword severed one of the hairy legs, and again he barely saved himself as the monstrosity swerved at him, fangs clicking fiendishly. But the creature did not press the pursuit; turning, it scuttled across the crystal floor and ran up the wall to the ceiling, where it crouched for an instant, glaring down at him with its fiendish red eyes. Then without warning it launched itself through space, trailing a strand of slimy grayish stuff.

Conan stepped back to avoid the hurtling body—then ducked frantically, just in time to escape being snared by the flying web-rope. He saw the monster's intent and sprang toward the door, but it was quicker, and a sticky strand cast across the door made him a prisoner. He dared not try to cut it with his sword; he knew the stuff would cling to the blade; and, before he could shake it loose, the fiend would be sinking its fangs into his back.

Then began a desperate game, the wits and quickness

of the man matched against the fiendish craft and speed of the giant spider. It no longer scuttled across the floor in a direct charge, or swung its body through the air at him. It raced about the ceiling and the walls, seeking to snare him in the long loops of sticky gray web-strands, which it flung with a devilish accuracy. These strands were thick as ropes, and Conan knew that once they were coiled about him, his desperate strength would not be enough to tear him free before the monster struck.

All over the chamber went on that devil's dance, in utter silence except for the quick breathing of the man, the low scuff of his bare feet on the shining floor, the castanet rattle of the monstrosity's fangs. The gray strands lay in coils on the floor; they were looped along the walls; they overlaid the jewel-chests and silken couches, and hung in dusky festoons from the jeweled ceiling. Conan's steel-trap quickness of eye and muscle had kept him untouched, though the sticky loops had passed him so closed they rasped his naked hide. He knew he could not always avoid them; he not only had to watch the strands swinging from the ceiling, but to keep his eye on the floor, lest he trip in the coils that lay there. Sooner or later a gummy loop would writhe about him, pythonlike, and then, wrapped like a cocoon, he would lie at the monster's mercy.

The spider raced across the chamber floor, the gray rope waving out behind it. Conan leaped high, clearing a couch —with a quick wheel the fiend ran up the wall, and the strand, leaping off the floor like a live thing, whipped about the Cimmerian's ankle. He caught himself on his hands as he fell, jerking frantically at the web which held him like a pliant vise, or the coil of a python. The hairy devil was racing down the wall to complete its capture. Stung to frenzy, Conan caught up a jewel chest and hurled it with all his strength. Full in the midst of the branching black legs the massive missile struck, smashing against the wall with a muffled sickening crunch. Blood and greenish slime spattered, and the shattered mass fell with the burst gem-chest to the floor. The crushed black body lay among the flaming riot of jewels that spilled over it; the hairy legs moved aimlessly, the dying eyes glittered redly among the twinkling gems.

Conan glared about, but no other horror appeared, and he set himself to working free of the web. The substance clung tenaciously to his ankle and his hands, but at last he was free, and taking up his sword, he picked his way among the gray coils and loops to the inner door. What horrors lay within he did not know. The Cimmerian's blood was up and, since he had come so far and overcome so much peril, he was determined to go through to the grim finish of the adventure, whatever that might be. And he felt that the jewel he sought was not among the many so carelessly strewn about the gleaming chamber.

Stripping off the loops that fouled the inner door, he found that it, like the other, was not locked. He wondered if the soldiers below were still unaware of his presence. Well, he was high above their heads, and if tales were to be believed, they were used to strange noises in the tower above them—sinister sounds, and screams of agony and horror.

Yara was on his mind, and he was not altogether comfortable as he opened the golden door. But he saw only a flight of silver steps leading down, dimly lighted by what means he could not ascertain. Down these he went silently, gripping his sword. He heard no sound and came presently to an ivory door, set with bloodstones. He listened, but no sound came from within; only thin wisps of smoke drifted lazily from beneath the door, bearing a curious exotic odor unfamiliar to the Cimmerian. Below him the silver stair wound down to vanish in the dimness, and up that shadowy well no sound floated; he had an eery feeling that he was alone in a tower occupied only by ghosts and phantoms.

3

Cautiously he pressed against the ivory door, and it swung silently inward. On the shimmering threshold Conan stared like a wolf in strange surroundings, ready to fight or flee on the instant. He was looking into a large chamber with a domed golden ceiling; the walls were of green jade, the floor of ivory, partly covered with thick rugs. Smoke and exotic scent of incense floated up from a brazier on a golden tripod, and behind it sat an idol on a sort of marble couch. Conan stared aghast; the image had the body of a man, naked, and green in color; but the head was one of nightmare and madness. Too large for the human body, it had no attributes of humanity. Conan stared at the wide flaring ears, the curling proboscis, on either side of which stood white tusks tipped with round golden balls. The eyes were closed, as if in sleep.

This then, was the reason for the name, the Tower of the Elephant, for the head of the thing was much like that of the beasts described by the Shemitish wanderer. This was Yara's god; where then should the gem be, but concealed in the idol, since the stone was called the Elephant's Heart?

As Conan came forward, his eyes fixed on the motionless idol, the eyes of the thing opened suddenly! The Cimmerian froze in his tracks. It was no image—it was a living thing, and he was trapped in its chamber!

That he did not instantly explode in a burst of murderous frenzy is a fact that measured his horror, which paralyzed him where he stood. A civilized man in his position would have sought doubtful refuge in the conclusion that he was insane; it did not occur to the Cimmerian to doubt his senses. He knew he was face to face with a demon of the Elder World, and the realization robbed him of all his faculties except sight.

The trunk of the horror was lifted and quested about, the topaz eyes stared unseeingly, and Conan knew the monster was blind. With the thought came a thawing of his frozen nerves, and he began to back silently toward the door. But the creature heard. The sensitive trunk stretched toward him, and Conan's horror froze him again when the being spoke, in a strange, stammering voice that never changed its key or timbre. The Cimmerian knew that those jaws were never built or intended for human speech.

"Who is here? Have you come to torture me again, Yara? Will you never be done? Oh, Yag-kosha, is there no end to agony?"

Tears rolled from the sightless eyes, and Conan's gaze strayed to the limbs stretched on the marble couch. And he knew the monster would not rise to attack him. He knew the marks of the rack, and the searing brand of the flame, and tough-souled as he was, he stood aghast at the ruined deformities which his reason told him had once been limbs as comely as his own. And suddenly all fear and repulsion went from him to be replaced by a great pity. What this monster was, Conan could not know, but the evidences of its sufferings were so terrible and pathetic that a strange aching sadness came over the Cimmerian, he knew not why. He only felt that he was looking upon a cosmic tragedy, and he shrank with shame, as if the guilt of a whole race were laid upon him.

"I am not Yara," he said. "I am only a thief. I will not harm you."

"Come near that I may touch you," the creature faltered, and Conan came near unfearingly, his sword hanging forgotten in his hand. The sensitive trunk came out and groped over his face and shoulders, as a blind man gropes, and its touch was light as a girl's hand.

"You are not of Yara's race of devils," sighed the creature. "The clean, lean fierceness of the wastelands marks you. I know your people from of old, whom I knew by another name in the long, long ago when another world lifted its jeweled spires to the stars. There is blood on your fingers."

"A spider in the chamber above and a lion in the garden," muttered Conan.

"You have slain a man too, this night," answered the other. "And there is death in the tower above. I feel; I know."

"Aye," muttered Conan. "The prince of all thieves lies there dead from the bite of a vermin."

"So—and so!" the strange inhuman voice rose in a sort of low chant. "A slaying in the tavern and a slaying on the roof—I know; I feel. And the third will make the magic of which not even Yara dreams—oh, magic of deliverance, green gods of Yag!"

Again tears fell as the tortured body was rocked to and fro in the grip of varied emotions. Conan looked on, bewildered.

Then the convulsions ceased; the soft, sightless eyes were turned toward the Cimmerian, the trunk beckoned.

"O man, listen," said the strange being. "I am foul and monstrous to you, am I not? Nay, do not answer; I know. But you would seem as strange to me, could I see you. There are many worlds besides this earth, and life takes many shapes. I am neither god nor demon, but flesh and blood like yourself, though the substance differ in part, and the form be cast in different mold.

"I am very old, O man of the waste countries; long and long ago I came to this planet with others of my world, from the green planet Yag, which circles for ever in the outer fringe of this universe. We swept through space on mighty wings that drove us through the cosmos quicker than light, because we had warred with the kings of Yag and were defeated and outcast. But we could never return, for on earth our wings withered from our shoulders. Here we abode apart from earthly life. We fought the strange and terrible forms of life which then walked the earth, so that we became feared and were not molested in the dim jungles of the East where we had our abode.

"We saw men grow from the ape and build the shining cities of Valusia, Kamelia, Commoria, and their sisters. We saw them reel before the thrusts of the heathen Atlanteans and Picts and Lemurians. We saw the oceans rise and engulf Atlantis and Lemuria, and the isles of the Picts, and the shining cities of civilization. We saw the survivors of Pictdom and Atlantis build their stone-age empire and go down to ruin, locked in bloody wars. We saw the Picts sink into abysmal savagery, the Atlanteans into apedom again. We saw new savages drift southward in conquering waves from the Arctic Circle to build a new civilization, with new kingdoms called Nemedia, and Koth, and Aquilonia, and their sisters. We saw your people rise under a new name from the jungles of the apes that had been Atlanteans. We saw the descendants of the Lemurians, who had survived the cataclysm, rise again through savagery and ride westward, as Hyrkanians. And we saw this race of devils, survivors of the ancient civilization that was before Atlantis sank, come once more into culture and power—this accursed kingdom of Zamora.

"All this we saw, neither aiding nor hindering the immutable cosmic law, and one by one we died; for we of Yag are not immortal, though our lives are as the lives of planets and constellations. At last I alone was left, dreaming of old times among the ruined temples of jungle-lost Khitai, worshipped as a god by an ancient yellow-skinned race. Then came Yara, versed in dark knowledge handed down through the days of barbarism, since before Atlantis sank.

"First he sat at my feet and learned wisdom. But he was not satisfied with what I taught him, for it was white magic, and he wished evil lore, to enslave kings and glut a fiendish ambition. I would teach him none of the black secrets I had gained, through no wish of mine, through the eons.

"But his wisdom was deeper than I had guessed; with guile gotten among the dusky tombs of dark Stygia, he trapped me into divulging a secret I had not intended to bare; and turning my own power upon me, he enslaved me. Ah, gods of Yag, my cup has been bitter since that hour!

"He brought me up from the lost jungles of Khitai where the gray apes danced to the pipes of the yellow priests, and offerings of fruit and wine heaped my broken altars. No more was I a god to kindly junglefolk—I was slave to a devil in human form."

Again tears stole from the unseeing eyes.

"He pent me in this tower, which at his command I built for him in a single night. By fire and rack he mastered me, and by strange unearthly tortures you would not understand. In agony I would long ago have taken my own life, if I could. But he kept me alive—mangled, blinded, and broken—to do his foul bidding. And for three hundred years I have done his bidding, from this marble couch, blackening my soul with cosmic sins, and staining my wisdom with crimes, because I had no other choice. Yet not all my ancient secrets has he wrested from me, and my last gift shall be the sorcery of the Blood and the Jewel.

"For I feel the end of time draw near. You are the hand of Fate. I beg of you, take the gem you will find on yonder altar."

Conan turned to the gold and ivory altar indicated, and took up a great round jewel, clear as crimson crystal; and he knew that this was the Heart of the Elephant.

"Now for the great magic, the mighty magic, such as earth has not seen before, and shall not see again, through a million million of millenniums. By my life-blood I conjure it, by blood born on the green breast of Yag, dreaming far-poised in the great, blue vastness of Space.

"Take your sword, man, and cut out my heart; then squeeze it so that the blood will flow over the red stone. Then go you down these stairs and enter the ebony chamber where Yara sits wrapped in lotus dreams of evil. Speak his name and he will awaken. Then lay this gem before him, and say, 'Yag-kosha gives you a last gift and a last enchantment.' Then get you from the tower quickly; fear not, your way shall be made clear. The life of man is not the life of Yag, nor is human death the death of Yag. Let me be free of this cage of broken, blind flesh, and I will once more be Yogah of Yag, morning-crowned and shining, with wings to fly, and feet to dance, and eyes to see, and hands to break."

Uncertainly Conan approached, and Yag-kosha, or Yogah, as if sensing his uncertainty, indicated where he should strike. Conan set his teeth and drove the sword deep. Blood streamed over the blade and his hand, and the monster started convulsively, then lay back quite still. Sure that life had fled, at least life as he understood it, Conan set to work on his grisly task and quickly brought forth something that he felt must be the strange being's heart, though it differed curiously from any he had ever seen. Holding the still pulsing organ over the blazing jewel, he pressed it with both hands, and a rain of blood fell on the stone. To his surprise, it did not run off, but soaked into the gem, as water is absorbed by a sponge.

Holding the jewel gingerly, he went out of the fantastic chamber and came upon the silver steps. He did not look back; he instinctively felt that some form of transmutation was taking place in the body on the marble couch, and he further felt that it was of a sort not to be witnessed by human eyes.

He closed the ivory door behind him and without hesitation descended the silver steps. It did not occur to him to ignore the instructions given him. He halted at an ebony door, in the center of which was a grinning silver skull, and pushed it open. He looked into a chamber of ebony and jet and saw, on a black silken couch, a tall, spare form reclining. Yara the priest and sorcerer lay before him, his eyes open and dilated with the fumes of the yellow lotus, far-staring, as if fixed on gulfs and nighted abysses beyond human ken.

"Yara!" said Conan, like a judge pronouncing doom. "Awaken!"

The eyes cleared instantly and became cold and cruel as a vulture's. The tall, silken-clad form lifted erect and towered gauntly above the Cimmerian.

"Dog!" His hiss was like the voice of a cobra. "What do you here?"

Conan laid the jewel on the great ebony table.

"He who sent this gem bade me say, 'Yag-kosha gives a last gift and a last enchantment.' "

Yara recoiled, his dark face ashy. The jewel was no longer crystal-clear; its murky depths pulsed and throbbed, and curious smoky waves of changing color passed over its smooth surface. As if drawn hypnotically, Yara bent over the table and gripped the gem in his hands, staring into its shadowed depths, as if it were a magnet to draw the shuddering soul from his body. And as Conan looked, he thought that his eyes must be playing him tricks. For when Yara had risen up from his couch, the priest had seemed gigantically tall; yet now he saw that Yara's head would scarcely come to his shoulder. He blinked, puzzled, and for the first time that night doubted his own senses. Then with a shock he realized that the priest was shrinking in stature—was growing smaller before his very gaze.

With a detached feeling he watched, as a man might watch a play; immersed in a feeling of overpowering unreality, the Cimmerian was no longer sure of his own identity; he only knew that he was looking upon the external evidences of the unseen play of vast Outer forces, beyond his understanding.

Now Yara was no bigger than a child; now like an infant he sprawled on the table, still grasping the jewel. And now the sorcerer suddenly realized his fate, and he sprang up, releasing the gem. But still he dwindled, and Conan saw a tiny, pigmy figure rushing wildly about the ebony table-top, waving tiny arms and shrieking in a voice that was like the squeak of an insect.

Now he had shrunk until the great jewel towered above him like a hill, and Conan saw him cover his eyes with his hands, as if to shield them from the glare, as he staggered about like a madman. Conan sensed that some unseen magnetic force was pulling Yara to the gem. Thrice he raced wildly about it in a narrowing circle, thrice he strove to turn and run out across the table; then with a scream that echoed faintly in the ears of the watcher, the priest threw up his arms and ran straight toward the blazing globe.

Bending close, Conan saw Yara clamber up the smooth, curving surface, impossibly, like a man climbing a glass mountain. Now the priest stood on the top, still with tossing arms, invoking what grisly names only the gods know. And suddenly he sank into the very heart of the jewel, as a man sinks into a sea, and Conan saw the smoky waves close over his head. Now he saw him in the crimson heart of the jewel, once more crystal-clear, as a man sees a scene far away, tiny with great distance. And into the heart came a green, shining winged figure with body of a man and the head of an elephant—no longer blind or crippled. Yara threw up his arms and fled as a madman flees, and on his heels came the avenger. Then, like the bursting of a bubble, the great jewel vanished in a rainbow burst of iridescent gleams, and the ebony table-top lay bare and deserted—as bare, Conan somehow knew, as the marble couch in the chamber above, where the body of that strange transcosmic being called Yag-kosha and Yogah had lain.

The Cimmerian turned and fled from the chamber,

down the silver stairs. So mazed was he that it did not occur to him to escape from the tower by the way he had entered it. Down that winding, shadowy silver well he ran, and came into a larger chamber at the foot of the gleaming stairs. There he halted for an instant; he had come into the room of the soldiers. He saw the glitter of their silver corselets, the sheen of their jeweled sword-hilts. They sat slumped at the banquet board, their dusky plumes waving somberly above their drooping helmeted heads; they lay among their dice and fallen goblets on the wine-stained, lapis-lazuli floor. And he knew that they were dead. The promise had been made, the word kept; whether sorcery or magic or the falling shadow of great green wings had stilled the revelry, Conan could not know, but his way had been made clear. And a silver door stood open, framed in the whiteness of dawn.

Into the waving green gardens came the Cimmerian and, as the dawn wind blew upon him with the cool fragrance of luxuriant growths, he started like a man waking from a dream. He turned back uncertainly, to stare at the cryptic tower he had just felt. Was he bewitched and enchanted? Had he dreamed all that had seemed to have passed? As he looked he saw the gleaming tower sway against the crimson dawn, its jewel-crusted rim sparkling in the growing light, and crash into shining shards.

The Hall of the Dead

Becoming fed up with the City of Thieves (and vice versa*) Conan wanders westward to the capital of Zamora, Shadizar the Wicked. Here, he hopes, the pickings will be richer. For a time he is, indeed, more successful in his thievery than he had been in Arenjun—although the women of Shadizar quickly relieve him of his gains in return for initiating him into the arts of love. Rumors of treasure send him to the nearby ruins of ancient Larsha, just ahead of the squad of soldiers sent to arrest him.*

THE GORGE WAS DARK, although the setting sun had left a band of orange and yellow and green along the western horizon. Against this band of color, a sharp eye could still discern, in black silhouette, the domes and spires of Shadizar the Wicked, the city of dark-haired women and towers of spider-haunted mystery—the capital of Zamora.

As the twilight faded, the first few stars appeared overhead. As if answering a signal, lights winked on in the distant domes and spires. While the light of the stars was pale and wan, that of the windows of Shadizar was a sultry amber, with a hint of abominable deeds.

The gorge was quiet save for the chirping of nocturnal insects. Presently, however, this silence was broken by the sound of moving men. Up the gorge came a squad of Zamorian soldiers—five men in plain steel caps and leather jerkins, studded with bronze buttons, led by an officer in a polished bronze cuirass and a helmet with a towering horsehair crest. Their bronze-greaved legs swished through the long, lush grass that covered the floor of the gorge. Their harness creaked and their weapons clanked and tinkled. Three of them bore bows and the other two, pikes; short swords hung at their sides and bucklers were slung across their backs. The officer was armed with a long sword and a dagger.

One of the soldiers muttered: "If we catch this Conan fellow alive, what will they do with him?"

"Send him to Yezud to feed to the spider god, I'll warrant," said another. "The question is, shall we be alive to collect that reward they promised us?"

"Not afraid of him, are you?" said a third.

"Me?" The second speaker snorted. "I fear naught, including death itself. The question is, whose death? This thief is not a civilized man but a wild barbarian, with the strength of ten. So I went to the magistrate to draw up my will—"

"It is cheering to know that your heirs will get the reward," said another. "I wish I had thought of that."

"Oh," said the first man who had spoken, "they'll find some excuse to cheat us of the reward, even if we catch the rascal."

"The prefect himself has promised," said another. "The rich merchants and nobles whom Conan has been robbing raised a fund. I saw the money—a bag so heavy with gold that a man could scarce lift it. After all that public display, they'd not dare to go back on their word."

"But suppose we catch him not," said the second speaker. "There was something about paying for it with our heads." The speaker raised his voice. "Captain Nestor! What was that about our heads—"

"Hold your tongues, all of you!" snapped the officer. "You can be heard as far as Arenjun. If Conan is within a mile, he'll be warned. Cease your chatter, and try to move without so much clangor."

The officer was a broad-shouldered man of medium height and powerful build; daylight would have shown his eyes to be gray and his hair light brown, streaked with gray. He was a Gunderman, from the northernmost province of Aquilonia, fifteen hundred miles to the west. His mission—to take Conan dead or alive—troubled him. The prefect had warned him that, if he failed, he might expect severe punishment—perhaps even the headsman's block. The king himself had demanded that the outlaw be taken, and the king of Zamora had a short way with servants who failed their missions. A tip from the underworld had revealed that Conan was seen heading for this gorge earlier that day, and Nestor's commander had hastily dispatched him with such troopers as could be found in the barracks.

Nestor had no confidence in the soldiers that trailed behind him. He considered them braggarts who would flee in the face of danger, leaving him to confront the barbarian alone. And, although the Gunderman was a brave man, he did not deceive himself about his chances with this ferocious, gigantic young savage. His armor would give him no more than a slight edge.

As the glow in the western sky faded, the darkness deepened and the walls of the gorge became narrower, steeper, and rockier. Behind Nestor, the men began to murmur again:

"I like it not. This road leads to the ruins of Larsha the Accursed, where the ghosts of the ancients lurk to devour passers-by. And in that city, 'tis said, lies the Hall of the Dead—"

"Shut up!" snarled Nestor, turning his head. "If—"

At that instant, the officer tripped over a rawhide rope stretched across the path and fell sprawling in the grass. There was the snap of a spring pole released from its lodgment, and the rope went slack.

With a rumbling roar, a mass of rocks and dirt cascaded down the left-hand slope. As Nestor scrambled to his feet, a stone the size of a man's head struck his corselet and knocked him down again. Another knocked off his helmet, while smaller stones stung his limbs. Behind him sounded a multiple scream and the clatter of stone striking metal. Then silence fell.

Nestor staggered to his feet, coughed the dust out of his lungs, and turned to see what had befallen. A few paces behind him, a rock slide blocked the gorge from wall to wall. Approaching, he made out a human hand and a foot projecting from the rubble. He called but received no reply. When he touched the protruding members, he found no life. The slide, set off by the pull on the rope, had wiped out his entire squad.

Nestor flexed his joints to learn what harm he had suffered. No bones appeared to be broken, although his corselet was dented and he bore several bruises. Burning with wrath, he found his helmet and took up the trail alone. Failing to catch the thief would have been bad enough; but if he also had to confess to the loss of his men, he foresaw a lingering and painful death. His only chance now was to bring back Conan—or at least his head.

Sword in hand, Nestor limped on up the endless windings of the gorge. A light in the sky before him showed that the moon, a little past full, was rising. He strained his eyes, expecting the barbarian to spring upon him from behind every bend in the ravine.

The gorge became shallower and the walls less steep. Gullies opened into the gorge to right and left, while the bottom became stony and uneven, forcing Nestor to scramble over rocks and underbrush. At last the gorge gave out completely. Climbing a short slope, the Gunderman found himself on the edge of an upland plateau, surrounded by distant mountains. A bowshot ahead, bone-white in the light of the moon, rose the walls of Larsha. A massive gate stood directly in front of him. Time had bitten scallops out of the walls, and over it rose half-ruined roofs and towers.

Nestor paused. Larsha was said to be immensely old. According to the tales, it went back to Cataclysmic times, when the forebears of the Zamorians, the Zhemri, formed an island of semi-civilization in a sea of barbarism.

Stories of the death that lurked in these ruins were rife in the bazaars of Shadizar. As far as Nestor had been able to learn, not one of the many men who, in historic times, had invaded the ruins searching for the treasure rumored to exist there, had ever returned. None knew what form the danger took, because no survivor had lived to carry the tale.

A decade before, King Tiridates had sent a company of his bravest soldiers, in broad daylight, into the city, while the king himself waited outside the walls. There had been screams and sounds of flight, and then—nothing. The men who waited outside had fled, and Tiridates perforce had fled with them. That was the last attempt to unlock the mystery of Larsha by main force.

Although Nestor had all the usual mercenary's lust for unearned wealth, he was not rash. Years of soldiering in the kingdoms between Zamora and his homeland had taught him caution. As he paused, weighing the dangers of his alternatives, a sight made him stiffen. Close to the wall, he sighted the figure of a man, slinking toward the gate. Although the man was too far away to recognize faces in the moonlight, there was no mistaking that panther-like stride. Conan!

Filled with rising fury, Nestor started forward. He walked swiftly, holding his scabbard to keep it from clanking. But, quietly though he moved, the keen ears of the barbarian warned him. Conan whirled, and his sword whispered from its sheath. Then, seeing that only a single foe pursued him, the Cimmerian stood his ground.

As Nestor approached, he began to pick out details of the other's appearance. Conan was well over six feet tall, and his threadbare tunic failed to mask the hard lines of his mighty thews. A leathern sack hung by a strap from his shoulder. His face was youthful but hard, surmounted by a square-cut mane of thick black hair.

Not a word was spoken. Nestor paused to catch his breath and cast aside his cloak, and in that instant Conan hurled himself upon the older man.

Two swords glimmered like lightnings in the moonlight as the clang and rasp of blades shattered the graveyard silence. Nestor was the more experienced fighter, but the reach and blinding speed of the other nullified this advantage. Conan's attack was as elemental and irresistible as a hurricane. Parrying shrewdly, Nestor was forced back, step after step. Narrowly he watched his opponent, waiting for the other's attack to slow from sheer fatigue. But the Cimmerian seemed not to know what fatigue was.

Making a backhand cut, Nestor slit Conan's tunic over the chest but did not quite reach the skin. In a blinding return thrust, Conan's point glanced off Nestor's breastplate, plowing a groove in the bronze.

As Nestor stepped back from another furious attack, a stone turned under his foot. Conan aimed a terrific cut at the Gunderman's neck. Had it gone as intended, Nestor's head would have flown from his shoulders; but, as he stumbled, the blow hit his crested helm instead. It struck with a heavy clang, bit into the iron, and hurled Nestor to the ground.

Breathing deeply, Conan stepped forward, sword ready. His pursuer lay motionless with blood seeping from his cloven helmet. Youthful overconfidence in the force of his own blows convinced Conan that he had slain his antagonist. Sheathing his sword, he turned back toward the city of the ancients.

The Cimmerian approached the gate. This consisted of two massive valves, twice as high as a man, made of foot-thick timbers sheathed in bronze. Conan pushed against the valves, grunting, but without effect. He drew his sword and struck the bronze with the pommel. From the way the gates sagged, Conan guessed that the wood of the doors had rotted away; but the bronze was too thick to hew through without spoiling the edge of his blade. And there was an easier way.

Thirty paces north of the gate, the wall had crumbled so that its lowest point was less than twenty feet above the ground. At the same time, a pile of tailings against the foot of the wall rose to within six or eight feet of the broken edge.

Conan approached the broken section, drew back a few paces, and then ran forward. He bounded up the slope of the tailings, leaped into the air, and caught the broken edge of the wall. A grunt, a heave, and a scramble, and he was over the edge, ignoring scratches and bruises. He stared down into the city.

Inside the wall was a cleared space, where for centuries plant life had been waging war upon the ancient pavement. The paving slabs were cracked and up-ended. Between them, grass, weeds, and a few scrubby trees had forced their way.

Beyond the cleared area lay the ruins of one of the poorer districts. Here the one-story hovels of mud brick had slumped into mere mounds of dirt. Beyond them, white in the moonlight, Conan discerned the better-preserved buildings of stone—the temples, the palaces, and the houses of the nobles and the rich merchants. As with many ancient ruins, an aura of evil hung over the deserted city.

Straining his ears, Conan stared right and left. Nothing moved. The only sound was the chirp of crickets.

Conan, too, had heard the tales of the doom that haunted Larsha. Although the supernatural roused panicky, atavistic fears in his barbarian's soul, he hardened himself with the thought that, when a supernatural being took material form, it could be hurt or killed by material weapons, just like any earthly man or monster. He had not come this far to be stopped from a try at the treasure by man, beast, or demon.

According to the tales, the fabled treasure of Larsha lay in the royal palace. Gripping his scabbarded sword in his left hand, the young thief dropped from the inner side of the broken wall. An instant later, he was threading his way through the winding streets toward the center of the city. He made no more noise than a shadow.

Ruin encompassed him on every side. Here and there the front of a house had fallen into the street, forcing Conan to detour or to scramble over piles of broken brick and marble. The gibbous moon was now high in the sky, washing the ruins in an eery light. On the Cimmerian's right rose a temple, partly fallen but with the portico, upheld by four massive marble columns, still intact. Along the edge of the roof, a row of marble gargoyles peered down—statues of monsters of bygone days, half demon and half beast.

Conan tried to remember the scraps of legend that he had overheard in the wineshops of the Maul, concerning the abandonment of Larsha. There was something about a curse sent by an angered god, many centuries before, in punishment for deeds so wicked that they made the crimes and vices of Shadizar looks like virtues . . .

He started for the center of the city again but now noticed something peculiar. His sandals tended to stick to the shattered pavement, as if it were covered with warm pitch. The soles made sucking noises as he raised his feet.

He stooped and felt the ground. It was coated with a film of a colorless, sticky substance, now nearly dry.

Hand on hilt, Conan glared about him in the moonlight. But no sound came to his ears. He resumed his advance. Again his sandals made sucking noises as he raised them. He halted, turning his head. He could have sworn that similar sucking noises came to his ears from a distance. For an instant, he thought they might be the echoes of his own footsteps. But he had passed the half-ruined temple, and now no walls rose on either side of him to reflect the sound.

Again he advanced, then halted. Again he heard the sucking sound, and this time it did not cease when he froze to immobility. In fact, it became louder. His keen hearing located it as coming from directly in front of him. Since he could see nothing moving in the street before him, the source of the sound must be in a side street or in one of the ruined buildings.

The sound increased to an indescribable slithering, gurgling hiss. Even Conan's iron nerves were shaken by the strain of waiting for the unknown source of the sound to appear.

At last, around the next corner poured a huge, slimy mass, leprous gray in the moonlight. It glided into the street before him and swiftly advanced upon him, silent save for the sucking sound of its peculiar method of locomotion. From its front end rose a pair of hornlike projections, at least ten feet long, with a shorter pair below. The long horns bent this way and that, and Conan saw that they bore eyes on their ends.

The creature was, in fact, a slug, like the harmless garden slug that leaves a trail of slime in its nightly wanderings. This slug, however, was fifty feet long and as thick through the middle as Conan was tall. Moreover, it moved as fast as a man could run. The fetid smell of the thing wafted ahead of it.

Momentarily paralyzed with astonishment, Conan stared at the vast mass of rubbery flesh bearing down upon him. The slug emitted a sound like that of a man spitting, but magnified many times over.

Galvanized into action at last, the Cimmerian leaped sideways. As he did so, a jet of liquid flashed through the night air, just where he had stood. A tiny droplet struck his shoulder and burned like a coal of fire.

Conan turned and ran back the way he had come, his long legs flashing in the moonlight. Again he had to bound over piles of broken masonary. His ears told him that the slug was close behind. Perhaps it was gaining. He dared not turn to look, lest he trip over some marble fragment and go sprawling; the monster would be upon him before he could regain his feet.

Again came that spitting sound. Conan leaped frantically to one side; again the jet of liquid flashed past him. Even if he kept ahead of the slug all the way to the city wall, the next shot would probably hit its mark.

Conan dodged around a corner to put obstacles between himself and the slug. He raced down a narrow zigzag street, then around another corner. He was lost in the maze of streets, he knew; but the main thing was to keep turning corners so as not to give his pursuer another clear shot at him. The sucking sounds and the stench indicated that it was following his trail. Once, when he paused to catch his breath, he looked back to see the slug pouring around the last corner he had turned.

On and on he went, dodging this way and that through the maze of the ancient city. If he could not outrun the slug, perhaps he could tire it. A man, he knew, could outlast almost any animal in a long-distance run. But the slug seemed tireless.

Something about the buildings he was passing struck him as familiar. Then he realized that he was coming to the half-ruined temple he had passed just before he met the slug. A quick glance showed him that the upper parts of the building could be reached by an active climber.

Conan bounded up a pile of rubbish to the top of the broken wall. Leaping from stone to stone, he made his way up the jagged profile of the wall to an unruined section facing the street. He found himself on a stretch of roof behind the row of marble gargoyles. He approached them, treading softly lest the half-ruined roof collapse beneath him and detouring around holes through which a man could fall into the chambers below.

The sound and smell of the slug came to him from the street. Realizing that it had lost his trail and uncertain as to which way to turn, the creature had evidently stopped in front of the temple. Very cautiously—for he was sure the slug could see him in the moonlight—Conan peered past one of the statues and down into the street.

There lay the great, grayish mass, on which the moon shone moistly. The eye stalks wavered this way and that, seeking the creature's prey. Beneath them, the shorter horns swept back and forth a little above the ground, as if smelling for the Cimmerian's trail.

Conan felt certain that the slug would soon pick up his trail. He had no doubt that it could slither up the sides of the building quite as readily as he had climbed it.

He put a hand against a gargoyle—a nightmarish statue with a humanoid body, bat's wings, and a reptilian head—and pushed. The statue rocked a trifle with a faint crunching noise.

At the sound, the horns of the slug whipped upward toward the roof of the temple. The slug's head came around, bending its body into a sharp curve. The head approached the front of the temple and began to slide up one of the huge pillars, directly below the place where Conan crouched with bared teeth.

A sword, Conan thought, would be of little use against such a monstrosity. Like other lowly forms of life, it could survive damage that would instantly destroy a higher creature.

Up the pillar came the slug's head, the eyes on their stalks swiveling back and forth. At the present rate, the monster's head would reach the edge of the roof while most of its body still lay in the street below.

Then Conan saw what he must do. He hurled himself at the gargoyle. With a mighty heave, he sent it tumbling over the edge of the roof. Instead of the crash that such a mass of marble would ordinarily make on striking the pavement, there floated up the sound of a moist, squashy impact, followed by a heavy thud as the forward part of the slug's body fell back to earth.

When Conan risked a glance over the parapet, he saw that the statue had sunk into the slug's body until it was almost buried. The great, gray mass writhed and lashed like a worm on a fisherman's hook. A blow of the tail made the front of the temple tremble; somewhere in the interior a few loose stones fell clattering. Conan wondered if the whole structure were about to collapse beneath him, burying him in the débris.

"So much for you!" snarled the Cimmerian.

He went along the row of gargoyles until he found another that was loose and directly over part of the slug's body. Down it went with another squashing impact. A third missed and shattered on the pavement. A fourth and smaller statue he picked bodily up and, muscles cracking with the strain, hurled outward so that it fell on the writhing head.

As the beast's convulsions slowly subsided, Conan pushed over two more gargoyles to make sure. When the body no longer writhed, he clambered down to the street. He approached the great, stinking mass cautiously, sword out. At last, summoning all his courage, he slashed into the rubbery flesh. Dark ichor oozed out, and rippling motions ran through the wet, gray skin. But, even though parts might retain signs of independent life, the slug as a whole was dead.

Conan was still slashing furiously when a voice made him whirl about. It said:

"I've got you this time!"

It was Nestor, approaching sword in hand, with a blood-stained bandage around his head in place of his helmet. The Gunderman stopped at the sight of the slug. "Mitra! What is this?"

"It's the spook of Larsha," said Conan, speaking Zamorian with a barbarous accent. "It chased me over half the city before I slew it." As Nestor stared incredulously, the Cimmerian continued: "What do you here? How many times must I kill you before you stay dead?"

"You shall see how dead I am," grated Nestor, bringing his sword up to guard.

"What happened to your soldiers?"

"Dead in that rock slide you rigged, as you soon shall be —"

"Look, you fool," said Conan, "why waste your strength on sword strokes, when there's more wealth here than the pair of us can carry away—if the tales are true? You are a good man of your hands; why not join me to raid the treasure of Larsha instead?"

"I must do my duty and avenge my men! Defend yourself, dog or a barbarian!"

"By Crom, I'll fight if you like!" growled Conan, bringing up his sword. "But think, man! If you go back to Shadizar, they'll crucify you for losing your command—even if you took my head with you, which I do not think you can do. If one tenth of the stories are true, you'll get more from your share of the loot than you'd earn in a hundred years as a mercenary captain."

Nestor had lowered his blade and stepped back. Now he stood mute, thinking deeply. Conan added: "Besides, you'll never make real warriors of these poltroons of Zamorians!"

The Gunderman sighed and sheathed his sword. "You are right, damn you. Until this venture is over, we'll fight back to back and go equal shares on the loot, eh?" He held out his hand.

"Done!" said Conan, sheathing likewise and clasping the other's hand. "If we have to run for it and get separated, let's meet at the fountain of Ninus."

The royal palace of Larsha stood in the center of the city, in the midst of a broad plaza. It was the one structure that had not crumbled with age, and this for a simple reason. It was carved out of a single crag or hillock of rock that once broke the flatness of the plateau on which Larsha stood. So meticulous had been the construction of this building, however, that close inspection was needed to show that it was not an ordinary composite structure. Lines engraved in the black, basaltic surface imitated the joints between building stones.

Treading softly, Conan and Nestor peered into the dark interior. "We shall need light," said Nestor. "I do not care to walk into another slug like that in the dark."

"I don't smell another slug," said Conan, "but the treasure might have another guardian."

He turned back and hewed down a pine sapling that thrust up through the broken pavement. Then he lopped its limbs and cut it into short lengths. Whittling a pile of shavings with his sword, he started a small fire with flint and steel. He split the ends of two of the billets until they were frayed out and then ignited them. The resinous wood burned vigorously. He handed one torch to Nestor, and each of them thrust half the spare billets through his girdle. Then, swords out, they again approached the palace.

Inside the archway, the flickering yellow flames of the

torches were reflected from polished walls of black stone; but underfoot the dust lay inches thick. Several bats, hanging from bits of stone carving overhead, squeaked angrily and whirred away into deeper darkness.

They passed between statues of horrific aspect, set in niches on either side. Dark hallways opened on either hand. They crossed a throne room. The throne, carved of the same black stone as the rest of the building, still stood. Other chairs and divans, being made of wood, had crumbled into dust, leaving a litter of nails, metallic ornaments, and semi-precious stones on the floor.

"It must have stood vacant for thousands of years," whispered Nestor.

They traversed several chambers, which might have been a king's private apartments; but the absence of perishable furnishings made it impossible to tell. They found themselves before a door. Conan put his torch close to it.

It was a stout door, set in an arch of stone and made of massive timbers, bound together with brackets of green-filmed copper. Conan poked the door with his sword. The blade entered easily; a little shower of dusty fragments, pale in the torchlight, sifted down.

"It's rotten," growled Nestor, kicking out. His boot went into the wood almost as easily as Conan's sword had done. A copper fitting fell to the floor with a dull clank.

In a moment they had battered down the rotten timbers in a shower of wood dust. They stooped, thrusting their torches ahead of them into the opening. Light, reflected from silver, gold, and jewels, winked back at them.

Nestor pushed through the opening, then backed out so suddenly that he bumped into Conan. "There are men in there!" he hissed.

"Let's see." Conan thrust his head into the opening and peered right and left. "They're dead. Come on!"

Inside, they stared about them until their torches burned down to their hands and they had to light a new pair. Around the room, seven giant warriors, each at least seven feet tall, sprawled in chairs. Their heads lay against the chair backs and their mouths hung open. They wore the trappings of a bygone era; their plumed copper helmets and the copper scales on their corselets were green with age. Their skins were brown and waxy-looking, like those of mummies, and grizzled beards hung down to their waists. Copper-bladed bills and pikes leaned against the wall beside them or lay on the floor.

In the center of the room rose an altar, of black basalt like the rest of the palace. Near the altar, on the floor, several chests of treasure had lain. The wood of these chests had rotted away; the chests had burst open, letting a glittering drift of treasure pour out on the floor.

Conan stepped close to one of the immobile warriors and touched the man's leg with the point of his sword. The body lay still. He murmured:

"The ancients must have mummified them, as they tell me the priests do with the dead in Stygia."

Nestor looked uneasily at the seven still forms. The feeble flames of the torches seemed unable to push the dense darkness back to the sable walls and roof of the chamber.

The block of black stone in the middle of the room rose to waist height. On its flat, polished top, inlaid in narrow strips of ivory, was a diagram of interlaced circles and triangles. The whole formed a seven-pointed star. The spaces between the lines were marked by symbols in some form of writing that Conan did not recognize. He could read Zamorian and write it after a fashion, and he had smatterings of Hyrkanian and Corinthian; but these cryptic glyphs were beyond him.

In any case, he was more interested in the things that lay on top of the altar. On each point of the star, winking in the ruddy, wavering light of the torches, lay a great, green jewel, larger than a hen's egg. At the center of the diagram stood a green statuette of a serpent with upreared head, apparently carved from jade.

Conan moved his torch close to the seven great, glowing gems. "I want those," he grunted. "You can have the rest."

"No, you don't!" snapped Nestor. "Those are worth more than all the other treasure in this room put together. I will have them!"

Tension crackled between the two men, and their free hands stole toward their hilts. For a space they stood silently, glaring at each other. Then Nestor said:

"Then let us divide them, as we agreed to do."

"You cannot divide seven by two," said Conan. "Let us flip one of these coins for them. The winner takes the seven jewels, while the other man has his pick of the rest. Does that suit you?"

Conan picked a coin out of one of the heaps that marked the places where the chests had lain. Although he had acquired a good working knowledge of coins in his career as a thief, this was entirely unfamiliar. One side bore a face, but whether of a man, a demon, or an owl he could not tell. The other side was covered with symbols like those on the altar.

Conan showed the coin to Nestor. The two treasure hunters grunted agreement. Conan flipped the coin into the air, caught it, and slapped it down on his left wrist. He extended the wrist, with the coin still covered, toward Nestor.

"Heads," said the Gunderman.

Conan removed his hand from the coin. Nestor peered and growled: "Ishtar curse the thing! You win. Hold my torch a moment."

Conan, alert for any treacherous move, took the torch. But Nestor merely untied the strap of his cloak and spread the garment on the dusty floor. He began shoveling handfuls of gold and gems from the heaps on the floor into a pile on the cloak.

"Don't load yourself so heavily that you can't run," said Conan. "We are not out of this yet, and it's a long walk back to Shadizar."

"I can handle it," said Nestor. He gathered up the corners of the cloak, slung the improvised bag over his back, and held out a hand for his torch.

Conan handed it to him and stepped to the altar. One by one he took the great, green jewels and thrust them into the leathern sack that hung from his shoulders.

When all seven had been removed from the altar top, he paused, looking at the jade serpent. "This will fetch a pretty price," he said. Snatching it up, he thrust it, too, into his booty bag.

"Why not take some of the remaining gold and jewels, too?" asked Nestor. "I have all I can carry."

"You've got the best stuff," said Conan. "Besides, I don't need any more. Man, with these I can buy a kingdom! Or a dukedom, anyway, and all the wine I can drink and women I—"

A sound caused the plunderers to whirl, staring wildly. Around the walls, the seven mummified warriors were coming to life. Their heads came up, their mouths closed, and air hissed into their ancient, withered lungs. Their joints creaked like rusty hinges as they picked up their pikes and bills and rose to their feet.

"Run!" yelled Nestor, hurling his torch at the nearest giant and snatching out his sword.

The torch struck the giant in the chest, fell to the floor, and went out. Having both hands free, Conan retained his torch while he drew his sword. The light of the remaining torch flickered feebly on the green of the ancient copper harness as the giants closed in on the pair.

Conan ducked the sweep of a bill and knocked the thrust of a pike aside. Between him and the door, Nestor engaged a giant who was moving to block their escape. The Gunderman parried a thrust and struck a fierce, backhanded blow at his enemy's thigh. The blade bit, but only a little way; it was like chopping wood. The giant staggered, and Nestor hewed at another. The point of a pike glanced off his dented cuirass.

The giants moved slowly, or the treasure hunters would have fallen before their first onset. Leaping, dodging, and whirling, Conan avoided blows that would have stretched him senseless on the dusty floor. Again and again his blade bit into the dry, woody flesh of his assailants. Blows that would have decapitated a living man only staggered these creatures from another age. He landed a chop on the hand of one attacker, maiming the member and causing the giant to drop his pike.

He dodged the thrust of another pike and put every ounce of strength into a low forehand cut at the giant's ankle. The blade bit half through, and the giant crashed to the floor.

"Out!" bellowed Conan, leaping over the fallen body.

He and Nestor raced out the door and through halls and chambers. For an instant Conan feared they were lost, but he caught a glimpse of light ahead. The two dashed out the main portal of the palace. Behind them came the clatter and tramp of the guardians. Overhead, the sky had paled and the stars were going out with the coming of dawn.

"Head for the wall," panted Nestor. "I think we can outrun them."

As they reached the far side of the plaza, Conan glanced back. "Look!" he cried.

One by one, the giants emerged from the palace. And one by one, as they came into the growing light, they sank to the pavement and crumbled into dust, leaving their plumed copper helmets, their scaled cuirasses, and their other accouterments in heaps on the ground.

"Well, that's that," said Nestor. "But how shall we get back into Shadizar without being arrested? It will be daylight long before we get there."

Conan grinned. "There's a way of getting in that we thieves know. Near the northeast corner of the wall stands a clump of trees. If you poke around among the shrubs that mask the wall, you will find a kind of culvert—I suppose to let the water out of the city in heavy rains. It used to be closed by an iron grating, but that has rusted away. If you are not too fat, you can worm your way through it. You come out in a lot where people dump rubbish from houses that have been torn down."

"Good," said Nestor. "I'll—"

A deep rumble cut off his words. The earth heaved and rocked and trembled, throwing him to the ground and staggering the Cimmerian.

"Look out!" yelled Conan.

As Nestor started to scramble up, Conan caught his arm and dragged him back toward the center of the plaza. As he did so, the wall of a nearby building fell over into the plaza. It smashed down just where the two had been standing, but its mighty crash was lost in the thunder of the earthquake.

"Let's get out of here!" shouted Nestor.

Steering by the moon, now low in the western sky, they ran zigzag through the streets. On either side of them, walls and columns leaned, crumbled, and crashed. The noise was deafening. Clouds of dust arose, making the fugitives cough.

Conan skidded to a halt and leaped back to avoid being crushed under the front of a collapsing temple. He staggered as fresh tremors shook the earth beneath him. He scrambled over piles of ruin, some old and some freshly made. He leaped madly out from under a falling column drum. Fragments of stone and brick struck him; one laid open a cut along his jaw. Another glanced from his shin, making him curse by the gods of all the lands he had visited.

At last he reached the city wall. It was a wall no longer, having been shaken down to a low ridge of broken stone.

Limping, coughing, and panting, Conan climbed the ridge and turned to look back. Nestor was no longer with him. Probably, he thought, the Gunderman had been caught under a falling wall. Conan listened but could hear no cry for help.

The rumble of quaking earth and falling masonry died away. The light of the low moon glistened on the vast cloud of dust that covered the city. Then a dawn breeze sprang up and slowly wafted the dust away.

Sitting on the crest of the ridge of ruin that marked the site of the wall, Conan stared back across the site of Larsha. The city bore an aspect entirely different from when he had entered it. Not a single building remained upright. Even the monolithic palace of black basalt, where he and Nestor had found their treasure, had crumbled into a heap of broken blocks. Conan gave up thoughts of going back to the palace on some future occasion to collect the rest of the treasure. An army of workmen would have to clear away the wreckage before the valuables could be salvaged.

All of Larsha had fallen into heaps of rubble. As far as he could see in the growing light, nothing moved in the city. The only sound was the belated fall of an occasional stone.

Conan felt his booty bag, to make sure that he still had his loot, and turned his face westward, towards Shadizar. Behind him, the rising sun shot a spear of light against his broad back.

The following night, Conan swaggered into his favorite tavern, that of Abuletes, in the Maul. The low, smoke-stained room stank of sweat and sour wine. At crowded tables, thieves and murderers drank ale and wine, diced, argued, sang, quarreled, and blustered. It was deemed a dull evening here when at least one customer was not stabbed in a brawl.

Across the room, Conan sighted his sweetheart of the moment, drinking alone at a small table. This was Semiramis, a strongly-built, black-haired woman several years older than the Cimmerian.

"Ho there, Semiramis!" roared Conan, pushing his way across. "I've got something to show you! Abuletes! A jug of your best Kyrian! I'm in luck tonight!"

Had Conan been older, caution would have stopped him from openly boasting of his plunder, let alone displaying it. As it was, he strode up to Semiramis' table and up-ended the leathern sack containing the seven great, green gems.

The jewels cascaded out of the bag, thumped the wine-wet table top—and crumbled instantly into fine green powder, which sparkled in the candlelight.

Conan dropped the sack and stood with his mouth agape, while nearby drinkers burst into raucous laughter.

"Crom and Mannanan!" the Cimmerian breathed at last. "This time, it seems, I was too clever for my own good." Then he bethought him of the jade serpent, still in the bag. "Well, I have something that will pay for a few good carousals, anyway."

Moved by curiosity, Semiramis picked up the sack from the table. Then she dropped it with a scream.

"It's—it's alive!" she cried.

"What—" began Conan, but a shout from the doorway cut him off:

"There he is, men! Seize him!"

A fat magistrate had entered the tavern, followed by a

squad of the night watch, armed with bills. The other customers fell silent, staring woodenly into space as if they knew nothing of Conan or of any of the other riff-raff who were Abuletes' guests.

The magistrate pushed toward Conan's table. Whipping out his sword, the Cimmerian put his back against the wall. His blue eyes blazed dangerously, and his teeth showed in the candle light.

"Take me if you can, dogs!" he snarled. "I've done nothing against your stupid laws!" Out of the side of his mouth, he muttered to Semiramis: "Grab the bag and get out of here. If they get me, it's yours."

"I—I'm afraid of it!" whimpered the woman.

"Oh-ho!" chortled the magistrate, coming forward. "Nothing, eh? Nothing but to rob our leading citizens blind! There's evidence enough to lop your head off a hundred times over! And then you slew Nestor's soldiers and persuaded him to join you in a raid on the ruins of Larsha, eh? We found him earlier this evening, drunk and boasting of his feat. The villain got away from us, but you shan't!"

As the watchmen formed a half-circle around Conan, bills pointing toward his breast, the magistrate noticed the sack on the table. "What's this, your latest loot? We'll see—"

The fat man thrust a hand into the sack. For an instant he fumbled. Then his eyes widened; his mouth opened to emit an appalling shriek. He jerked his hand out of the bag. A jade-green snake, alive and writhing, had thrown a loop around his wrist and had sunk its fangs into his hand.

Cries of horror and amazement arose. A watchman sprang back and fell over a table, smashing mugs and splashing liquors. Another stepped forward to catch the magistrate as he tottered and fell. A third dropped his bill and, screaming hysterically, broke for the door.

Panic seized the customers. Some jammed themselves

into the door, struggling to get out. A couple started fighting with knives, while another thief, locked in combat with a watchman, rolled on the floor. One of the candles was knocked over; then another, leaving the room but dimly lit by the little earthenware lamp over the counter.

In the gloom, Conan caught Semiramis' wrist and hauled her to her feet. He beat the panic-stricken mob aside with the flat of his sword and forced his way through the throng to the door. Out in the night, the two ran, rounding several corners to throw off pursuit. Then they stopped to breathe. Conan said:

"This city will be too cursed hot for me after this. I'm on my way. Good-bye, Semiramis."

"Would you not care to spend a last night with me?"

"Not this time. I must try to catch that rascal Nestor. If the fool hadn't blabbed, the law would not have gotten on my trail so quickly. He has all the treasure a man can carry, while I ended up with naught. Maybe I can persuade him to give me half; if not—" He thumbed the edge of his sword.

Semiramis sighed. "There will always be a hideout for you in Shadizar, while I live. Give me a last kiss."

They embraced briefly. Then Conan was gone, like a shadow in the night.

On the Corinthian Road that leads west from Shadizar, three bowshots from the city walls, stands the fountain of Ninus. According to the story, Ninus was a rich merchant who suffered from a wasting disease. A god visited him in his dreams and promised him a cure if he would build a fountain on the road leading to Shadizar from the west, so that travelers could wash and quench their thirst before entering the city. Ninus built the fountain, but the tale does not tell whether he recovered from his sickness.

Half an hour after his escape from Abuletes' tavern,

Conan found Nestor, sitting on the curbing of Ninus' fountain.

"How did you make out with your seven matchless gems?" asked Nestor.

Conan told what had befallen his share of the loot. "Now," he said, "since—thanks to your loose tongue—I must leave Shadizar, and since I have none of the treasure left, it would be only right for you to divide your remaining portion with me."

Nestor gave a barking, mirthless laugh. "My share? Boy, here is half of what I have left." From his girdle he brought out two pieces of gold and tossed one to Conan, who caught it. "I owe it to you for pulling me away from that falling wall."

"What happened to you?"

"When the watch cornered me in the dive, I managed to cast a table and bowl a few over. Then I picked up the bright stuff in my cloak, slung it over my back, and started for the door. One who tried to halt me I cut down; but another landed a slash on my cloak. The next thing I knew, the whole mass of gold and jewels spilled out on the floor, and everybody—watchmen, magistrate, and customers—joined in a mad scramble for them." He held up the cloak, showing a two-foot rent in the fabric. "Thinking that the treasure would do me no good if my head were adorning a spike over the West Gate, I left while the leaving was good. When I got outside the city, I looked in my mantle, but all I found were those two coins, caught in a fold. You're welcome to one of them."

Conan stood scowling for a moment. Then his mouth twitched into a grin. A low laugh rumbled in his throat; his head went back as he burst into a thunderous guffaw. "A fine pair of treasure-seekers we are! Crom, but the gods have had sport with us! What a joke!"

Nestor smiled wryly. "I am glad you see the amusing

side of it. But after this I do not think Shadizar will be safe for either of us."

"Whither are you bound?" asked Conan.

"I'll head east, to seek a mercenary post in Turan. They say King Yildiz is hiring fighters to whip his raggle-taggle horde into a real army. Why not come with me, lad? You're cut out for a soldier."

Conan shook his head. "Not for me, marching back and forth on the drill ground all day while some fatheaded officer bawls: 'Forward, *march!* Present, *pikes!*' I hear there are good pickings in the West; I'll try that for a while."

"Well, may your barbarous gods go with you," said Nestor. "If you change your mind, ask for me in the barracks at Aghrapur. Farewell!"

"Farewell!" replied Conan. Without further words, he stepped out on the Corinthian Road and soon was lost to view in the night.

The God in the Bowl

Conan's grim adventures in the Tower of the Elephant and in the ruins of Larsha leave him with an aversion to the sorcery of the East. He flees northwestward through Corinthia into Nemedia, the second most powerful of the Hyborian kingdoms after Aquilonia. In the city of Numalia, he resumes his professional activities as a thief.

ARUS THE WATCHMAN grasped his crossbow with shaky hands and felt beads of clammy perspiration ooze out upon his skin, as he stared at the unlovely corpse that sprawled on the polished floor before him. It is not pleasant to come upon Death in a lonely place at midnight.

The watchman stood in a vast corridor lighted by huge candles set in niches along the walls. Between the niches, these walls were covered with black velvet wall-hangings, and between the hangings hung shields and crossed weapons of fantastic make. Here and there, too, stood figures of curious gods—images carved of stone or rare woods, or cast in bronze, iron, or silver—dimly mirrored in the gleaming black floor.

Arus shuddered. He had never become used to the place, although he had worked there as watchman for some months. It was a fantastic establishment, the great museum and antique house that men called Kallian Publico's Temple, with its rarities from all over the world—and now, in the lonesomeness of midnight, Arus stood in the great silent hall and stared at the sprawling corpse that had been the Temple's rich and powerful owner.

It entered even the dull brain of the watchman that the man looked strangely different, now, from the way he had when he rode along the Palian Way in his gilded chariot, arrogant and domineering, with his dark eyes glinting with magnetic vitality. Men who had hated Kallian Publico would scarcely have recognized him now as he lay like a disintegrated tun of fat, his rich robe half torn from him and his purple tunic awry. His face was blackened, his eyes started from his head, and his tongue lolled from his gaping mouth. His fat hands were thrown out as in a gesture of curious futility. On the thick fingers, gems glittered.

"Why did they not take his rings?" muttered the watchman uneasily. Then he started and stared, the short hairs prickling at the nape of his neck. Through the dark silken hangings that masked one of the many doorways, opening into the hall, came a figure.

Arus saw a tall, powerfully-built youth, naked but for a loincloth and sandals strapped high about his ankles. His skin was burned brown as by the suns of the wastelands, and Arus glanced nervously at his broad shoulders, massive chest, and heavy arms. A single look at the moody, broad-browed features told the watchman that the man was no Nemedian. From under a mop of unruly black hair smoldered a pair of dangerous blue eyes. A long sword hung in a leather scabbard from his girdle.

Arus felt his skin crawl. He fingered his crossbow tensely, of half a mind to drive a bolt through the stranger's body without parley, yet fearful of what might happen if he failed to inflict death at the first shot.

The stranger looked at the body on the floor more in curiosity than surprise.

"Why did you kill him?" asked Arus nervously.

The other shook his touseled head. "I did not kill him," he answered, speaking Nemedian with a barbaric accent. "Who is he?"

"Kallian Publico," replied Arus, edging back.

A flicker of interest showed in the moody blue eyes. "The owner of the house?"

"Aye." Arus had edged his way to the wall. Now he took hold of a thick velvet rope, which hung there, and jerked it violently. From the street outside sounded the strident clang of the bell that hung before all shops and establishments to summon the watch.

The stranger started. "Why did you do that?" he asked. "It will fetch the watchman!"

"I am the watchman, knave!" answered Arus, bracing his courage. "Stand where you are. Do not move or I'll loose a bolt through you!"

His finger touched the trigger of his arbalest; the wicked square head of the quarrel pointed straight at the other's broad breast. The stranger scowled, his dark face lowering. He showed no fear but seemed to hesitate, whether to obey the command or to chance a sudden break. Arus licked his lips and his blood turned cold as he plainly saw caution struggle with murderous intent in the foreigner's cloudy eyes.

Then he heard a door crash open and a medley of voices, and he drew a deep breath of grateful amazement. The stranger tensed and glared with the worried look of a startled beast of prey as half a dozen men entered the hall. All but one wore the scarlet tunic of the Numalian police. They were girt with short stabbing swords and carried bills—long-shafted weapons, half pike, half ax.

"What devil's work is this?" exclaimed the foremost man, whose cold gray eyes and lean, keen features, no less than his civilian garments, set him apart from his burly companions.

"By Mitra, Demetrio!" exclaimed Arus. "Fortune is assuredly with me tonight. I had no hope that the watch would answer the summons so swiftly—or that you would be among them!"

"I was making the rounds with Dionus," answered Demetrio. "We were just passing the Temple when the watch-bell clanged. But who is this? Ishtar! The master of the Temple himself!"

"None other," replied Arus, "and foully murdered. It is my duty to walk about the building steadily all night, because, as you know, there is an immense amount of wealth stored here. Kallian Publico had rich patrons—scholars, princes, and wealthy collectors of rarities. Well, only a few minutes ago I tried the door that opens on the portico and found it only bolted, not locked. The door is provided with a bolt, which works from either side, and also a great lock, which can be worked only from without. Only Kallian Publico had a key to that, the very key that now hangs at his girdle.

"I knew something was amiss, for Kallian always locked the door with the great lock when he closed the Temple, and I had not seen him since he left at close of day for his villa in the suburbs. I have a key that works the bolt; I entered and found the body lying as you see it. I have not touched it."

"So." Demetrio's keen eyes swept the somber stranger. "And who is this?"

"The murderer, without doubt!" cried Arus. "He came from that door yonder. He is a northern barbarian of some sort—perhaps a Hyperborean or a Bossonian."

"Who are you?" asked Demetrio.

"I am Conan, a Cimmerian," answered the barbarian.

"Did you kill this man?"

The Cimmerian shook his head.

"Answer me!" snapped the questioner.

An angry glint rose in the moody blue eyes. "I am no dog, to be spoken to thus!"

"Oh, an insolent fellow!" sneered Demetrio's companion, a big man wearing the insignia of prefect of police. "An independent cur! I'll soon knock the impudence out of him. Here, you! Speak up! Why did you murder—"

"Just a moment, Dionus," ordered Demetrio. "Fellow, I am chief of the Inquisitorial Council of the city of Numalia. You had best tell me why you are here and, if you are not the murderer, prove it."

The Cimmerian hesitated. He showed no fear but rather a slight bewilderment, as a barbarian does when confronted by the complexities of civilized systems, the workings of which are so baffling and mysterious to him.

"While he thinks it over," rapped Demetrio, turning to Arus, "tell me: Did you see Kallian Publico leave the Temple this evening?"

"No, my lord; but he's usually gone when I arrive to begin my sentry-go. The great door was bolted and locked."

"Could he have entered the building again without your having seen him?"

"Why, it is possible but hardly probable. If he had returned from his villa, he would of course have come in his chariot, for the way is long—and whoever heard of Kallian Publico traveling otherwise? Even if I had been on the other side of the Temple, I should have heard the wheels of the chariot on the cobblestones. And I've heard no such thing."

"And the door was locked earlier in the night?"

"I'll swear to it. I try all doors several times during the night. The door was locked on the outside until perhaps half an hour ago—that was the last time I tried it ere I found it unlocked."

"You heard no cries or sounds of struggle?"

"No, sir. But that's not strange, for the walls of the Temple are so thick that no sound can pass through them."

"Why go to all this trouble of questions and speculations?" complained the burly prefect. "Here's our man, no doubt about it. Let's take him to the Court of Justice—I'll wring a confession from him if I have to smash his bones to a pulp."

Demetrio looked at the barbarian. "You understand what he said?" asked the inquisitor. "What have you to say?"

"That any man who touches me will quickly be greeting his ancestors in Hell," the Cimmerian ground between his powerful teeth, his eyes glinting angry flames.

"Why did you come here, if not to kill this man?" pursued Demetrio.

"I came to steal," sullenly answered the other.

"To steal what?"

Conan hesitated. "Food."

"That's a lie!" said Demetrio. "You knew there was no food here. Tell me the truth or—"

The Cimmerian laid his hand on his sword hilt, and the gesture was as fraught with menace as the lifting of a tiger's lip to bare its fangs. "Save your bullying for the cowards who fear you," he growled. "I'm no city-bred Nemedian to cringe before your hired dogs. I've slain better men than you for less than this."

Dionus, who had opened his mouth to bellow in wrath, closed it again. The watchmen shifted their bills uncertainly and glanced at Demetrio for orders. Speechless at hearing the all-powerful police thus defied, they expected a command to seize the barbarian. But Demetrio did not give it. Arus glanced from one to the other, wondering what was going on in the keen brain behind Demetrio's hawk face. Perhaps the magistrate feared to arouse the barbaric frenzy of the Cimmerian, or perhaps there was an honest doubt in his mind.

"I have not accused you of killing Kallian," he snapped. "But you must admit that appearances are against you. How did you enter the Temple?"

"I hid in the shadows of the warehouse behind this building," Conan answered grudgingly. "When this dog," he jerked a thumb at Arus, "passed by and rounded the corner, I ran to the wall and scaled it—"

"A lie!" broke in Arus. "No man could climb that straight wall!"

"Have you never seen a Cimmerian scale a sheer cliff?" asked Demetrio. "I am conducting this investigation. Go on, Conan."

"The corner is decorated with carvings," said the Cimmerian. "It was easy to climb. I gained the roof before this dog came around the building again. I found a trap door, fastened with an iron bolt that went through it and was locked on the inside. I hewed the bolt in twain—"

Arus, remembering the thickness of the bolt, gasped and moved back from the barbarian, who scowled abstractedly at him and continued:

"I passed through the trap door and entered an upper chamber. I did not pause but came straightway to the stair—"

"How did you know where the stair was? Only Kallian's servants and his rich patrons were ever allowed in those upper rooms."

Conan stared in stubborn silence.

"What did you do after you reached the stair?" demanded Demetrio.

"I came straight down it," muttered the Cimmerian. "It let into the chamber behind yonder curtained door. As I came down the stairs, I heard the opening of another door. When I looked through the hanging, I saw this dog standing over the dead man."

"Why did you come from your hiding place?"

"Because at first I thought him another thief, come to steal that which—" The Cimmerian checked himself.

"—That which you yourself had come after!" finished

Demetrio. "You did not tarry in the upper rooms, where the richest goods are stored. You were sent here by someone who knows the Temple well, to steal some special thing!"

"And to kill Kallian Publico!" exclaimed Dionus. "By Mitra, we've hit it! Seize him, men—we'll have a confession before morning!"

With a foreign curse Conan leaped back, whipping out his sword with a viciousness that made the keen blade hum.

"Back, if you value your curs' lives!" he snarled. "Because you dare to torture shopkeepers and strip and beat harlots to make them talk, don't think you can lay your fat paws on a hillman! Fumble with your bow, watchman, and I'll burst your guts with my heel!"

"Wait!" said Demetrio. "Call off your dogs, Dionus. I'm still not convinced that he is the murderer." Demetrio leaned towards Dionus and whispered something that Arus could not catch, but which he suspected of being a plan to trick Conan into parting with his sword.

"Very well," grunted Dionus. "Fall back, men, but keep an eye on him."

"Give me your sword," said Demetrio to Conan.

"Take it if you can!" snarled Conan.

The inquisitor shrugged. "Very well. But do not try to escape. Men with crossbows watch the house on the outside."

The barbarian lowered his blade, although he relaxed only slightly the tense watchfulness of his attitude. Demetrio turned again to the corpse.

"Strangled," he muttered. "Why strangle him when a sword stroke is so much quicker and surer? These Cimmerians are born sword in hand, as it were; I never heard of their killing a man in this manner."

"Perhaps to divert suspicion," said Dionus.

"Possibly." Demetrio felt the body with experienced hands. "Dead at least half an hour. If Conan tells the truth about when he entered the Temple, he could hardly have slain the man before Arus entered. True, he might be lying—he might have broken in earlier."

"I climbed the wall after Arus made his last round," growled Conan.

"So you say." Demetrio brooded over the dead man's throat, which had been crushed to a pulp of purplish flesh. The head sagged awry on splintered vertebrae. Demetrio shook his head in doubt. "Why should a murderer use a cable thicker than a man's arm? And what terrible constriction could have so crushed his neck?"

He rose and walked to the nearest door opening into the corridor.

"Here is a bust knocked from a stand near the door," he said, "and here the floor is scratched, and the hangings in the doorway are pulled awry . . . Kallian Publico must have been attacked in that room. Perhaps he broke away from his assailant, or dragged the fellow with him as he fled. Anyway, he staggered out into the corridor, where the murderer must have followed and finished him."

"And if this heathen isn't the murderer, then where is he?" demanded the prefect.

"I have not exonerated the Cimmerian yet," said the inquisitor. "But we'll investigate that room—"

He halted and wheeled, listening. From the street sounded a rattle of chariot wheels, which approached and then abruptly ceased.

"Dionus!" barked the inquisitor. "Send two men to find that chariot. Bring the driver here."

"From the sound," said Arus, who was familiar with all the noises of the street, "I should say that it stopped in front of Promero's house, just on the other side of the silk merchant's shop."

"Who is Promero?" asked Demetrio.

"Kallian Publico's chief clerk."

"Fetch him here with the driver," said Demetrio.

Two guardsmen clomped away. Demetrio still studied the body; Dionus, Arus, and the remaining policemen watched Conan, who stood sword in hand like a bronze figure of brooding menace. Presently sandaled feet echoed outside, and the two guardsmen entered with a strongly-built, dark-skinned man in the leather helmet and long tunic of a charioteer, with a whip in his hand, and a small, timid-looking individual typical of that class which, risen from the ranks of artisans, supplies right-hand men for wealthy merchants and traders. The small man recoiled with a cry from the sprawling bulk on the floor.

"Oh, I knew evil would come of this!" he wailed.

Demetrio said: "You are Promero, the chief clerk, I suppose. And you?"

"Enaro, Kallian Publico's charioteer."

"You do not seem overly moved at the sight of his corpse," observed Demetrio.

The dark eyes flashed. "Why should I be moved? Someone has only done that which I longed to do but dared not."

"So!" murmured the inquisitor. "Are you a free man?"

Enaro's eyes were bitter as he drew aside his tunic, showing the brand of the debtor slave on his shoulder.

"Did you know your master was coming here tonight?"

"Nay. I brought the chariot to the Temple this evening as usual. He entered it, and I drove toward his villa. However, before we came to the Palian Way, he ordered me to turn and drive him back. He seemed much agitated."

"And did you drive him back to the Temple?"

"No. He bade me stop at Promero's house. There he

dismissed me, ordering me to return for him shortly after midnight."

"What time was this?"

"Shortly after dusk. The streets were almost deserted."

"What did you do then?"

"I returned to the slave quarters, where I remained until it was time to go to Promero's house. I drove straight there, and your men seized me as I talked with Promero in his door."

"Have you no idea why Kallian went to Promero's house?"

"He didn't speak of his business to his slaves."

Demetrio turned to Promero. "What do you know about this?"

"Naught." The clerk's teeth chattered as he spoke.

"Did Kallian Publico come to your house as the charioteer says?"

"Aye, sir."

"How long did he stay?"

"Only a short while. Then he left."

"Did he go from your house to the Temple?"

"I do not know!" The clerk's voice was shrill.

"Why did he come to your house?"

"To—to talk matters of business with me."

"You lie," said Demetrio. "*Why did he come to your house?*"

"I don't know! I know nothing!" Promero's voice became hysterical. "I had nothing to do with it—"

"Make him talk, Dionus," snapped Demetrio. Dionus grunted and nodded to one of his men who, grinning savagely, moved toward the two captives.

"Do you know who I am?" he growled, thrusting his head forward and staring at his shrinking prey.

"You're Posthumo," answered the clerk sullenly. "You gouged out a girl's eye in the Court of Justice because she would not incriminate her lover."

"I always get what I go after!" bellowed the guardsman. The veins in his thick neck swelled and his face grew purple as he seized the wretched clerk by the collar of his tunic, twisting it so that the man was half strangled.

"Speak up, rat!" he growled. "Answer the inquisitor!"

"Oh, Mitra, mercy!" screamed the wretch. "I swear—"

Posthumo slapped him terrifically, first on one side of the face and then on the other, then flung him to the floor and kicked him with vicious accuracy.

"Mercy!" moaned the victim. "I'll tell—I'll tell anything—"

"Then get up, you cur!" roared Posthumo. "Don't lie there whining!"

Dionus shot a quick glance at Conan to see if he were properly impressed. "You see what happens to those who cross the police," he said.

Conan spat with a sneer of contempt. "He's a weakling and a fool," he growled. "Let one of you touch me, and I'll spill his guts on the floor."

"Are you ready to talk?" asked Demetrio wearily.

"All I know," sobbed the clerk as he dragged himself to his feet, whimpering like a beaten dog, "is that Kallian came to my house shortly after I arrived—I left the temple when he did—and sent his chariot away. He threatened me with dismissal if I ever spoke of it. I am a poor man, my lords, without friends or favor. Without my position with him, I shall starve."

"What's that to me?" said Demetrio. "How long did he remain at your house?"

"Until perhaps half an hour before midnight. Then he left, saying that he was going to the Temple and would return after he had done what he wished to do there."

"What did he mean to do there?"

Promero hesitated, but a shuddering glance at the grinning Posthumo, doubling his huge first, soon opened his lips. "There was something in the Temple he wished to examine."

"But why should he come here alone, and in such secrecy?"

"Because the thing was not his property. It arrived at dawn, in a caravan from the south. The men of the caravan knew nothing of it, except that it had been placed with them by the men of a caravan from Stygia and was meant for Caranthes of Hanumar, priest of Ibis. The master of the caravan had been paid by these other men to deliver it directly to Caranthes, but the rascal wished to proceed straight to Aquilonia by the road on which Hanumar does not lie. So he asked if he might leave it in the Temple until Caranthes could send for it.

"Kallian agreed and told him that he himself would send a servant to inform Caranthes. But, after the men had gone and I spoke of the runner, Kallian forbade me to send him. He sat brooding over what the men had left."

"And what was that?"

"A sort of sarcophagus, such as is found in ancient Stygian tombs. But this one was round, like a covered metal bowl. Its composition was like copper, but harder, and it was carved with hieroglyphics like those on ancient menhirs in southern Stygia. The lid was made fast to the body by carven copperlike bands."

"What was in it?"

"The men of the caravan did not know. They only said that those who gave it to them said that it was a priceless relic found among the tombs far beneath the pyramids and sent to Caranthes 'because of the love which the sender bore the priest of Ibis.' Kallian Publico believed that it contained the diadem of the giant-kings, of the people who dwelt in that dark land before the ancestors of the Stygians came there. He showed me a design carved on the lid, which he swore was the shape of the diadem that legend tells us the monster-kings wore.

"He determined to open the bowl to see what it contained. He became like a madman when he thought of the fabled diadem, set with strange jewels known only to the ancient race, a single one of which would be worth more than all the jewels of the modern world.

"I warned him against it. But, a short time before midnight, he went alone to the Temple, hiding in the shadows until the watchman had passed to the other side of the building, then letting himself in with his belt key. I watched him from the shadows of the silk shop until he entered, then returned to my own house. If the diadem, or anything else of great value, were in the bowl, he intended hiding it elsewhere in the Temple and slipping out again. Then on the morrow he would raise a great hue and cry, saying that thieves had broken into his house and stolen Caranthes' property. None would know of his prowlings but the charioteer and I, and neither of us would betray him."

"But the watchman?" objected Demetrio.

"Kallian did not intend to be seen by him; he planned to have him crucified as an accomplice of the thieves," answered Promero. Arus gulped and turned pale as the duplicity of his employer came home to him.

"Where is this sarcophagus?" asked Demetrio. Promero pointed, the inquisitor grunted. "So! The very room in which Kallian must have been attacked."

Promero twisted his thin hands. "Why should a man in Stygia send Caranthes a gift? Ancient gods and queer mummies have come up the caravan roads before, but who loves the priest of Ibis so well in Stygia, where they still worship the arch-demon Set, who coils among the tombs in the darkness? The god Ibis has fought Set since the first dawn of the earth, and Caranthes has fought Set's priests all his life. There is something dark and hidden here."

"Show us this sarcophagus," commanded Demetrio, and Promero hesitantly led the way. All followed, including Conan, who was apparently heedless of the wary eye the guardsmen kept upon him and seemed merely curious. They passed through the torn hangings and entered the room, which was more dimly lit than the corridor. Doors on either side gave into other chambers, and the walls were lined with fantastic images, gods of strange lands and far peoples. Promero cried out sharply.

"Look! The bowl! It's open—and empty!"

In the center stood a strange black cylinder, nearly four feet in height and perhaps three feet in diameter at its widest circumference, which was halfway between the top and the bottom. The heavy, carven lid lay on the floor, and beside it a hammer and a chisel. Demetrio looked inside, puzzled an instant over the dim hieroglyphs, and turned to Conan.

"Is this what you came to steal?"

The barbarian shook his head. "How could one man bear it away?"

"The bands were cut with this chisel," mused Demetrio, "and in haste. There are marks where misstrokes of the hammer dinted the metal. We may assume that Kallian opened the bowl. Someone was hiding nearby—possibly in the hangings of the doorway. When Kallian had the bowl open, the murderer sprang upon him—or he might have killed Kallian and opened the bowl himself."

"This is a grisly thing," shuddered the clerk. "It is too ancient to be holy. Whoever saw metal like that? It seems harder than Aquilonian steel, yet see how it is corroded and eaten away in spots. And look—here on the lid!" Promero pointed a shaky finger. "What would you say that was?"

Demetrio bent closer to the carven design. "I should say it represented a crown of some sort," he grunted.

"No!" exclaimed Promero. "I warned Kallian, but he would not believe me! It is a scaled serpent coiled with its tail in its mouth. It is the sign of Set, the Old Serpent, the god of the Stygians! This bowl is too old for a human world—it is a relic of the time when Set walked the earth in the form of a man. Perhaps the race that sprang from his loins laid the bones of their kings away in such cases as this!"

"And you'll say that those moldering bones rose up, strangled Kallian Publico, and then walked away?"

"It was no man who was laid to rest in that bowl," whispered the clerk, his eyes wide and staring. "What man could lie in it?"

Demetrio swore. "If Conan is not the murderer, the slayer is still somewhere in this building. Dionus and Arus, remain here with me, and you three prisoners stay here, too. The rest of you, search the house! The murderer—if he got away before Arus found the body—could only have escaped by the way Conan used in entering, and in that case the barbarian would have seen him—if he is telling the truth."

"I saw no one but this dog," growled Conan, indicating Arus.

"Of course not, because you're the murderer," said Dionus. "We're wasting time, but we'll search as a formality. And if we find no one, I promise that you shall burn! Remember the law, my black-haired savage: For slaying an artisan you go to the mines; a tradesman, you hang; a gentleman, you burn!"

Conan bared his teeth for answer. The men began their search. The listeners in the chamber heard them stamping upstairs and down, moving objects, opening doors, and bellowing to one another through the rooms.

"Conan," said Demetrio, "you know what it means if they find no one."

"I did not kill him," snarled the Cimmerian. "If he had sought to hinder me I'd have split his skull; but I did not see him until I sighted his corpse."

"Someone sent you here to steal, at least," said Demetrio, "and by your silence you incriminate yourself in this murder as well. The mere fact of your being here is enough to send you to the mines, whether you admit your guilt or not. But, if you tell the whole tale, you may save yourself from the stake."

"Well," answered the barbarian grudgingly, "I came here to steal the Zamorian diamond goblet. A man gave me a diagram of the Temple and told me where to look for it. It is kept in that room," Conan pointed, "in a niche in the floor under a copper Shemitish god."

"He speaks truth there," said Promero. "I thought not half a dozen men in the world knew the secret of that hiding place."

"And if you had secured it," Dionus sneered, "would you really have taken it to the man who hired you?"

Again the smoldering eyes flashed resentment. "I am no dog," the barbarian muttered. "I keep my word."

"Who sent you here?" Demetrio demanded, but Conan kept a sullen silence. The guardsmen straggled back from their search.

"There's no man hiding in this house," they said. "We've ransacked the place. We found the trap door in the roof through which the barbarian entered, and the bolt he cut in half. A man escaping that way would have been seen by our guards, unless he fled before we came. Besides, he would have had to stack furniture to reach the trap door from below, and that has not been done. Why could he not have gone out the front door just before Arus came around the building?"

"Because," said Demetrio, "the door was bolted on the inside, and the only keys that will work that bolt are the one belonging to Arus and the one that still hangs on the girdle of Kallian Publico."

Another said: "I think I saw the rope used by the murderer."

"Where is it, fool?" exclaimed Dionus.

"In the chamber adjoining this one," answered the guard. "It is a thick black cable wrapped about a marble pillar. I couldn't reach it."

He led the way into a room filled with marble statuary and pointed to a tall column. Then he halted and stared.

"It's gone!" he cried.

"It was never there," snorted Dionus.

"By Mitra, it was! Coiled about the pillar just above those carven leaves. It is so shadowy up there that I could not tell much—but it was there."

"You're drunk," said Demetrio, turning away. "That's too high for a man to reach, and nobody could climb that smooth pillar."

"A Cimmerian could," muttered one of the men.

"Possibly. Say that Conan strangled Kallian, tied the cable around the pillar, crossed the corridor, and hid in the room where the stair is. How, then could he have removed it after you saw it? He has been among us ever since Arus found the body. No, I tell you that Conan did not commit the murder. I believe the real slayer killed Kallian to secure whatever was in the bowl and is hiding now in some secret nook of the Temple. If we cannot find him, we shall have to blame the barbarian, to satisfy justice, but—where is Promero?"

They had straggled back to the silent body in the corridor. Dionus bellowed for Promero, who came from the room in which stood the empty bowl. He was shaking and his face was white.

"What now, man?" exclaimed Demetrio irritably.

"I found a symbol on the bottom of the bowl!" chattered Promero. "Not an ancient hieroglyphic, but a symbol freshly carved! The mark of Thoth-Amon, the Stygian sorcerer, Caranthes' deadly foe! He must have found the bowl in some grisly cavern below the haunted pyramids! The gods of old times did not die as men die—they fell into long slumbers, and their worshipers locked them in sarcophagi, so that no alien hand might break their sleep! Thoth-Amon sent death to Caranthes—Kallian's greed caused him to loose this horror—and it is lurking somewhere near us—even now it may be creeping upon us—"

"You gibbering fool!" roared Dionus, striking Promero heavily across the mouth. "Well, Demetrio," he said, turning to the inquisitor, "I see nought for it but to arrest this barbarian—"

The Cimmerian cried out, glaring toward the door of a chamber that adjoined the room of statues. "Look!" he exclaimed. "I saw something move in that room—I saw it through the hangings. Something that crossed the floor like a dark shadow."

"Bah;" snorted Posthumo. "We searched that room—"

"He saw something!" Promero's voice shrilled and cracked with hysterical excitement. "This place is accursed! Something came out of the sarcophagus and killed Kallian Publico! It hid where no man could hide, and now it lurks in that chamber! Mitra defend us from the powers of darkness!" He caught Dionus' sleeve with claw-like fingers. "Search that room again, my lord!"

As the prefect shook off the clerk's frenzied grip, Posthumo said: "You shall search it yourself, clerk!" Grasping Promero by neck and girdle, he propelled the screaming wretch before him to the door, where he paused and hurled him into the room so violently that the clerk fell and lay half stunned.

"Enough," growled Dionus, eyeing the silent Cimmerian. The prefect lifted his hand, and tension crackled in the air, when an interruption came. A guardsman entered, dragging a slender, richly-dressed figure.

"I saw him slinking about the back of the Temple," quoth the guard, looking for commendation. Instead, he received curses that lifted his hair.

"Release that gentleman, you bungling fool!" shouted the prefect. "Know you not Aztrias Petanius, the nephew of the governor?"

The abashed guard fell away, while the foppish young nobleman fastidiously brushed his embroidered sleeve.

"Save your apologies, good Dionus," he lisped. "All in line of duty, I know. I was returning from a late revel and walking to rid my brain of the fumes of the wine. What have we here? By Mitra, is it murder?"

"Murder it is, my lord," answered the prefect. "But we have a suspect who, though Demetrio seems to have doubts on the matter, will doubtless go to the stake for it."

"A vicious-looking brute," murmured the young aristocrat. "How can any doubt his guilt? Never before have I seen such a villainous countenance."

"Oh, yes you have, you scented dog," snarled the Cimmerian, "when you hired me to steal the Zamorian goblet for you. Revels, eh? Bah! You were waiting in the shadows for me to hand you the loot. I would not have revealed your name if you had given me fair words. Now tell these dogs that you saw me climb the wall after the watchman made his last round, so they shall know I had no time to kill this fat swine before Arus entered and found the body."

Demetrio looked quickly at Aztrias, who did not change color. "If what he says is true, my lord," said the inquisitor, "it clears him of the murder, and we can easily hush up the matter of attempted theft. The Cimmerian merits ten years at hard labor for housebreaking; but, if you say the word, we'll arrange for him to escape, and none but us shall ever know about it. I understand—you wouldn't be the first young nobleman who had to resort to such means to pay gambling debts and the like—but you can rely on our discretion."

Conan looked expectantly at the young noble, but Aztrias shrugged his slender shoulders and covered a yawn with a delicate white hand.

"I know him not," he answered. "He is mad to say I hired him. Let him take his just deserts. He has a strong back, and the toil in the mines will be good for him."

Conan, eyes blazing, started as if stung. The guards tensed, gripping their bills; then relaxed as he dropped his head, as if in sullen resignation. Arus could not tell whether or not he was watching them from under his heavy black brows.

The Cimmerian struck with no more warning than a striking cobra; his sword flashed in the candlelight. Aztrias began a shriek that ended as his head flew from his shoulders in a shower of blood, the features frozen into a white mask of horror.

Demetrio drew a dagger and stepped forward for a stab. Catlike, Conan wheeled and thrust murderously for the inquisitor's groin. Demetrio's instinctive recoil barely deflected the point, which sank into his thigh, glanced from the bone, and plowed out through the outer side of his leg. Demetrio sank to one knee with a groan of agony.

Conan did not pause. The bill that Dionus flung up saved the prefect's skull from the whistling blade, which turned slightly as it cut through the shaft, glanced from the side of his head, and sheared off his right ear. The blinding speed of the barbarian paralyzed the police. Half of them would have been down before they had a chance to fight back except that the burly Posthumo, more by luck than by skill, threw his arms around the Cimmerian, pinioning his sword arm. Conan's left hand leaped to the guard's head, and Posthumo fell away shrieking, clutching a gaping red socket where an eye had been.

Conan bounded back from the waving bills. His leap carried him outside the ring of his foes to where Arus had bent over to re-cock his crossbow. A savage kick in the belly dropped him, green-faced and gagging, and Conan's sandaled heel crunched square in the watchman's mouth. The wretch screamed through a ruin of splintered teeth, blowing bloody froth from his mangled lips.

Then all were frozen in their tracks by the soul-shaking horror of a scream, which rose from the chamber into which Posthumo had hurled Promero. From the velvet-hung door the clerk came reeling and stood, shaking with great silent sobs, tears running down his pasty face and dripping from his loose, sagging lips, like an idiot-babe weeping.

All halted to stare at him aghast—Conan with his dripping sword, the police with their lifted bills, Demetrio crouching on the floor and striving to staunch the blood that jetted from the great gash in his thigh, Dionus clutching the bleeding stump of his severed ear, Arus weeping and spitting out fragments of broken teeth—even Posthumo ceased his howls and blinked with his good eye.

Promero reeled out into the corridor and fell stiffly before them, screeching in an unbearable high-pitched laughter of madness: "The god has a long reach; ha-ha-ha! Oh, a cursed long reach!" Then, with a frightful convulsion, he stiffened and lay grinning vacantly at the shadowy ceiling.

"He's dead!" whispered Dionus in tones of awe, forgetting his own hurt and the barbarian who stood with dripping sword so near him. He bent over the body, then straightened, his pig's eyes popping. "He's not wounded. In Mitra's name, *what is in that chamber?*"

Then horror swept over them, and they ran screaming for the outer door. The guards, dropping their bills, jammed into it in a clawing and shrieking mob and burst through like madmen. Arus followed, and the half-blind

Posthumo blundered blindly after his fellows, squealing like a wounded pig and begging them not to leave him behind. He fell among the rearmost, and they knocked him down and trampled him, screaming in their fear. He crawled after them, and behind him came Demetrio, limping along and grasping his blood-spurting thigh. Police, charioteer, watchman, and officials, wounded or whole, they burst screaming into the street, where the men watching the house took panic and joined in the flight, not waiting to ask why.

Conan stood in the great corridor alone, save for the three corpses on the floor. The barbarian shifted his grip on his sword and strode into the chamber. It was hung with rich silken tapestries. Silken cushions and couches lay strewn about in careless profusion, and over a heavy, gilded screen a Face looked at the Cimmerian.

Conan stared in wonder at the cold, classic beauty of that countenance, whose like he had never seen among the sons of men. Neither weakness, nor mercy, nor cruelty, nor kindness, nor any other human emotion showed in those features. They might have been the marble mask of a god, carved by a master hand, except for the unmistakable life in them—life cold and strange, such as the Cimmerian had never known and could not understand. He thought fleetingly of the marble perfection of the body concealed by the screen; it must be perfect, he thought, since the face was so inhumanly beautiful.

But he could see only the finely-molded head, which swayed from side to side. The full lips opened and spoke a single word, in a rich, vibrant tone like the golden chimes that ring in the jungle-lost temples of Khitai. It was an unknown tongue, forgotten before the kingdoms of man arose, but Conan knew that it meant: "Come!"

And the Cimmerian came, with a desperate leap and humming slash of his sword. The beautiful head flew from the body, struck the floor to one side of the screen, and rolled a little way before coming to rest.

Then Conan's skin crawled, for the screen shook and heaved with the convulsions of something behind. He had seen and heard men die by the scores, and never had he heard a human being make such sounds in his death-throes. There was a thrashing, floundering noise. The screen shook, swayed, tottered, leaned forward, and fell with a metallic crash at Conan's feet. He looked beyond it.

Then the full horror of it rushed over the Cimmerian. He fled, nor did he slacken his headlong flight until the spires of Numalia faded into the dawn behind him. The thought of Set was like a nightmare, and the children of Set who once ruled the earth and who now slept in their nighted caverns below the black pyramids. Behind that gilded screen had lain no human body—only the shimmering, headless coils of a gigantic serpent.

Rogues in the House

Somewhat disillusioned about the possibility of avoiding supernatural obstacles to the orderly pursuit of his calling, and having made Nemedia much too hot to hold him, Conan drifts south again into Corinthia, where, in one of the small city-states making up that country, he continues to occupy himself with the unlawful appropriation of private property. He is about nineteen at this time, harder and more experienced if not more given to unprofitable caution than when he first appeared in the southern kingdoms.

"One fled, one dead, one sleeping in a golden bed."

—Old Rime

1

At a court festival, Nabonidus, the Red Priest, who was the real ruler of the city, touched Murilo, the young aristocrat, courteously on the arm. Murilo turned to meet the priest's enigmatic gaze, and to wonder at the hidden meaning therein. No words passed between them, but Nabonidus bowed and handed Murilo a small gold cask. The young nobleman, knowing that Nabonidus did nothing without reason, excused himself at the first opportunity and returned hastily to his chamber. There he opened the cask and found within a human ear, which he recognized by a peculiar scar upon it. He broke into a profuse sweat and was no longer in doubt about the meaning in the Red Priest's glance.

But Murilo, for all his scented black curls and foppish

apparel, was no weakling to bend his neck to the knife without a struggle. He did not know whether Nabonidus was merely playing with him or giving him a chance to go into voluntary exile, but the fact that he was still alive and at liberty proved that he was to be given at least a few hours, probably for meditation. However, he needed no meditation for decision; what he needed was a tool. And Fate furnished that tool, working among the dives and brothels of the squalid quarters even while the young nobleman shivered and pondered in the part of the city occupied by the purple-towered marble and ivory palaces of the aristocracy.

There was a priest of Anu whose temple, rising at the fringe of the slum district, was the scene of more than devotions. The priest was fat and full-fed, and he was at once a fence for stolen articles and a spy for the police. He worked a thriving trade both ways, because the district on which he bordered was the Maze, a tangle of muddy, winding alleys and sordid dens, frequented by the boldest thieves in the kingdom. Daring above all were a Gunderman deserter from the mercenaries and a barbaric Cimmerian. Because of the priest of Anu, the Gunderman was taken and hanged in the market square. But the Cimmerian fled, and learning in devious ways of the priest's treachery, he entered the temple of Anu by night and cut off the priest's head. There followed a great turmoil in the city, but search for the killer proved fruitless until a woman betrayed him to the authorities and led a captain of the guard and his squad to the hidden chamber where the barbarian lay drunk.

Waking to stupefied but ferocious life when they seized him, he disemboweled the captain, burst through his assailants, and would have escaped but for the liquor that still clouded his senses. Bewildered and half blinded, he missed the open door in his headlong flight and dashed his head against the stone wall so terrifically that he knocked himself senseless. When he came to, he was in the strongest dungeon in the city, shackled to the wall with chains not even his barbaric thews could break.

To this cell came Murilo, masked and wrapped in a wide black cloak. The Cimmerian surveyed him with interest, thinking him the executioner sent to dispatch him. Murilo set him at rights and regarded him with no less interest. Even in the dim light of the dungeon, with his limbs loaded with chains, the primitive power of the man was evident. His mighty body and thick-muscled limbs combined the strength of a grizzly with the quickness of a panther. Under his tangled black mane his blue eyes blazed with unquenchable savagery.

"Would you like to live?" asked Murilo. The barbarian grunted, new interest glinting in his eyes.

"If I arrange for your escape, will you do a favor for me?" the aristocrat asked.

The Cimmerian did not speak, but the intentness of his gaze answered for him.

"I want you to kill a man for me."

"Who?"

Murilo's voice sank to a whisper. "Nabonidus, the king's priest!"

The Cimmerian showed no sign of surprise or perturbation. He had none of the fear or reverence for authority that civilization instills in men. King or beggar, it was all one to him. Nor did he ask why Murilo had come to him, when the quarters were full of cutthroats outside prisons.

"When am I to escape?" he demanded.

"Within the hour. There is but one guard in this part of the dungeon at night. He can be bribed; he *has* been bribed. See, here are the keys to your chains. I'll remove them and, after I have been gone an hour, the guard, Athicus, will unlock the door to your cell. You will bind him with strips torn from your tunic; so when he is found, the authorities will think you were rescued from the outside and will not suspect him. Go at once to the house of the Red Priest and kill him. Then go to the Rat's Den, where a man will meet you and give you a pouch of gold and a horse. With those you can escape from the city and flee the country."

"Take off these cursed chains now," demanded the Cimmerian. "And have the guard bring me food. By Crom, I have lived on moldy bread and water for a whole day, and I am nigh to famishing."

"It shall be done; but remember—you are not to escape until I have had time to reach my house."

Freed of his chains, the barbarian stood up and stretched his heavy arms, enormous in the gloom of the dungeon. Murilo again felt that if any man in the world could accomplish the task he had set, this Cimmerian could. With a few repeated instructions he left the prison, first directing Athicus to take a platter of beef and ale in to the prisoner. He knew he could trust the guard, not only because of the money he had paid, but also because of certain information he possessed regarding the man.

When he returned to his chamber, Murilo was in full control of his fears. Nabonidus would strike through the king—of that he was certain. And since the royal guardsmen were not knocking at his door, it was as certain that the priest had said nothing to the king, so far. Tomorrow he would speak, beyond a doubt—if he lived to see tomorrow.

Murilo believed the Cimmerian would keep faith with him. Whether the man would be able to carry out his purpose remained to be seen. Men had attempted to assassinate the Red Priest before, and they had died in hideous and nameless ways. But they had been products of the cities of men, lacking the wolfish instincts of the barbarian. The instant that Murilo, turning the gold cask with its severed ear in his hands, had learned through his secret channels that the Cimmerian had been captured, he had seen a solution of his problem.

In his chamber again, he drank a toast to the man, whose name was Conan, and to his success that night. And while he was drinking, one of his spies brought him the news that Athicus had been arrested and thrown into prison. The Cimmerian had not escaped.

Murilo felt his blood turn to ice again. He could see in this twist of fate only the sinister hand of Nabonidus, and an eery obsession began to grow on him that the Red Priest was more than human—a sorcerer who read the minds of his victims and pulled strings on which they danced like puppets. With despair came desperation. Girding a sword beneath his black cloak, he left his house by a hidden way and hurried through the deserted streets. It was just at midnight when he came to the house of Nabonidus, looming blackly among the walled gardens that separated it from the surrounding estates.

The wall was high but not impossible to negotiate. Nabonidus did not put his trust in mere barriers of stone. It was what was inside the wall that was to be feared. What these things were Murilo did not know precisely. He knew there was at least a huge savage dog that roamed the gardens and had on occasion torn an intruder to pieces as a hound rends a rabbit. What else there might be he did not care to conjecture. Men who had been allowed to enter the house on brief, legitimate business, reported that Nabonidus dwelt among rich furnishings, yet simply, attended by a surprisingly small number of servants. Indeed, they mentioned only one as having been visible—a tall, silent man called Joka. Some one else, presumably a slave, had been heard moving about in the recesses of the house, but this person no one had ever seen. The greatest mystery of that mysterious house was Nabonidus himself, whose power of intrigue and grasp on international politics had made him the strongest man in the kingdom. People, chancellor and king moved puppetlike on the strings he worked.

Murilo scaled the wall and dropped down into the gardens, which were expanses of shadow, darkened by clumps of shrubbery and waving foliage. No light shone in the windows of the house, which loomed so blackly among the trees. The young nobleman stole stealthily yet swiftly through the shrubs. Momentarily he expected to hear the baying of the great dog and to see its giant body hurtle through the shadows. He doubted the effectiveness of his sword against such an attack, but he did not hesitate. As well die beneath the fangs of a beast as the ax of the headsman.

He stumbled over something bulky and yielding. Bending close in the dim starlight, he made out a limp shape on the ground. It was the dog that guarded the gardens, and it was dead. Its neck was broken and it bore what seemed to be the marks of great fangs. Murilo felt that no human being had done this. The beast had met a monster more savage than itself. Murilo glared nervously at the cryptic masses of bush and shrub; then, with a shrug of his shoulders, he approached the silent house.

The first door he tried proved to be unlocked. He entered warily, sword in hand, and found himself in a long, shadowy hallway dimly illumined by a light that gleamed through the hangings at the other end. Complete silence hung over the whole house. Murilo glided along the hall and halted to peer through the hangings. He looked into a lighted room, over the windows of which velvet curtains were drawn so closely as to allow no beam to shine through. The room was empty, in so far as human life was concerned, but it had a grisly occupant, nevertheless. In the midst of a wreckage of furniture and torn hangings that told of a fearful struggle, lay the body of a man. The form lay on its belly, but the head was twisted about so that the chin rested behind a shoulder. The features, contorted into an awful grin, seemed to leer at the horrified nobleman.

For the first time that night, Murilo's resolution wavered. He cast an uncertain glance back the way he had come. Then the memory of the headsman's block and ax steeled him, and he crossed the room, swerving to avoid the grinning horror sprawled in its midst. Though he had never seen the man before, he knew from former descriptions that it was Joka, Nabonidus' saturnine servant.

He peered through a curtained door into a broad circular chamber, banded by a gallery half-way between the polished floor and the lofty ceiling. This chamber was furnished as if for a king. In the midst of it stood an ornate mahogany table, loaded with vessels of wine and rich viands. And Murilo stiffened. In a great chair whose broad back was toward him, he saw a figure whose habiliments were familiar. He glimpsed an arm in a red sleeve resting on the arm of the chair; the head, clad in the familiar scarlet hood of the gown, was bent forward as if in meditation. Just so had Murilo seen Nabonidus sit a hundred times in the royal court.

Cursing the pounding of his own heart, the young nobleman stole across the chamber, sword extended, his whole frame poised for the thrust. His prey did not move, nor seem to hear his cautious advance. Was the Red Priest asleep, or was it a corpse which slumped in that great chair? The length of a single stride separated Murilo from his enemy, when suddenly the man in the chair rose and faced him.

The blood went suddenly from Murilo's features. His sword fell from his fingers and rang on the polished floor. A terrible cry broke from his livid lips; it was followed by the thud of a falling body. Then once more silence reigned over the house of the Red Priest.

2

Shortly after Murilo left the dungeon where Conan the Cimmerian was confined, Athicus brought the prisoner a platter of food which included, among other things, a huge joint of beef and a tankard of ale. Conan fell to voraciously, and Athicus made a final round of the cells, to see that all was in order, and that none should witness the pretended prison break. It was while he was so occupied that a squad of guardsmen marched into the prison and placed him under arrest. Murilo had been mistaken when he assumed this arrest denoted discovery of Conan's planned escape. It was another matter; Athicus had become careless in his dealings with the underworld, and one of his past sins had caught up with him.

Another jailer took his place, a stolid, dependable creature whom no amount of bribery could have shaken from his duty. He was unimaginative, but he had an exalted idea of the importance of his job.

After Athicus had been marched away to be formally arraigned before a magistrate, this jailer made the rounds of the cells as a matter of routine. As he passed that of Conan, his sense of propriety was shocked and outraged to see the prisoner free of his chains and in the act of gnawing the last shreds of meat from a huge beefbone. The jailer was so upset that he made the mistake of entering the cell alone, without calling guards from other parts of the prison. It was his first mistake in the line of duty, and his last. Conan brained him with the beef bone, took his poniard and his keys, and made a leisurely departure. As Murilo had said, only one guard was on duty there at night. The Cimmerian passed himself outside the walls by means of the keys he had taken and presently emerged into the outer air, as free as if Murilo's plan had been successful.

In the shadows of the prison walls, Conan paused to decide his next course of action. It occurred to him that since he had escaped through his own actions, he owed nothing to Murilo; yet it had been the young nobleman who had removed his chains and had the food sent to him, without either of which his escape would have been impossible. Conan decided that he was indebted to Murilo and, since he was a man who discharged his obligations eventually, he determined to carry out his promise to the young aristocrat. But first he had some business of his own to attend to.

He discarded his ragged tunic and moved off through the night naked but for a loincloth. As he went he fingered the poniard he had captured—a murderous weapon with a broad, double-edged blade nineteen inches long. He slunk along alleys and shadowed plazas until he came to the district which was his destination—the Maze. Along its labyrinthian ways he went with the certainty of familiarity. It was indeed a maze of black alleys and enclosed courts and devious ways; of furtive sounds, and stenches. There was no paving on the streets; mud and filth mingled in an unsavory mess. Sewers were unknown; refuse was dumped into the alleys to form reeking heaps and puddles. Unless a man walked with care he was likely to lose his footing and plunge waist-deep into nauseous pools. Nor was it uncommon to stumble over a corpse lying with its throat cut or its head knocked in, in the mud. Honest folk shunned the Maze with good reason.

Conan reached his destination without being seen, just

as one he wished fervently to meet was leaving it. As the Cimmerian slunk into the courtyard below, the girl who had sold him to the police was taking leave of her new lover in a chamber one flight up. This young thug, her door closed behind him, groped his way down a creaking flight of stairs, intent on his own meditations, which, like those of most of the denizens of the Maze, had to do with the unlawful acquirement of property. Part-way down the stairs, he halted suddenly, his hair standing up. A vague bulk crouched in the darkness before him, a pair of eyes blazed like the eyes of a hunting beast. A beastlike snarl was the last thing he heard in life, as the monster lurched against him and a keen blade ripped through his belly. He gave one gasping cry and slumped down limply on the stairway.

The barbarian loomed above him for an instant, ghoul-like, his eyes burning in the gloom. He knew the sound was heard, but the people in the Maze were careful to attend to their own business. A death cry on darkened stairs was nothing unusual. Later, some one would venture to investigate, but only after a reasonable lapse of time.

Conan went up the stairs and halted at a door he knew well of old. It was fastened within, but his blade passed between the door and the jamb and lifted the bar. He stepped inside, closing the door after him, and faced the girl who had betrayed him to the police.

The wench was sitting cross-legged in her shift on her unkempt bed. She turned white and stared at him as if at a ghost. She had heard the cry from the stairs, and she saw the red stain on the poniard in his hand. But she was too filled with terror on her own account to waste any time lamenting the evident fate of her lover. She began to beg for her life, almost incoherent with terror. Conan did not reply; he merely stood and glared at her with his burning eyes, testing the edge of his poniard with a callused thumb.

At last he crossed the chamber, while she cowered back against the wall, sobbing frantic pleas for mercy. Grasping her yellow locks with no gentle hand, he dragged her off the bed. Thrusting his blade back in its sheath, he tucked his squirming captive under his left arm and strode to the window. As in most houses of that type, a ledge encircled each story, caused by the continuance of the window ledges. Conan kicked the window open and stepped out on that narrow band. If any had been near or awake, they would have witnessed the bizarre sight of a man moving carefully along the ledge, carrying a kicking, half-naked wench under his arm. They would have been no more puzzled than the girl.

Reaching the spot he sought, Conan halted, gripping the wall with his free hand. Inside the building rose a sudden clamor, showing that the body had at last been discovered. His captive whimpered and twisted, renewing her importunities. Conan glanced down into the muck and slime of the alleys below; he listened briefly to the clamor inside and the pleas of the wench; then he dropped her with great accuracy into a cesspool. He enjoyed her kickings and flounderings and the concentrated venom of her profanity for a few seconds, and even allowed himself a low rumble of laughter. Then he lifted his head, listened to the growing tumult within the building, and decided it was time for him to kill Nabonidus.

3

It was a reverberating clang of metal that roused Murilo. He groaned and struggled dazedly to a sitting position. About him all was silence and darkness, and for an instant he was sickened with the fear that he was blind. Then he remembered what had gone before, and his flesh crawled. By the sense of touch he found that he was lying on a floor of evenly joined stone slabs. Further groping discovered a wall of the same material. He rose and leaned against it, trying in vain to orient himself. That he was in some sort of a prison seemed certain, but where and how long he was unable to guess. He remembered dimly a clashing noise and wondered if it had been the iron door of his dungeon closing on him, or if it betokened the entrance of an executioner.

At this thought he shuddered profoundly and began to feel his way along the wall. Momentarily he expected to encounter the limits of his prison, but after a while he came to the conclusion that he was travelling down a corridor. He kept to the wall, fearful of pits or other traps, and was presently aware of something near him in the blackness. He could see nothing, but either his ears had caught a stealthy sound, or some subconscious sense warned him. He stopped short, his hair standing on end; as surely as he lived, he felt the presence of some living creature crouching in the darkness in front of him.

He thought his heart would stop when a voice hissed in a barbaric accent: "Murilo! Is it you?"

"Conan!" Limp from the reaction, the young nobleman groped in the darkness, and his hands encountered a pair of great naked shoulders.

"A good thing I recognized you," grunted the barbarian. "I was about to stick you like a fattened pig."

"Where are we, in Mitra's name?"

"In the pits under the Red Priest's house; but why—"

"What is the time?"

"Not long after midnight."

Murilo shook his head, trying to assemble his scattered wits.

"What are you doing here?" demanded the Cimmerian.

"I came to kill Nabonidus. I heard they had changed the guard at your prison—"

"They did," growled Conan. "I broke the new jailer's head and walked out. I would have been here hours agone, but I had some personal business to attend to. Well, shall we hunt for Nabonidus?"

Murilo shuddered. "Conan, we are in the house of the archfiend! I came seeking a human enemy; I found a hairy devil out of hell!"

Conan grunted uncertainly; fearless as a wounded tiger as far as human foes were concerned, he had all the superstitious dreads of the primitive.

"I gained access to the house," whispered Murilo, as if the darkness were full of listening ears. "In the outer gardens I found Nabonidus' dog mauled to death. Within the house I came upon Joka, the servant. His neck had been broken. Then I saw Nabonidus himself seated in his chair, clad in his accustomed garb. At first I thought he, too, was dead. I stole up to stab him. He rose and faced me. God!" The memory of that horror struck the young nobleman momentarily speechless as he re-lived that awful instant.

"Conan," he whispered, "it was no *man* that stood before me! In body and posture it was not unlike a man, but from the scarlet hood of the priest grinned a face of madness and nightmare! It was covered with black hair, from which small piglike eyes glared redly; its nose was flat, with great flaring nostrils; its loose lips writhed back, disclosing huge yellow fangs, like the teeth of a dog. The hands that hung from the scarlet sleeves were misshapen and likewise covered with black hair. All this I saw in one glance, and then I was overcome with horror; my senses left me and I swooned."

"What then?" muttered the Cimmerian uneasily.

"I recovered consciousness only a short time ago; the

monster must have thrown me into these pits. Conan, I have suspected that Nabonidus was not wholly human! He is a demon—a were-thing! By day he moves among humanity in the guise of men, and by night he takes on his true aspect."

"That's evident," answered Conan. "Everyone knows there are men who take the form of wolves at will. But why did he kill his servants?"

"Who can delve the mind of a devil?" replied Murilo. "Our present interest is in getting out of this place. Human weapons cannot harm a were-man. How did you get in here?"

"Through the sewer. I reckoned on the gardens' being guarded. The sewers connect with a tunnel that lets into these pits. I thought to find some door leading up into the house unbolted."

"Then let us escape by the way you came!" exclaimed Murilo. "To the devil with it! Once out of this snake-den, we'll take our chance with the king's guardsmen and risk a flight from the city. Lead on!"

"Useless," grunted the Cimmerian. "The way to the sewers is barred. As I entered the tunnel, an iron grille crashed down from the roof. If I had not moved quicker than a flash of lightning, its spearheads would have pinned me to the floor like a worm. When I tried to lift it, it wouldn't move. An elephant couldn't shake it. Nor could anything bigger than a rabbit squirm between the bars."

Murilo cursed, an icy hand playing up and down his spine. He might have known Nabonidus would not leave any entrance into his house unguarded. Had Conan not possessed the steel-spring quickness of a wild thing, that falling portcullis would have skewered him. Doubtless his walking through the tunnel had sprung some hidden catch that released it from the roof. As it was, both were trapped living.

"There's but one thing to do," said Murilo, sweating profusely. "That's to search for some other exit; doubtless they're all set with traps, but we have no other choice."

The barbarian grunted agreement, and the companions began groping their way at random down the corridor. Even at that moment, something occurred to Murilo.

"How did you recognize me in this blackness?" he demanded.

"I smelled the perfume you put on your hair, when you came to my cell," answered Conan. "I smelled it again a while ago, when I was crouching in the dark and preparing to rip you open."

Murilo put a lock of his black hair to his nostrils; even so the scent was barely apparent to his civilized senses, and he realized how keen must be the organs of the barbarian.

Instinctively his hand went to his scabbard as they groped onward, and he cursed to find it empty. At that moment a faint glow became apparent ahead of them, and presently they came to a sharp bend in the corridor, about which the light filtered grayly. Together they peered around the corner, and Murilo, leaning against his companion, felt his huge frame stiffen. The young nobleman had also seen it—the body of a man, half naked, lying limply in the corridor beyond the bend, vaguely illumined by a radiance which seemed to emanate from a broad silver disk on the farther wall. A strange familiarity about the recumbent figure, which lay face down, stirred Murilo with inexplicable and monstrous conjectures. Motioning the Cimmerian to follow him, he stole forward and bent above the body. Overcoming a certain repugnance, he grasped it and turned it on its back. An incredulous oath escaped him; the Cimmerian grunted explosively.

"Nabonidus! The Red Priest!" ejaculated Murilo, his brain a dizzy vortex of whirling amazement. "Then who—what—?"

The priest groaned and stirred. With catlike quickness Conan bent over him, poniard poised above his heart. Murilo caught his wrist.

"Wait! Don't kill him yet—"

"Why not?" demanded the Cimmerian. "He has cast off his were-guise, and sleeps. Will you awaken him to tear us to pieces?"

"No, wait!" urged Murilo, trying to collect his jumbled wits. "Look! He is not sleeping—see that great blue welt on his shaven temple? He has been knocked senseless. He may have been lying here for hours."

"I thought you swore you saw him in beastly shape in the house above," said Conan.

"I did! Or else—he's coming to! Keep back your blade, Conan; there is a mystery here even darker than I thought. I must have words with this priest, before we kill him."

Nabonidus lifted a hand vaguely to his bruised temple, mumbled, and opened his eyes. For an instant they were blank and empty of intelligence; then life came back to them with a jerk, and he sat up, staring at the companions. Whatever terrific jolt had temporarily addled his razor-keen brain, it was functioning with its accustomed vigor again. His eyes shot swiftly about him, then came back to rest on Murilo's face.

"You honor my poor house, young sir," he laughed coolly, glancing at the great figure that loomed behind the young nobleman's shoulder. "You have brought a bravo, I see. Was your sword not sufficient to sever the life of my humble self?"

"Enough of this," impatiently returned Murilo. "How long have you lain here?"

"A peculiar question to put to a man just recovering consciousness," answered the priest. "I do not know what time it now is. But it lacked an hour or so of midnight when I was set upon."

"Then who is it that masquerades in your own gown in the house above?" demanded Murilo.

"That will be Thak," answered Nabonidus, ruefully fingering his bruises. "Yes, that will be Thak. And in my gown? The dog!"

Conan, who comprehended none of this, stirred restlessly, and growled something in his own tongue. Nabonidus glanced at him whimsically.

"Your bully's knife yearns for my heart, Murilo," he said. "I thought you might be wise enough to take my warning and leave the city."

"How was I to know that was to be granted me?" returned Murilo. "At any rate, my interests are here."

"You are in good company with that cutthroat," murmured Nabonidus. "I had suspected you for some time. That was why I caused that pallid court secretary to disappear. Before he died he told me many things, among others the name of the young nobleman who bribed him to filch state secrets, which the nobleman in turn sold to rival powers. Are you not ashamed of yourself, Murilo, you white-handed thief?"

"I have no more cause for shame than you, you vulture-hearted plunderer," answered Murilo promptly. "You exploit a whole kingdom for your personal greed; and, under the guise of disinterested statemanship, you swindle the king, beggar the rich, oppress the poor, and sacrifice the whole future of the nation for your ruthless ambition. You are no more than a fat hog with his snout in the trough. You are a greater thief than I am. This Cimmerian is the most honest man of the three of us, because he steals and murders openly."

"Well, then, we are all rogues together," agreed Nabonidus equably. "And what now? My life?"

"When I saw the ear of the secretary that had disappeared, I knew I was doomed," said Murilo abruptly, "and

I believed you would invoke the authority of the king. Was I right?"

"Quite so," answered the priest. "A court secretary is easy to do away with, but you are a bit too prominent. I had intended telling the king a jest about you in the morning."

"A jest that would have cost me my head," muttered Murilo. "Then the king is unaware of my foreign enterprises?"

"As yet," sighed Nabonidus. "And now, since I see your companion has his knife, I fear that jest will never be told."

"You should know how to get out of these rat-dens," said Murilo. "Suppose I agree to spare your life. Will you help us to escape, and swear to keep silent about my thievery?"

"When did a priest keep an oath?" complained Conan, comprehending the trend of the conversation. "Let me cut his throat; I want to see what color his blood is. They say in the Maze that his heart is black, so his blood must be black, too—"

"Be quiet," whispered Murilo. "If he does not show us the way out of these pits, we may rot here. Well, Nabonidus, what do you say?"

"What does a wolf with his leg in the trap say?" laughed the priest. "I am in your power, and, if we are to escape, we must aid one another. I swear, if we survive this adventure, to forget all your shifty dealings. I swear by the soul of Mitra!"

"I am satisfied," muttered Murilo. "Even the Red Priest would not break that oath. Now to get out of here. My friend here entered by way of the tunnel, but a grille fell behind him and blocked the way. Can you cause it to be lifted?"

"Not from these pits," answered the priest. "The control lever is in the chamber above the tunnel. There is only one other way out of these pits, which I will show you. But tell me, how did you come here?"

Murilo told him in a few words, and Nabonidus nodded, rising stiffly. He limped down the corridor, which here widened into a sort of vast chamber, and approached the distant silver disk. As they advanced the light increased, though it never became anything but a dim shadowy radiance. Near the disk they saw a narrow stair leading upward.

"That is the other exit," said Nabonidus. "And I strongly doubt if the door at the head is bolted. But I have an idea that he who would go through that door had better cut his own throat first. Look into the disk."

What had seemed a silver plate was in reality a great mirror set in the wall. A confusing system of copperlike tubes jutted out from the wall above it, bending down toward it at right angles. Glancing into these tubes, Murilo saw a bewildering array of smaller mirrors. He turned his attention to the larger mirror in the wall, and ejaculated in amazement. Peering over his shoulder, Conan grunted.

They seemed to be looking through a broad window into a well-lighted chamber. There were broad mirrors on the walls, with velvet hangings between; there were silken couches, chairs of ebony and ivory, and curtained doorways leading off from the chamber. And before one doorway which was not curtained, sat a bulky black object that contrasted grotesquely with the richness of the chamber.

Murilo felt his blood freeze again as he looked at the horror which seemed to be staring directly into his eyes. Involuntarily he recoiled from the mirror, while Conan thrust his head truculently forward, till his jaws almost touched the surface, growling some threat or defiance in his own barbaric tongue.

"In Mitra's name, Nabonidus," gasped Murilo, shaken, "what is it?"

"That is Thak," answered the priest, caressing his temple. "Some would call him an ape, but he is almost as different from a real ape as he is different from a real man. His people dwell far to the east, in the mountains that fringe the eastern frontiers of Zamora. There are not many of them; but, if they are not exterminated, I believe they will become human beings in perhaps a hundred thousand years. They are in the formative stage; they are neither apes, as their remote ancestors were, nor men, as their remote descendants may be. They dwell in the high crags of well-nigh inaccessible mountains, knowing nothing of fire or the making of shelter or garments, or the use of weapons. Yet they have a language of a sort, consisting mainly of grunts and clicks.

"I took Thak when he was a cub, and he learned what I taught him much more swiftly and thoroughly than any true animal could have done. He was at once bodyguard and servant. But I forgot that being partly a man, he could not be submerged into a mere shadow of myself, like a true animal. Apparently his semi-brain retained impressions of hate, resentment, and some sort of bestial ambition of its own.

"At any rate, he struck when I least expected it. Last night he appeared to go suddenly mad. His actions had all the appearance of bestial insanity, yet I know that they must have been the result of long and careful planning.

"I heard a sound of fighting in the garden, and going to investigate—for I believed it was yourself, being dragged down by my watchdog—I saw Thak emerge from the shrubbery dripping with blood. Before I was aware of his intention, he sprang at me with an awful scream and struck me senseless. I remember no more, but can only surmise that, following some whim of his semi-human brain, he stripped me of my gown and cast me still living into the pits—for which reason, only the gods can guess. He must have killed the dog when he came from the garden, and after he struck me down, he evidently killed Joka, as you saw the man lying dead in the house. Joka would have come to my aid, even against Thak, whom he always hated."

Murilo stared in the mirror at the creature which sat with such monstrous patience before the closed door. He shuddered at the sight of the great black hands, thickly grown with hair that was almost furlike. The body was thick, broad, and stooped. The unnaturally wide shoulders had burst the scarlet gown, and on these shoulders Murilo noted the same thick growth of black hair. The face peering from the scarlet hood was utterly bestial, and yet Murilo realized that Nabonidus spoke truth when he said that Thak was not wholly a beast. There was something in the red murky eyes, something in the creature's clumsy posture, something in the whole appearance of the thing that set it apart from the truly animal. That monstrous body housed a brain and soul that were just budding awfully into something vaguely human. Murilo stood aghast as he recognized a faint and hideous kinship between his kind and that squatting monstrosity, and he was nauseated by a fleeting realization of the abysses of bellowing bestiality up through which humanity had painfully toiled.

"Surely he sees us," muttered Conan. "Why does he not charge us? He could break this window with ease."

Murilo realized that Conan supposed the mirror to be a window through which they were looking.

"He does not see us," answered the priest. "We are looking into the chamber above us. That door that Thak is guarding is the one at the head of these stairs. It is simply an arrangement of mirrors. Do you see those mirrors on the walls? They transmit the reflection of the room into these tubes, down which other mirrors carry it to reflect it at last on an enlarged scale in this great mirror."

Murilo realized that the priest must be centuries ahead of his generation, to perfect such an invention; but Conan put it down to witchcraft and troubled his head no more about it.

"I constructed these pits for a place of refuge as well as a dungeon," the priest was saying. "There are times when I have taken refuge here and, through these mirrors, watched doom fall upon those who sought me with ill intent."

"But why is Thak watching that door?" demanded Murilo.

"He must have heard the falling of the grating in the tunnel. It is connected with bells in the chambers above. He knows someone is in the pits, and he is waiting for him to come up the stairs. Oh, he has learned well the lessons I taught him. He has seen what happened to men who come through that door, when I tugged at the rope that hangs on yonder wall, and he waits to mimic me."

"And while he waits, what are we to do?" demanded Murilo.

"There is naught we can do, except watch him. As long as he is in that chamber, we dare not ascend the stairs. He has the strength of a true gorilla and could easily tear us all to pieces. But he does not need to exert his muscles; if we open that door he has but to tug that rope, and blast us into eternity."

"How?"

"I bargained to help you escape," answered the priest; "not to betray my secrets."

Murilo started to reply, then stiffened suddenly. A stealthy hand had parted the curtains of one of the doorways. Between them appeared a dark face whose glittering eyes fixed menacingly on the squat form in the scarlet robe.

"Petreus!" hissed Nabonidus. "Mitra, what a gathering of vultures this night is!"

The face remained framed between the parted curtains. Over the intruder's shoulder other faces peered—dark, thin faces, alight with sinister eagerness.

"What do they here?" muttered Murilo, unconsciously lowering his voice, although he knew they could not hear him.

"Why, what would Petreus and his ardent young nationalists be doing in the house of the Red Priest?" laughed Nabonidus. "Look how eagerly they glare at the figure they think is their arch-enemy. They have fallen into your error; it should be amusing to watch their expressions when they are disillusioned."

Murilo did not reply. The whole affair had a distinctly unreal atmosphere. He felt as if he were watching the play of puppets, or as a disembodied ghost himself, impersonally viewing the actions of the living, his presence unseen and unsuspected.

He saw Petreus put his finger warningly to his lips, and nod to his fellow-conspirators. The young nobleman could not tell if Thak was aware of the intruders. The ape-man's position had not changed, as he sat with his back toward the door through which the men were gliding.

"They had the same idea you had," Nabonidus was muttering at his ear. "Only their reasons were patriotic rather than selfish. Easy to gain access to my house, now that the dog is dead. Oh, what a chance to rid myself of their menace once and for all! If I were sitting where Thak sits—a leap to the wall—a tug on that rope—"

Petreus had placed one foot lightly over the threshold of the chamber; his fellows were at his heels, their daggers glinting dully. Suddenly Thak rose and wheeled toward him. The unexpected horror of his appearance, where they had thought to behold the hated but familiar countenance of Nabonidus, wrought havoc with their nerves, as the same spectacle had wrought upon Murilo. With a shriek Petreus recoiled, carrying his companions backward with him. They stumbled and floundered over each other; and in that instant Thak, covering the distance in one prodigious, grotesque leap, caught and jerked powerfully at a thick velvet rope which hung near the doorway.

Instantly the curtains whipped back on either hand, leaving the door clear, and down across it something flashed with a peculiar silvery blur.

"He remembered!" Nabonidus was exulting. "The beast is half a man! He had seen the doom performed, and he remembered! Watch, now! Watch! Watch!"

Murilo saw that it was a panel of heavy glass that had fallen across the doorway. Through it he saw the pallid faces of the conspirators. Petreus, throwing out his hands as if to ward off a charge from Thak, encountered the transparent barrier, and from his gestures, said something to his companions. Now that the curtains were drawn back, the men in the pits could see all that took place in the chamber that contained the nationalists. Completely unnerved, these ran across the chamber toward the door by which they had apparently entered, only to halt suddenly, as if stopped by an invisible wall.

"The jerk of the rope sealed that chamber," laughed Nabonidus. "It is simple; the glass panels work in grooves in the doorways. Jerking the rope trips the spring that holds them. They slide down and lock in place, and can only be worked from outside. The glass is unbreakable; a man with a mallet could not shatter it. Ah!"

The trapped men were in a hysteria of fright; they ran wildly from one door to another, beating vainly at the crystal walls, shaking their fists wildly at the implacable black shape which squatted outside. Then one threw back his head, glared upward, and began to scream, to judge from the working of his lips, while he pointed toward the ceiling.

"The fall of the panels released the clouds of doom," said the Red Priest with a wild laugh. "The dust of the gray lotus, from the Swamps of the Dead, beyond the land of Khitai."

In the middle of the ceiling hung a cluster of gold buds; these had opened like the petals of a great carven rose, and from them billowed a gray mist that swiftly filled the chamber. Instantly the scene changed from one of hysteria to one of madness and horror. The trapped men began to stagger; they ran in drunken circles. Froth dripped from their lips, which twisted as in awful laughter. Raging, they fell upon one another with daggers and teeth, slashing, tearing, slaying in a holocaust of madness. Murilo turned sick as he watched and was glad that he could not hear the screams and howls with which that doomed chamber must be ringing. Like pictures thrown on a screen, it was silent.

Outside the chamber of horror Thak was leaping up and down in brutish glee, tossing his long hairy arms on high. At Murilo's shoulder Nabonidus was laughing like a fiend.

"Ah, a good stroke, Petreus! That fairly disemboweled him! Now one for you, my patriotic friend! So! They are all down, and the living tear the flesh of the dead with their slavering teeth."

Murilo shuddered. Behind him the Cimmerian swore softly in his uncouth tongue. Only death was to be seen in the chamber of the gray mist; torn, gashed, and mangled, the conspirators lay in a red heap, gaping mouths and blood-dabbled faces staring blankly upward through the slowly swirling eddies of gray.

Thak, stooping like a giant gnome, approached the wall where the rope hung, and gave it a peculiar sidewise pull.

"He is opening the farther door," said Nabonidus. "By Mitra, he is more of a human than even I had guessed! See, the mist swirls out of the chamber and is dissipated. He waits, to be safe. Now he raises the other panel. He is cautious—he knows the doom of the gray lotus, which brings madness and death. By Mitra!"

Murilo jerked about at the electric quality of the exclamation.

"Our one chance!" exclaimed Nabonidus. "If he leaves

the chamber above for a few minutes, we will risk a dash up those stairs."

Suddenly tense, they watched the monster waddle through the doorway and vanish. With the lifting of the glass panel, the curtains had fallen again, hiding the chamber of death.

"We must chance it!" gasped Nabonidus, and Murilo saw perspiration break out on his face. "Perhaps he will be disposing of the bodies as he has seen me do. Quick! Follow me up those stairs!"

He ran toward the steps and up them with an agility that amazed Murilo. The young nobleman and the barbarian were close at his heels, and they heard his gusty sigh of relief as he threw open the door at the top of the stairs. They burst into the broad chamber they had seen mirrored below. Thak was nowhere to be seen.

"He's in that chamber with the corpses!" exclaimed Murilo. "Why not trap him there as he trapped them?"

"No, no!" gasped Nabonidus, an unaccustomed pallor tingeing his features. "We do not know that he is in there. He might emerge before we could reach the trap rope, anyway! Follow me into the corridor; I must reach my chamber and obtain weapons which will destroy him. This corridor is the only one opening from this chamber which is not set with a trap of some kind."

They followed him swiftly through a curtained doorway opposite the door of the death chamber and came into a corridor, into which various chambers opened. With fumbling haste Nabonidus began to try the doors on each side. They were locked, as was the door at the other end of the corridor.

"My god!" The Red Priest leaned against the wall, his skin ashen. "The doors are locked, and Thak took my keys from me. We are trapped, after all."

Murilo stared appalled to see the man in such a state of

nerves, and Nabonidus pulled himself together with an effort.

"That beast has me in a panic," he said. "If you had seen him tear men as I have seen—well, Mitra aid us, but we must fight him now with what the gods have given us. Come!"

He led them back to the curtained doorway, and peered into the great chamber in time to see Thak emerge from the opposite doorway. It was apparent that the beast-man had suspected something. His small, close-set ears twitched; he glared angrily about him and, approaching the nearest doorway, tore aside the curtains to look behind them.

Nabonidus drew back, shaking like a leaf. He gripped Conan's shoulder. "Man, do you dare pit your knife against his fangs?"

The Cimmerian's eyes blazed in answer.

"Quick!" the Red Priest whispered, thrusting him behind the curtains, close against the wall. "As he will find us soon enough, we will draw him to us. As he rushes past you, sink your blade in his back if you can. You, Murilo, show yourself to him and then flee up the corridor. Mitra knows, we have no chance with him in hand-to-hand combat, but we are doomed anyway when he finds us."

Murilo felt his blood congeal in his veins, but he steeled himself and stepped outside the doorway. Instantly Thak, on the other side of the chamber, wheeled, glared, and charged with a thunderous roar. His scarlet hood had fallen back, revealing his black misshapen head; his black hands and red robe were splashed with a brighter red. He was like a crimson and black nightmare as he rushed across the chamber, fangs bared, his bowed legs hurtling his enormous body along at a terrifying gait.

Murilo turned and ran back into the corridor and, quick as he was, the shaggy horror was almost at his heels. Then as the monster rushed past the curtains, from among them catapulated a great form that struck full on the ape-man's shoulders, at the same instant driving the poniard into the brutish back. Thak screamed horribly as the impact knocked him off his feet, and the combatants hit the floor together. Instantly there began a whirl and thrash of limbs, the tearing and rending of a fiendish battle.

Murilo saw that the barbarian had locked his legs about the ape-man's torso and was striving to maintain his position on the monster's back while he butchered it with his poniard. Thak, on the other hand, was striving to dislodge his clinging foe, to drag him around within reach of the giant fangs that gaped for his flesh. In a whirlwind of blows and scarlet tatters they rolled along the corridor, revolving so swiftly that Murilo dared not use the chair he had caught up, lest he strike the Cimmerian. And he saw that in spite of the handicap of Conan's first hold, and the voluminous robe that lashed and wrapped about the ape-man's limbs and body, Thak's giant strength was swiftly prevailing. Inexorably he was dragging the Cimmerian around in front of him. The ape-man had taken punishment enough to have killed a dozen men. Conan's poniard had sunk again and again into his torso, shoulders, and bull-like neck; he was streaming blood from a score of wounds; but, unless the blade quickly reached some absolutely vital spot, Thak's inhuman vitality would survive to finish the Cimmerian and, after him, Conan's companions.

Conan was fighting like a wild beast himself, in silence except for his gasps of effort. The black talons of the monster and the awful grasp of those misshapen hands ripped and tore at him, the grinning jaws gaped for his throat. Then Murilo, seeing an opening, sprang and swung the chair with all his power, and with force enough to have brained a human being. The chair glanced from Thak's slanted black skull; but the stunned monster momentarily relaxed his rending grasp, and in that instant Conan, gasping and streaming blood, plunged forward and sank his poniard to the hilt in the ape-man's heart.

With a convulsive shudder, the beast-man stared from the floor, then sank limply back. His fierce eyes set and glazed, his thick limbs quivered and became rigid.

Conan staggered dizzily up, shaking the sweat and blood out of his eyes. Blood dripped from his poniard and fingers, and trickled in rivulets down his thighs, arms, and breast. Murilo caught at him to support him, but the barbarian shook him off impatiently.

"When I cannot stand alone, it will be time to die," he mumbled, through mashed lips. "But I'd like a flagon of wine."

Nabonidus was staring down at the still figure as if he could not believe his own eyes. Black, hairy, abhorrent, the monster lay, grotesque in the tatters of the scarlet robe; yet more human than bestial, even so, and possessed somehow of a vague and terrible pathos.

Even the Cimmerian sensed this, for he panted: "I have slain a *man* tonight, not a *beast*. I will count him among the chiefs whose souls I've sent into the dark, and my women will sing of him."

Nabonidus stooped and picked up a bunch of keys on a golden chain. They had fallen from the ape-man's girdle during the battle. Motioning his companions to follow him, he led them to a chamber, unlocked the door, and led the way inside. It was illumined like the others. The Red Priest took a vessel of wine from a table and filled crystal beakers. As his companions drank thirstily, he murmured: "What a night! It is nearly dawn, now. What of you, my friends?"

"I'll dress Conan's hurts, if you will fetch me bandages and the like," said Murilo, and Nabonidus nodded, and moved toward the door that led into the corridor. Something about his bowed head caused Murilo to watch him sharply. At the door the Red Priest wheeled suddenly. His face had undergone a transformation. His eyes gleamed with his old fire, his lips laughed soundlessly.

"Rogues together!" his voice rang with its accustomed mockery. "But not fools together. You are the fool, Murilo!"

"What do you mean?" The young nobleman started forward.

"Back!" Nabonidus's voice cracked like a whip. "Another step and I will blast you!"

Murilo's blood turned cold as he saw that the Red Priest's hand grasped a thick velvet rope, which hung among the curtains just outside the door.

"What treachery is this?" cried Murilo. "You swore—"

"I swore I would not tell the king a jest concerning you! I did not swear not to take matters into my own hands if I could. Do you think I would pass up such an apportunity? Under ordinary circumstances I would not dare to kill you myself, without sanction of the king, but now none will ever know. You will go into the acid vats along with Thak and the nationalist fools, and none will be the wiser. What a night this has been for me! If I have lost some valuable servants, I have nevertheless rid myself of various dangerous enemies. Stand back! I am over the threshold, and you cannot possibly reach me before I tug this cord and send you to Hell. Not the gray lotus, this time, but something just as effective. Nearly every chamber in my house is a trap. And so, Murilo, fool that you are—"

Too quickly for the sight to follow, Conan caught up a stool and hurled it. Nabonidus instinctively threw up his arm with a cry, but not in time. The missile crunched against his head, and the Red Priest swayed and fell face-down in a slowly widening pool of dark crimson.

"His blood was red, after all," grunted Conan.

Murilo raked back his sweat-plastered hair with a shaky

hand as he leaned against the table, weak from the reaction of relief.

"It is dawn," he said. "Let us get out of here, before we fall afoul of some other doom. If we can climb the outer wall without being seen, we shall not be connected with this night's work. Let the police write their own explanation."

He glanced at the body of the Red Priest where it lay etched in crimson, and shrugged his shoulders.

"He was the fool, after all; had he not paused to taunt us, he could have trapped us easily."

"Well," said the Cimmerian tranquilly, "he's travelled the road all rogues must walk at last. I'd like to loot the house, but I suppose we'd best go."

As they emerged from the dimness of the dawn-whitened garden, Murilo said: "The Red Priest has gone into the dark, so my road is clear in the city, and I have nothing to fear. But what of you? There is still the matter of that priest in the Maze, and—"

"I'm tired of this city anyway," grinned the Cimmerian. "You mentioned a horse waiting at the Rats' Den. I'm curious to see how fast that horse can carry me into another kingdom. There's many a highway I want to travel before I walk the road Nabonidus walked this night."

The Hand of Nergal

Conan has enjoyed his taste of Hyborian intrigue. It is clear to him that there is no essential difference between the motives of the palace and those of the Rats' Den, whereas the pickings are better in higher places. With his own horse under him and a grubstake from the grateful—and thoughtful—Murilo, the Cimmerian sets out to look over the civilized world, with an eye to making it his oyster.

The Road of Kings, which winds through the Hyborian kingdoms, at last leads him eastward into Turan, where he takes service in the armies of King Yildiz. He does not at first find military services congenial, being too self-willed and hot-tempered to submit easily to discipline. Moreover, being at this time an indifferent horseman and archer, in a force of which the mounted bowman is the mainstay, he is relegated to a low-paid, irregular unit. Soon, however, a chance arises to show his true mettle.

1. *Black Shadows*

"*Crom!*"

The oath was torn from the young warrior's grim-set lips. He threw back his head, sending his tousled shock of black hair flying, and lifted his smouldering blue eyes skyward. They widened in sheer astonishment. An eery thrill of superstitious awe ran through his tall, powerfully-built body, which was burnt brown by fierce wasteland suns, broad-shouldered and deep-chested, lean of waist, long of leg, and naked save for a rag of cloth about his loins and high-strapped sandals.

He had entered the battle mounted, as one of a troop of irregular cavalry. But his horse, given him by the nobleman Murilo in Corinthia, had fallen to the foemen's arrows at the first onset and the youth had fought on afoot. His shield had been smashed by the enemy's blows; he had cast it aside and battled with sword alone.

Above, from the sunset-smouldering sky of this bleak, wind-swept Turanian steppe, where two great armies were locked in a fury of desperate battle, came horror.

The field was drenched in sunset fires and bathed in human blood. Here the mighty host of Yildiz, king of Turan, in whose army the youth served as a mercenary, had fought for five long hours against the iron-shod legions of Munthassem Khan, rebellious satrap of the Zamorian Marches of northern Turan. Now, circling slowly downwards from the crimson sky, came nameless things whose like the barbarian had never seen or heard of before in all his travels. They were black, shadowy monsters, hovering on broad, arch-ribbed wings like enormous bats.

The two armies fought on, unseeing. Only Conan, here on this low hill, ringed about with the bodies of men his sword had slain, saw them descending through the sunset sky.

Leaning on his dripping blade and resting his sinewy arms for a moment, he stared at the weird shadow-things. For they seemed to be more shadow than substance—translucent to the sight, like wisps of noisome black vapor or the shadowy ghosts of gigantic vampire bats. Evil, slitted eyes of green flame glared through their smoky forms.

And even as he watched, nape-hairs prickling with a barbarian's dread of the supernatural, they fell upon the battle like vultures on a field of blood—fell and slew.

Screams of pain and fear rose from the host of King

Yildiz, as the black shadows hurtled amongst their ranks. Wherever the shadow-devils swooped, they left a bloody corpse. By the hundred they came, and the weary ranks of the Turanian army fell back, stumbling, tossing away their weapons in panic.

"Fight, you dogs! Stand and fight!" Thundering angry commands in a stern voice, a tall, commanding figure on a great black mare sought to hold the crumbling line. Conan glimpsed the sparkles of silver-gilt chain mail under a rich blue cloak, and a hawk-nosed, black-bearded face, kingly and harsh under a spired steel helm that caught the crimson sun like a polished mirror. He knew the man for King Yildiz' general, Bakra of Akif.

With a ringing oath, the proud commander drew his tulwar and laid about him with the flat of the blade. Perhaps he could have rallied the ranks, but one of the devil-shadows swooped on him from behind. It folded vaporous, filming wings about him in a grisly embrace and he stiffened. Conan could see his face, suddenly pale with staring, frozen eyes of fear—and he saw the features through the enveloping wings, like a white mask behind a veil of thin, black lace.

The general's horse went mad and bolted in terror. But the phantom-thing plucked the general from his saddle. For a moment it bore him in mid-air on slowly beating wings, then let him fall, a torn and bloody thing in dripping rags. The face, which had stared at Conan through shadowy wings with eyes of glazing terror, was a red ruin. Thus ended the career of Bakra of Akif.

And thus ended his battle, as well.

With its commander gone, the army went mad. Conan saw seasoned veterans, with a score of campaigns under their belts, run shrieking from the field like raw recruits. He saw proud nobles fly screaming like craven serfs. And behind them, untouched by the flying phantoms, grinning with victory, the hosts of the rebel satrap pressed their weirdly-won advantage. The day was lost—unless one strong man should stand firm and rally the broken host by his example.

Before the foremost of the fleeing soldiers rose suddenly a figure so grim and savage that it checked their headlong, panic-stricken flight.

"Stand, you fatherless curs, or by Crom I'll fill your craven bellies with a foot of steel!"

It was the Cimmerian mercenary, his dark face like a grim mask of stone, cold as death. Fierce eyes under black, scowling brows, blazed with volcanic rage. Naked, splattered from head to heel with reeking gore, he held a mighty longsword in one great, scarred fist. His voice was like the deep growl of thunder.

"Back, if you set any value on your sniveling lives, you white-livered dogs—*back*—or I'll spill your cowardly guts at your feet! Lift that scimitar against me, you Hyrkanian pig, and I'll tear out your heart with my bare hands and make you eat it before you die. What! Are you women, to fly from shadows? But a moment ago, you were men—aye, fighting-men of Turan! You stood against foes armed with naked steel and fought them face to face. Now you turn and run like children from night-shadows, *faugh!* It makes me proud to be a barbarian—to see you city-bred weaklings cringe before a flight of bats!"

For a moment he held them—but for a moment only. A black-winged nightmare swooped upon him, and he—even he—stepped back from its grim, shadowy wings and the stench of its fetid breath.

The soldiers fled, leaving Conan to fight the thing alone. And fight he did. Setting his feet squarely, he swung the great sword, pivoting on slim hips, with the full strength of back, shoulders, and mighty arms behind the blow.

The sword flashed in a whistling arc of steel, cleaving the phantom in two. But it was, as he had guessed, a thing without substance, for his sword encountered no more resistance than the empty air. The force of the blow swung him off balance, and he fell sprawling on the stony plain.

Above him, the shadowy thing hovered. His sword had torn a great rent through it, as a man's hand breaks a thread of rising smoke. But, even as he watched, the vapory body reformed. Eyes like sparks of green hell-fire blazed down at him, alive with a horrible mirth and an inhuman hunger.

"*Crom!*" Conan gasped. It may have been a curse, but it sounded almost like a prayer.

He sought to lift the sword again, but it fell from nerveless hands. The instant the sword had slashed through the black shadow, it had gone cold, with an aching, stony, bone-deep chill like the interstellar gulfs that yawn blackly beyond the farthest stars.

The shadow-bat hovered on slowly beating wings, as if gloating over its fallen victim or savoring his superstitious fear.

With strengthless hands, Conan fumbled at his waist, where a strip of rawhide bound his loincloth to his middle. There a thin dagger hung beside a pouch. His fumbling fingers found the pouch, not the dagger hilt, and touched something smooth and warm within the leathern bag.

Suddenly, Conan jerked his hand away as a tingling electric warmth tore through his nerves. His fingers had brushed against that curious amulet he had found yesterday, when they lay encamped at Bahari. And, in touching the smooth stone, a strange force had been released.

The bat-thing veered suddenly away from him. A moment before, it had hovered so close that his flesh had crawled beneath the unearthly chill that seemed to radiate from its ghostly form. Now it tore madly away from him, wings beating in a frenzy.

Conan dragged himself to his knees, fighting the weakness that pervaded his limbs. First, the ghastly cold of the shadow's touch—then the tingling warmth that had seethed through his naked body. Between these two conflicting forces, he felt his strength draining away. His vision blurred; his mind wavered on the brink of darkness. Fiercely, he shook his head to clear his wits and gazed about him.

"Mitra! Crom and Mitra! Has the whole world gone mad?"

The grisly host of flying terrors had driven the army of General Bakra from the field, or slain those that did not flee fast enough. But the grinning host of Munthassem Khan they had not touched—had ignored, almost as if the soldiers of Yaralet and the shadowy nightmare-things had been partners in some unholy alliance of black sorcery.

But now it was the warriors of Yaralet who fled screaming before the shadowy vampires. Both armies broken and fled—had the world indeed gone mad, Conan wildly asked of the sunset sky?

As for the Cimmerian, strength and consciousness drained from him suddenly. He fell forward into black oblivion.

2. *Field of Blood*

The sun flamed like a crimson coal on the horizon. It glowered across the silent battlefield like the one red eye that blazes madly in a cyclops's misshapen brow. Silent as death, strewn with the wreckage of war, the battlefield stretched grim and still in the lurid rays. Here and there amidst the sprawled, unmoving bodies, scarlet pools of congealing gore lay like calm lakes reflecting the red-streamered sky.

Dark, furtive figures moved in the tall grasses, snuffling and whining at the heaped and scattered corpses. Their humped shoulders and ugly, doglike snouts marked them as hyenas from the steppes. For them, the battlefield would be a banquet table.

Down from the flaming sky flapped ungainly, black-winged vultures, come to feast on the slain. The grisly birds of prey dropped upon the mangled bodies with a rustle of dusky wings. But for these carrion-eaters, nothing moved on the silent, bloody field. It was still as death itself. No rumble of chariot wheels or peal of brazen trumpets broken the unearthly silence. The stillness of the dead followed fast on the thunder of battle.

Like eery harbingers of Fate, a wavering line of herons flapped slowly away down the sky toward the reed-grown banks of the river Nezvaya, whose turgid flood glinted dully crimson in the last light. Beyond the further shore, the black, walled bulk of the city of Yaralet loomed like a mountain of ebony into the dusk.

Yet one figure moved through that wide-strewn field of ruin, pygmylike against the glowing coals of sunset. It was the young Cimmerian giant with the wild black mane and the smouldering blue eyes. The black wings of interstellar cold had brushed him but lightly; life had stirred and consciousness returned. He wandered to and fro across the black field, limping slightly, for there was a ghastly wound in his thigh, taken in the fury of battle and only noticed and crudely bandaged as he had recovered consciousness and moved to arise.

Carefully yet impatiently he moved among the dead, bloody as were they. He was splashed with gore from head to foot, and the great sword he trailed in his right hand was stained crimson to the hilt. Bone-weary was Conan, and his gullet was desert-dry. He ached from a score of wounds—mere cuts and scratches, save for the great slash on his thigh—and he lusted for a skin of wine and a platter of beef.

As he prowled among the bodies, limping from corpse to corpse, he growled like a hungry wolf, swearing wrathfully. He had come into this Turanian war as a mercenary, owning naught but his horse—now slain—and the great sword in his hand. Now that the battle was lost, the war was ended, and he was marooned alone in the midst of the enemy land, he had at least hoped to loot the fallen of some choice pieces of gear they would no longer need. A gemmed dagger, a gold bracelet, a silver breastplate—a few such baubles and he could bribe his way out of the reach of Munthassem Khan and return to Zamora with a grub-stake.

Others had been here before him, either thieves slinking from the shadowy city or soldiers who crept back to the field from which they had fled. For the field was stripped; there was nothing left but broken swords, splintered javelins, dented helms and shields. Conan glared out across the littered plain, cursing sulphurously. He had lain in his swoon too long; even the looters had left. He was like the wolf who lingers so late at his blood-letting that jackals have stripped the prey; in this case, human jackals.

Straightening up from his fruitless quest, he gave over the search with the fatalism of the true barbarian. Time now to think of a plan. Brows knotted, scowling in thought, he glanced uncertainly afar off across the darkening plain. The square, flat-roofed towers of Yaralet stood black and solid against the dying gleam of sunset. No hope of refuge there, for one who had fought under the banners of King Yildiz! Yet no city, friend or enemy, lay nearer. And Yildiz's capital of Aghrapur was hundreds of leagues south . . .

Lost in his thoughts, he did not notice the approach of the great black figure until a faint, shuddering neigh reached his ears. He turned swiftly, favoring his injured leg, lifting the longsword threateningly—then relaxed, grinning.

"Crom! You startled me. So I am not the only survivor, eh?" Conan chuckled.

The tall black mare stood trembling, gazing at the

naked giant with wide, frightened eyes. It was the same mount that General Bakra had ridden—he who lay somewhere on the field, sprawled in a puddle of blood.

The mare whinnied, grateful for the sound of a friendly human voice. Although not a horseman, Conan could see that she was in sad condition. Her sides heaved, lathered with the sweat of fear, and her long legs trembled with exhaustion. The devil-bats had struck terror into her heart, too, Conan thought grimly. He spoke soothingly, calming her, and stepped gingerly nearer until he could reach out and stroke the panting beast, gentling her into submission.

In his far northern homeland, horses were rare. To the penniless barbarians of the Cimmerian tribes from whose loins he was sprung, only the chief of great wealth owned a fine steed, or the bold warrior who had taken one in battle. But despite his ignorance of the fine points of horsemanship, Conan quieted the great black mare and vaulted into the saddle. He sat astride the horse, fumbling with the reins, and rode slowly off the field, now a swamp of inky blackness in the darkness of night. He felt better. There were provisions in the saddlebags, and with a strong mare between his thighs he had a good chance of making it alone across the bleak and barren tundras to the borders of Zamora.

3. *Hildico*

A low, tortured moan reached his ears.

Conan jerked the reins, drawing the black mare to a halt, and peered about him suspiciously in the deep gloom. His scalp prickled in superstitious dread at the eery sound. Then he shrugged and spat an oath. No night-phantom, no hunting ghoul of the wastes; that was a cry of pain. This meant that still a third survivor of the doomed battle yet drew breath. And a living man might be presumed to be unlooted.

He swung from the saddle, wrapping the reins about the spokes of a broken chariot wheel. The cry had come from the left; here at the very edge of the battlefield, a wounded survivor might well have escaped the cunning eye of looters. Conan might ride into Zamora with a pouchful of gems yet.

The Cimmerian limped toward the source of the quavering moan, which came from the margin of the plain. He parted the straggling reeds that grew in shaggy clumps along the banks of the slow river and glared down at a pale figure, which writhed feebly at his very feet. It was a girl.

She lay there, half-naked, her white limbs cut and bruised. Blood was clotting in the foaming curls of her long, black hair, like a chain of rubies. There was unseeing agony in her lustrous dark eyes, and she moaned in delirium.

The Cimmerian stood looking down at her, noting almost absently the lithe beauty of her limbs and the rounded, lush young breasts. He was puzzled—what was a girl like this, a mere child, doing on a battlefield? She had not the sullen, flamboyant, sullied look of a camp trull about her. Her slim and graceful body denoted breeding, even nobility. Baffled, he shook his head, black mane swinging against brawny shoulders. At his feet, the girl stirred.

"*The Heart . . . the Heart . . . of Tammuz . . . O Master!*" she cried softly, her dark head turning restlessly from side to side, babbling as one in a fever.

Conan shrugged, and his eyes clouded momentarily by what, in another man, would have been an expression of pity. Wounded to the death, he thought grimly, and he lifted his sword to put the wench out of her misery.

As the blade hovered above her white breast, she whimpered again like a child in pain. The great sword halted in mid-air, and the Cimmerian stood for an instant, motionless as a bronze statue.

Then, in sudden decision, he slammed the sword back in its sheath and bent, lifting the girl effortlessly in his mighty arms. She struggled blindly, weakly, moaning in half-conscious protest.

Carrying her with careful tenderness, he limped toward the reed-masked riverbank and lay her down gently on the dry, cushioning reeds. Filling his cupped palms with river water, the barbarian bathed her white face and cleansed her cuts as gently as a mother might tend her child.

Her wounds proved superficial, mere bruises, save for the cut on her brow. And even that, although it had bled heavily, was far from mortal. Conan grunted with relief and bathed the girl's face and brow with cold, clear water. Then, awkwardly pillowing her head against his chest, he dribbled some of the water between her half-parted lips. She gasped, choked a little, and came awake—staring up at him from eyes like dark stars, clouded with bewilderment and the shadows of fear.

"Who—what—*the bats!*"

"They are gone now, girl," he said gruffly. "You have naught to fear. Came you hither from Yaralet?"

"Yes—yes—but who are you?"

"Conan, a Cimmerian. What is a lass like you doing on a battlefield?" he demanded.

But she seemed not to hear. Her brow frowned a little, as one in thought, and half under her breath she repeated his name.

"Conan—Conan—yes, that was the name!" Wonderingly she lifted her gaze to his scarred, brown face. "It was you I was sent to seek. How strange that you should find me!"

"And who sent you to seek me, wench?" he rumbled suspiciously.

"I am Hildico, a Brythunian, slave to the House of Atalis

the Far-seeing, who dwells yonder in Yaralet. My master sent me in secret to move among the warriors of King Yildiz, to seek one Conan, a mercenary of Cimmeria, and to bring him by a private way to his house within the city. You are the man I seek!"

"Aye? And what does your master want with me?"

The girl shook her dark head. "That I know not! But he said to tell you that he means no harm, and that much gold can be yours, if you will come."

"Gold, eh?" he mused, speculatively, helping her to her feet and steadying her with a brawny arm about her slim white shoulders as she staggered weakly.

"Yes. But I came not to the field in time to seek you before the battle. So I hid in the reeds along the river's edge to avoid the warriors. And then—the bats! Suddenly they were everywhere, swooping upon the fallen, killing—and one horseman fled from them into the reeds, trampling me under his hooves unawares—"

"What of this horseman?"

"Dead," she shuddered. "A bat tore him from the saddle and let his corpse fall into the river. I swooned, for in its panic, the horse struck me. . ." She lifted one small hand to her gashed brow.

"Lucky you were not slain," he growled. "Well, lass, we shall visit this master of yours, to learn what he wants of Conan—and how he knows my name!"

"You will come?" she asked breathlessly. He laughed and, vaulting astride the black mare, lifted her to the saddlebow before him with powerful arms.

"Aye! I am alone, amid enemies, in an alien land. My employment ended when Bakra's army was destroyed. Why should I scruple to meet a man who has picked me from ten thousand warriors, and who offers gold?"

They rode across the shallow ford of the river and across the gloom-drenched plain towards Yaralet, stronghold of Munthassem Khan. And Conan's heart, which never beat more joyously than when thrilled with the promise of excitement and adventure, sang.

4. *The House of Atalis*

A strange conclave was taking place in the small, velvet-hung, taper-lit chamber of Atalis, whom some men called a philosopher, others a seer, and others a rogue.

This figure of mystery was a slender man of medium height, with a splendid head and the ascetic features of a dedicated scholar, yet in his smooth face and keen eyes was something of the shrewd merchant. He was clad in a plain robe of rich fabric, and his head was shaven to denote devotion to study and the arts. As he talked in low tones with his companion, a third viewer—had any been present—might have observed something strange and curious about him. For Atalis, as he conversed, gestured with his left hand only. His right arm lay stretched across his lap at an unnatural angle. And from time to time his calm, clever features were hideously contorted with a sudden spasm of intense pain, at which time his right foot, hidden under his long robes, would twist back excruciatingly upon his ankle.

His companion was one whom the city of Yaralet knew and praised as Prince Than, scion of an ancient and noble house of Turan. The prince was a tall, lithe man, young and undeniably handsome. The firm, clean outline of his soldierly limbs and the steely quality of his cool gray eyes belied the foppishness of his curled and scented black locks and jewelled cloak.

Beside Atalis, who sat in a high-backed chair of dark wood carven by intricate skill with leering gargoyles and grinning faces, stood a small table of ebony inlaid with yellow ivory. Upon this rested a huge fragment of green crystal, as large as a human head. It flickered with a weird inward glow, and from time to time the philosopher would break off his low conversation to peer deeply within the glittering stone.

"Will she find him? And will he come?" Prince Than said, despairingly.

"He will come."

"But every moment that passes increases our danger. Even now Munthassem Khan may be watching, and it is dangerous for us to be together . . ."

"Munthassem Khan lies drugged with the dream lotus, for the Shadows of Nergal were abroad in the hour of sunset," said the philosopher. "And some danger we *must* risk, if ever the city is to be freed of this bloody-handed scourge!" His features knotted sickeningly in an involuntary grimace of intolerable pain, and then smoothed out again. He said grimly, "And you know, O Prince, how little time is left to us. Desperate measures for desperate men!"

Suddenly the prince's handsome face contorted with panic and he turned upon Atalis with eyes suddenly gone dead as cold marble. Almost as swiftly, light and animation returned to his gaze, and he sank back in his chair, pale and sweating.

"Very—little—time!" he gasped.

A hidden gong rang softly, somewhere within the dark and silent house of Atalis the Far-seeing. The philosopher raised his left hand to check the prince's involuntary start.

A moment later, one of the velvet wall-hangings drew aside, revealing a hidden door. And within the door, like a bloody apparition, stood the giant form of Conan with the half-fainting girl leaning on his arm.

With a little cry, the philosopher sprang to his feet and went toward the grim Cimmerian. "Welcome—thrice welcome, Conan! Come, enter. Here is wine—food—"

He gestured to a tabouret against the further wall and took the fainting girl from Conan. The Cimmerian's nostrils widened like those of some famished wolf at the scent of the food; but also, like a wolf, suspicious, wary of a trap, his smouldering blue eyes raked the smiling philosopher and the pale prince, and pried into every corner of the small chamber.

"See to the wench. She was trampled by a horse but brought me your message," he growled, and without ceremony he swaggered across the room, and poured and drained a goblet of strong red wine. Tearing a plump leg from a platter of roast fowl, he chewed hungrily. Atalis tugged a bell-rope and gave the girl into the keeping of a silent slave, who appeared from behind another hanging as if by magic.

"Now, what is this all about?" the Cimmerian demanded, seating himself on a low bench and wincing from the pain of his gashed thigh. "Who are you? How do you know my name? And what do you want of me?"

"We have time for talk, but later," Atalis replied. "Eat, drink, and rest You are wounded—"

"Crom take all this delay! We shall talk *now*."

"Very well. But you must let me cleanse and bind your wound while we talk!"

The Cimmerian shrugged impatiently and yielded with poor grace to the philosopher's swift ministrations. As Atalis sponged his gashed thigh, smeared the gaping wound with a scented salve, and bound it with a strip of clean cloth, Conan appeased his hunger by wolfing down the cold spiced meat and drinking deeply of the red wine.

"I know you, although we have never met," Atalis began in a smooth, soft voice, "because of my crystal—there, on yonder stand by the chair. Within its depths I can see and hear for a hundred leagues."

"Sorcery?" Conan spat sourly, having the warrior's contempt for all such magical mummery.

"If you like," Atalis smiled ingratiatingly. "But I am no sorceror—only a seeker after knowledge. A philisopher, some men call me—" His smile twisted into a terrible grin of agony, and with prickling scalp Conan watched the philosopher stagger as his foot bent horribly.

"Crom! Are you sick, man?"

Gasping from the pain, Atalis sank into his high-backed chair. "Not sick—cursed. By this fiend who rules us with a dread sceptre of hell-born magic. . ."

"Munthassem Khan?"

Atalis nodded wearily. "That I am no sorceror has spared my life—thus far. For the satrap slew all wizards in Yaralet; I, being but a humble philosopher, he let live. Yet he suspects that I know something of the Black Arts and has cursed me with this deadly scourge. It withers up my body and tortures my nerves, and will end in a convulsion of death, ere long!" He gestured at the unnaturally twisted limb that lay lifeless across his lap.

Prince Than gazed with wild eyes at Conan. "I, too, have been cursed by this hell-spawn, for that I am next to Munthassem Khan in rank and he thinks I may desire his throne. Me he has tortured in another way: a sickness of the brain—spasms of blindness that come and go—which will end by devouring my brain and leaving me a mindless, sightless, mewling thing!"

"Crom!" Conan swore softly. The philosopher gestured.

"You are our only hope! You alone can save our city from this black-hearted devil that torments and plagues us!"

Conan stared at him blankly. "I? But I am no wizard, man! What a warrior can do with cold steel, I can do; but how can I combat this devil's magic?"

"Listen, Conan of Cimmeria. I will tell you a strange and awful tale. . ."

5. *The Hand of Nergal*

In the city of Yaralet (said Atalis) when night falls, the people bar their windows, bolt their doors, and sit shuddering behind these barriers, praying in terror with candles burning before their household gods till the clean, wholesome light of dawn etches the squat towers of the city with living fire against the paling skies.

No archers guard the gates. No watchmen stride the lonely streets. No thief steals nimbly through the winding alleys, nor do painted sluts simper and beckon from the dark shadows. For in Yaralet, rogues and honest folk alike shun the night-shadows: thief, beggar, assassin, and bedizened wench seek haven in foul-smelling dens or dim-lit taverns. From dusk to dawn, Yaralet is a city of silence, her black ways empty and desolate.

It was not always thus. Once this was a bright and prosperous city, bustling with commerce, with shops and bazaars, filled with happy people who lived under the strong hand of a wise and gentle satrap—Munthassem Khan. He taxed them lightly, ruling with justice and mercy, busy with his private collection of antiquities and in the study of these ancient objects which absorbed his keen, questing mind. The caravans of slow-pacing camels that wound from the Desert Gate bore always with them, amongst the merchants, his agents seeking for rare and curious oddities to purchase for their master's private museum.

Then he changed, and a terrible shadow fell over Yaralet. The satrap was like one under a powerful and evil spell. Where he had been kind, he became cruel. Where generous, greedy. Where just and merciful, secretive, tyrannical, and savage.

Suddenly, the city guard seized men—nobles, wealthy merchants, priests, magicians—who vanished into the pits beneath the satrap's palace, never to be seen again.

Some whispered that a caravan from the far south had brought to him something from the depths of demon-haunted Stygia. Few had glimpsed it, and of those one said shudderingly that the thing was carven with strange, uncouth hieroglyphs like those seen on the dusty Stygian tombs. It seemed to cast an evil spell over the satrap, and it lent him amazing powers of black sorcery. Weird forces shielded him from those despairing patriots who sought to slay him. Strange crimson lights blazed in the windows of a tall tower of his palace, where men whispered that he had converted an empty suite into a grim temple to some dark and bloody god.

And terror walked the streets of nighted Yaralet, as if summoned from the realm of death by some awesome, devil-purchased lore.

Exactly what they feared at night, the people did not know. But it was no vain dream against which they soon came to bolt their doors. Men hinted at slinking, batlike forms glimpsed from barred windows—of hovering, shadowy horrors alien to human knowledge, deadly to human sanity. Tales spread of doorways splintered in the night, of sudden unearthly cries and shrieks torn from human throats—followed by significant, and utter, silence. And they dared to tell of the rising sun illuminating broken doors that swung in houses suddenly and unaccountably empty . . .

The thing from Stygia was the Hand of Nergal.

"It looks," said Atalis softly, "like a clawed hand carven of old ivory, worked all over with weird glyphs in a forgotten tongue. The claws clasp a sphere of shadowy, dim crystal. I know that the satrap has it: I have seen it here" —he gestured—"in my crystal. For, although no enchanter, I have learned some of the Dark Arts."

Conan stirred restlessly. "And you know of this thing?"

Atalis smiled faintly. "Know of it? Aye! Old books speak of it and whisper the dark legend of its bloody history. The blind seer who penned the *Book of Skelos* knew it well . . . Nergal's Hand they name it, shudderingly. They say it fell from the stars into the sunset isles of the uttermost west, ages upon ages before King Kull rose to bring the Seven Empires beneath his single standard. Centuries and ages beyond thought have rolled across the world since first bearded Pictish fishermen drew it dripping from the deep and stared wonderingly into its shadowy fires! They bartered it to greedy Atlantean merchants, and it passed east across the world. The withered, hoary-bearded mages of elder Thule and dark Grondar probed its mysteries in their towers of purple and silver. The serpent men of shadow-haunted Valusia peered into its glimmering depths. With it, Kom-Yazoth whelmed the Thirty Kings until the Hand turned upon and slew him. For the *Book of Skelos* says the Hand brings two gifts unto its possessor—first, power beyond all limit—then, death beyond all despair."

Only the calm voice of the philosopher droned through the hushed room, but the black-headed warrior thought he could hear, as in a dream, the faint echo of thundering chariots, the clash of steel, the cry of tormented kings drowned in the clangor of collapsing empires. . . .

"When all of the elder world was broken in the Cataclysm and the green sea rolled in restless fathoms above the shattered spires of lost Atlantis, and the nations sank one by one in red ruin, the Hand passed from the knowledge of men. For three thousand years the Hand slept, but when the young kingdoms of Koth and Ophir awoke and slowly emerged from the murk of barbarism, the talisman was found. The dark wizard-kings of grim Acheron plumbed its secrets, and when the lusty Hyborians broke that cruel kingdom beneath their heel, it passed southwards into dusty Stygia, where the bloody priests of that black land set it to terrible purposes in rites of which I dare not speak. It fell, when some swarthy sorceror was slain, and was buried with him, sleeping away the centuries . . . but now tomb robbers have roused the Hand of Nergal again, and it has come into the possession of Munthassem Khan. The temptation of ultimate and absolute power, which it holds out to all, has corrupted him, as countless others have been corrupted, who fell beneath its insidious spell. I fear me, Cimmerian, for all these lands, now that the Demon's Hand wakes and dark forces walk the earth again . . ."

Atalis' voice died away in whispering silence, and Conan growled uneasily, bristling.

"Well . . . Crom, man, what have I to do with such matters?" he rumbled.

"You alone can destroy the influence of the talisman over the satrap's mind!"

The smouldering blue eyes widened. "How?"

"You alone possess the counter-talisman."

"I? You are mad—I hold no truck with amulets and suchlike magical trash—!"

Atalis stilled him with a lifted palm. "Did you not find a curious golden object before the battle?" he queried, softly. Conan started.

"Aye, that I did—at Bahari, yestereve, as we lay in camp—" He plunged one hand into his pocket-pouch and drew out the smooth, glowing stone. The philosopher and the prince stared at it, drawing in their breaths.

"*The Heart of Tammuz!* Yes, the counter-talisman in very truth—!" Heart-shaped it was, and large as a child's fist, worked in golden amber or perhaps rare yellow jade. It lay there in the Cimmerian's hand, glowing with soft fires, and he remembered with a prickling of awe how the healing, tingling warmth of it had driven from his body the supernatural chill of the bat-winged shadows.

"Come, Conan! We shall accompany you. There is a secret passageway from this my chamber into the satrap's hall—an underground tunnel like that by which my slave, Hildico, led you under the city streets into my house. You, armed with the protection of the Heart, shall slay Munthassem Khan, or destroy the Hand of Nergal. There is no danger, for he lies deep in a magical slumber, which comes upon him whenever he has need to summon forth the Shadows of Nergal, as he has already done this night to overwhelm the Turanian army of King Yildiz. Come!"

Conan strode to the table and drained the last of the wine. Then, shrugging, muttering an oath to Crom, he followed the limping seer and the slim prince into a dark opening behind an arras.

In a moment they were gone, and the chamber lay empty and silent as a grave. The only motion came from flickering lights within the green, jagged crystal beside the chair. Within its depths one could see the small figure of Munthassem Khan, lying in a drugged sleep within his mighty hall.

6. *The Heart of Tammuz*

They strode through endless darkness. Water dripped from the roof of the rock-hewn tunnel, and now and then the red eyes of rats gleamed at them from the tunnel's floor, gleamed and were gone with squeaks of rage as the small scavengers fled before the footsteps of the strange beings who invaded their subterranean domain.

Atalis went first, trailing his one good hand along the wet, uneven cavern wall.

"I would not set this task on you, my young friend," he was saying in a low whisper. "But it was into your hands the Heart of Tammuz fell, and I sense a purpose—a destiny—in its choice. There is an affinity between opposed forces, such as the Dark Power we symbolize as 'Nergal' and the Power of Light we call 'Tammuz.' The Heart awoke and, in some manner beyond knowledge, caused itself to be found; for the Hand was also awake and working its dread purpose. Thus I commend you to this task, for the Powers seem to have singled you for this deed—*hush!* We are beneath the palace now. We are almost there—" He drew ahead and stroked one delicate hand over the rough surface of rock that closed off the passage. A mass of rock swung silently aside on secret counterweights. Light burst upon them.

They stood at one end of a vast, shadow-filled hall whose high, vaulted roof was lost in darkness overhead. In the center of the hall, which was otherwise empty save for rows of mighty columns, stood a square dais, and upon the dais, a massive throne of black marble, and upon the throne—Munthassem Khan.

He was of middle years, but thin and wasted, gaunt to the point of emaciation. Paper-white, unhealthy flesh and shrunken upon his skull-like face, and dark circles shadowed his hollow eyes. Clasped across his chest as he lay sprawled in the throne, he held an ivory rod, like a sceptre. Its end was worked into a demon's claw, grasping a smoky crystal that pulsed like a living heart with slow fires. Beside the throne, a dish of brass smoked with a narcotic incense: the dream lotus whose fumes empowered the sorceror to release the shadow-demons of Nergal. Atalis tugged at Conan's arm.

"See—he still sleeps! The Heart will protect you. Seize the ivory Hand from him, and all his power will be gone!" Conan growled reluctant consent, and started forward, his naked sword in one hand. There was something about this that he did not like. It was too easy . . .

"Ah, gentlemen. I have been expecting you."

On the dais, Munthassem Khan smiled down at them as they froze in astonishment. His tones were gentle, but a fury of mad rage flamed in his sick eyes. He lifted the ivory sceptre of power; he gestured . . .

The lights flickered eerily. And suddenly, shockingly, the limping seer screamed. His muscles contorted in a spasm of unendurable agony. He fell forward on the marble flags, writhing in pain.

"*Crom!*"

Prince Than plucked at his rapier, but a gesture of the

magic Hand stayed him. His eyes went blank and dead. Icy sweat started from his paling brow. He shrieked and sank to his knees, clawing frantically at his brow as pangs of blinding pain tore through his brain.

"And you, my young barbarian!"

Conan sprang. He moved like a striking panther, burly limbs a blur of speed. He was upon the first step of the dais before Munthassem Khan could move. His sword flashed up, wavered, and fell from strengthless hands. A wave of arctic cold numbed his limbs. It radiated from the cloudy gem within the ivory claw. He gasped for breath.

The burning eyes of Munthassem Khan blazed into his. The skull-like face chuckled with a ghastly imitation of mirth.

"The Heart protects, in very truth—but only him who knows how to invoke its power!" the satrap gloated, chuckling as the Cimmerian strove to summon strength into his iron limbs again. Conan set his jaw and fought grimly, savagely against the tide of chill and fetid darkness that poured in black rays from the demonic crystal and slowly blurred his mind. Strength drained from his limbs as wine from a slashed wineskin; he sank to his knees, then slumped at the foot of the dais. He felt his consciousness shrink to a tiny, lone point of light lost in a vast abyss of roaring darkness; the last spark of will wavered like a candle-flame in a gale. Hopeless, yet with the fierce, indominable determination of his savage breed, he fought on . . .

7. *Heart and Hand*

A woman screamed. Startled, Munthassem Khan jerked at the unexpected sound. His attention flickered away from Conan—his focus broke—and in that brief instant the slim white form of a nude girl with dark flashing eyes and a black torrent of foaming curls ran on swift feet across the pave from the shadow of a column to the side of the helpless Cimmerian.

Through the roaring haze, Conan gaped at her. Hildico?

Swift as thought, she knelt by his side. One white hand dipped into his pouch and emerged, clutching the Heart of Tammuz. She sprang lithely to her feet and hurled the counter-talisman at Munthassem Khan.

It caught him full between the eyes with an audible thud. Eyes filming, he sank bonelessly into the cushioned embrace of his black throne. The Hand of Nergal slid from nerveless fingers to clank against the marble step.

In the instant the talisman fell from the satrap's grip, the spell that bound Atalis and Prince Than in webs of scarlet agony snapped. Pale, shaken, exhausted, they were whole. And Conan's mighty strength poured back into his sprawled body. Cursing, he leapt to his feet. One hand caught Hildico's rounded shoulder and spun her away, out of danger, while with his other he snatched up his sword from the marble pave. Poised, he was ready to strike.

But he stopped, blinking with astonishment. At either side of the satrap's body lay the two talismans. And from both arose weird shapes of force.

From the Hand of Nergal, a darkly shimmering web of evil radiance spread—a glow of darkness, like the sheen of polished ebony. The foetor of the Pit was its unholy breath, and the bone-deep chill of interstellar space was its blighting touch. Before its subtle advance, the orange glare of the torches faded. It grew larger, fringed with writhing tentacles of radiant blackness.

But a nimbus of golden glory strengthened about the Heart of Tammuz and rose, forming a cloud of dazzling amber fire. The warmth of a thousand honey-hearted springs flowed from it, negating the arctic chill, and shafts of rich gold light cleaved the inky web of Nergal. The two cosmic forces met and fought. From this battle of the gods, Conan retreated with reluctant steps, joining his shaken comrades. He stood with them, staring with awe at the unimaginable conflict. Trembling, the nude form of Hildico shrank into the shelter of his arm.

"How did you get here, girl?" he demanded. She smiled wanly, with frightened eyes.

"I awoke, recovering from my swoon, and came into the Master's chamber, finding it empty. But within the Master's crystal of seership I saw your simulacra enter the satrap's hall and watched as he awoke and faced you. I, I followed—and finding you in his power, chanced all on a try for the Heart . . ."

"Lucky for all that you did," Conan acknowledged grimly. Atalis clutched his arm.

"*Look!*"

The golden fog of Tammuz was now a giant, flashing figure of intolerable light, dimly manlike in configuration but huge as those Colossi hewn from the stone cliffs of Shem by age-forgotten hands.

The dark shape of Nergal, too, had swelled into giant proportions. It was now a vast, ebon thing, brutal, hulking, misshapen, more like to some stupendous ape than manlike. In the foggy hump that was its brutlelike head, slitted eyes of malignant fire blazed like emerald stars.

The two forces came together with a thunderous, shattering roar like colliding worlds. The very walls shook at the fury of their meeting. Some half-forgotten sense within their flesh told the four that titanic cosmic forces strove and fought. The air was filled with the bitter stench of ozone. Foot-long sparks of electric fire crackled and snapped through the roiling fury as the golden god and the shadowy demon came together.

Shafts of unendurable brilliance tore through the clotted, struggling shadow-form. Bolts of blazing glory ripped it into shreds of drifting darkness. For a moment the dark web enshrouded, and dimmed, the golden flashing shape —but for a moment, only. Another roar of earth-shattering thunder, and the black one dissolved before the embrace of intolerable brightness. Then it was gone. And for a moment the figure of light towered above the dais, consuming it like a funeral pyre—then it, too, was gone.

Silence reigned in the thunder-riven hall of Munthassem Khan. Upon the blasted dais, both talismans had vanished —whether reduced to atoms by the fury of the cosmic forces that had been released here, or transported to some far place to await the next awakening of the beings they symbolized and contained, none could say.

And the body upon the dais? Naught of it was left, save for a handful of ashes.

"The heart is always stronger than the hand," Atalis said softly, in the ringing silence.

Conan reined the great black steed with a rough but masterly hand. It trembled, eager to be off, hooves ringing on the cobbles. He grinned, his barbaric blood thrilling to the might of the superb mare. A vast cloak of crimson silk belled from his broad shoulders, and his coat of silvered iron mesh mail glittered in the morning light.

"You are determined, then, to leave us, Conan?" asked Prince Than, resplendent in his robes as new satrap of Yaralet.

"Aye! The Satrap's Guard is a tame place, and I hunger for this new war King Yildiz is mounting against the hill tribes. A week of inaction, and I've had a bellyfull of peace! So fare you well, Than, Atalis!"

He tugged sharply on the reins, drawing the black mare about, and cantered out of the courtyard of the seer's house, while Atalis and the prince watched benignly.

"Odd that a mercenary like Conan would accept less in payment than he could get," the new satrap commented. "I offered him a chest full of gold—enough to support him for life. But he would take only one small sack, together with the horse he found on the battlefield and his pick of arms and garments. Too much gold, he said, would only slow him down."

Atalis shrugged—then smiled, pointing to the far end of the courtyard. A slim Brythunian girl with long mane of black curls appeared in a doorway. She came up to Conan, who drew the mare to a halt; he bent to speak with her. They exchanged a few words; then he reached down and caught her supple waist and swung her up before him onto the saddle. She sat sideways, clinging with both arms to his burly neck, her face buried in his breast.

He swung about, flung up one brawny arm, grinned back at them in farewell, and rode off with the lithe girl clasped before him.

Atalis chuckled. "Some men fight for things other than gold," he observed.

The City of Skulls

Conan remains in Turanian service for about two years, becoming an expert horseman and archer and traveling over the immense deserts, mountains, and jungles of Hyrkania, as far as the borders of Khitai. One such journey takes him to the fabled kingdom of Meru, a comparatively unknown land between Vendhya to the south, Hyrkania to the north and west, and Khitai to the east.

1. *Red Snow*

HOWLING LIKE WOLVES, a horde of squat, brown warriors swept down upon the Turanian troop from the foothills of the Talakma Mountains, where the hills flattened out into the broad, barren steppes of Hyrkania. The attack came at sunset. The western horizon streamed with scarlet banners, while to the south the invisible sun tinged the snows of the higher peaks with red.

For fifteen days, the escort of Turanians had jogged across the plain, fording the chill waters of the Zaporoska River, venturing deeper and ever deeper into the illimitable distances of the East. Then, without warning, came the attack.

Conan caught the body of Hormaz as the lieutenant slumped from his horse, a quivering, black-feathered arrow protruding from his throat. He lowered the body to the ground; then, shouting a curse, the young Cimmerian ripped his broad-bladed tulwar from its scabbard and turned with his comrades to meet the howling charge. For most of a month, he had ridden the dusty Hyrkanian plains as part of the escort. The monotony had long since begun to chafe him, and now his barbaric soul craved violent action to dispell his boredom.

His blade met the gilded scimitar of the foremost rider with such terrific force that the other's sword snapped near the hilt. Grinning like a tiger, Conan drew his sword in a back-handed slash across the bowlegged little warrior's belly. Howling like a doomed soul on the red-hot floors of Hell, his opponent fell twitching into a patch of blood-spattered snow.

Conan twisted in his saddle to catch another slashing sword on his shield. As he knocked the foeman's blade aside, he drove the point of his tulwar straight into the slant-eyed, yellowish face that snarled into his, watching the enemy's visage dissolve into a smear of ruined flesh.

Now the attackers were upon them in force. Dozens of small, dark men in fantastic, intricate armor of lacquered leather, trimmed with gold and flashing with gems, assailed them with demoniac frenzy. Bows twanged, lances thrust, and swords whirled and clashed.

Beyond the ring of his attackers, Conan saw his comrade Juma, a gigantic black from Kush, fighting on foot; his horse had fallen to an arrow at the first rush. The Kushite had lost his fur hat, so that the golden bangle in one ear winked in the fading light; but he had retained his lance. With this, he skewered three of the stocky attackers out of their saddles, one after another.

Beyond Juma, at the head of the column of King Yildiz's troop of picked warriors, the commander of the escort, Prince Ardashir, thundered commands from atop his mighty stallion. He wheeled his horse back and forth to keep between the foe and the horse-litter which bore his charge. This was Yildiz's daughter, Zosara. The troop were escorting the princess to her wedding with Kujula, the Great Khan of the Kuigar nomads.

Even as Conan watched, he saw Prince Ardashir clutch at his fur-cloaked chest. As if conjured up by magic, a black arrow had sprouted suddenly from his gemmed gorget. The prince gaped at the shaft; then, stiff as a statue, he toppled from horseback, his jewel-crusted, spiked helmet falling into the blood-spotted snow.

Thereafter, Conan became too busy to notice anything but the foes that swept howling around him. Although little more than a youth, the Cimmerian towered several inches above six feet. The swarthy attackers were dwarfed by comparison with his clean-limbed height. As they whirled around him in a snarling, yelping ring, they looked like a pack of hounds attempting to pull down a kingly tiger.

The battle swirled up and down the slope, like dead leaves whirled by autumnal gusts. Horses stamped, reared, and screamed; men hacked, cursed, and yelled. Here and there a pair of dismounted men continued their battle on foot. Bodies of men and horses lay in the churned mud and the trampled snow.

Conan, a red haze of fury thickening before his eyes, swung his tulwar with berserk fury. He would have preferred one of the straight broadswords of the West, to which he was more accustomed. Nevertheless, in the first few moments of the battle, he wreaked scarlet havoc with the unfamiliar weapon. In his flying hand, the glittering steel blade wove a shimmering web of razor-edged death about him. Into that web no less than nine of the sallow little men in lacquered leather ventured, to fall disemboweled or headless from their shaggy ponies. As he fought, the burly young Cimmerian bellowed a savage war chant of his primitive people; but soon he found that he needed every last bit of breath, for the battle grew rather than lessened in intensity.

Only seven months before, Conan had been the only warrior to survive the ill-fated punitive expedition that

King Yildiz had launched against a rebellious satrap of northern Turan, Munthassem Khan. By means of black sorcery, the satrap had smashed the force sent against him. He had—so he thought—wiped out the hostile army from its high-born general, Bakra of Akif, down to the lowliest mercenary foot soldier. Young Conan alone had survived. He lived to penetrate the city of Yaralet, which was writhing under the magic-maddened satrap's rule, and to bring a terrible doom on Munthassem Khan.

Returning in triumph to the glittering Turanian capital of Aghrapur, Conan received, as a reward, a place in this honor guard. At first he had had to endure the gibes of his fellow troopers at his clumsy horsemanship and indifferent skill with the bow. But the gibes soon died away as the other guardsmen learned to avoid provoking a swing of Conan's sledgehammer fists, and as his skill in riding and shooting improved with practice.

Now, Conan was beginning to wonder if this expedition could truly be called a reward. The light, leathern shield on his left arm was hacked into a shapeless ruin; he cast it aside. An arrow struck his horse's rump. With a scream, the beast brought its head down and bucked, lashing out with its heels. Conan went flying over its head; the horse bolted and disappeared.

Shaken and battered, the Cimmerian scrambled to his feet and fought on afoot. The scimitars of his foes slashed away his cloak and opened rents in his hauberk of chain mail. They slit the leathern jerkin beneath, until Conan bled from a dozen little superficial wounds.

But he fought on, teeth bared in a mirthless grin and eyes blazing a volcanic blue in a flushed, congested face framed by a square-cut black mane. One by one his fellows were cut down, until only he and the gigantic black, Juma, stood back to back. The Kushite howled wordlessly as he swung the butt of his broken lance like a club.

Then it seemed as if a hammer came up out of the red mist of berserk fury that clouded Conan's brain, as a heavy mace crashed against the side of his head, denting and cracking the spiked helm and driving the metal against his temple. His knees buckled and gave. The last thing he heard was the sharp, despairing cry of the princess as squat, grinning warriors tore her from the veiled palanquin down to the red snow that splotched the slope. Then, as he fell face down, he knew nothing.

2. *The Cup of the Gods*

A thousand red devils were beating against Conan's skull with red-hot hammers, and his cranium rang like a smitten anvil with every motion. As he slowly clambered out of black insensibility, Conan found himself dangling over one mighty shoulder of his comrade Juma, who grinned to see him awaken and helped him to stand. Although his head hurt abominably, Conan found he was strong enough to stay on his feet. Wondering, he looked about him.

Only he, Juma, and the girl Zosara had survived. The rest of the party—including Zosara's maid, slain by an arrow—were food for the gaunt, gray wolves of the Hyrkanian steppe. They stood on the northern slopes of the Talakmas, several miles south of the site of the battle. Stocky brown warriors in lacquered leather, many with bandaged wounds, surrounded them. Conan found that his wrists were stoutly manacled, and that massive iron chains linked the manacles. The princess, in silken coat and trousers, was also fettered; but her chains and fetters were much lighter and seemed to be made of solid silver.

Juma was also chained, upon him most of the attention of their captors was focused. They crowded around the Kushite, feeling his skin and then glancing at their fingers to see if his color had come off. One even moistened a piece of cloth in a patch of snow and then rubbed it against the back of Juma's hand. Juma grinned broadly and chuckled.

"It must be they've never seen a man like me," he said to Conan.

The officer in command of the victors snapped a command. His men swung into their saddles. The princess was bundled back into her horse litter. To Conan and Juma the commander said, in broken Hyrkanian:

"You two! You walk."

And walk they did, with the spears of the Azweri, as their captors were called, nudging them with frequent pricks between their shoulders. The litter of the princess swayed between its two horses in the middle of the column. Conan noted that the commander of the Azweri troop treated Zosara with respect; she did not appear to have been physically harmed. This chieftain did not seem to bear any grudge against Conan and Juma for the havoc they had wrought among his men, the death and wounds they had dealt.

"You damn good fighters!" he said with a grin.

On the other hand, he took no chances of letting his prisoners escape, or of letting them slow down the progress of his company by lagging. They were made to walk at a brisk pace from before dawn to after sunset, and any pause was countered by a prod with a lance. Conan set his jaw and obeyed for the moment.

For two days they wended over a devious trail through the heart of the mountain range. They crossed passes where they had to plow through deep snow, still unmelted from the previous winter. Here the breath came short from the altitude, and sudden storms whipped their ragged garments and drove stinging particles of snow and hail against their faces. Juma's teeth chattered. The black man found the cold much harder to endure than Conan, who had been reared in a northerly clime.

They came forth on the southern slopes of the Talakmas at last, to look upon a fantastic sight—a vast, green valley that sloped down and away before them. It was as if they stood on the lip of a stupendous dish. Below them, little clouds crept over leagues of dense, green jungle. In the midst of this jungle, a great lake or inland sea reflected the azure of the clear, bright sky.

Beyond this body of water, the green continued on until it was lost in a distant purple haze. And above the haze, jagged and white, standing out sharply against the blue, rose the peaks of the mighty Himelias, hundreds of miles further south. The Himelias formed the other lip of the dish, which was encircled by the vast crescent of the Talakmas to the north and the Himelias to the south.

Conan spoke to the officer: "What valley is this?"

"Meru," said the chief. "Men call it, Cup of Gods."

"Are we going down there?"

"Aye. You go to great city, Shamballah."

"Then what?"

"That for *rimpoche*—for god-king to decide."

"Who's he?"

"Jalung Thongpa, Terror of Men and Shadow of Heaven. You move along now, white-skinned dog. No time for talk."

Conan growled deep in his throat as a spear prick urged him on, silently vowing some day to teach this god-king the meaning of terror. He wondered if this ruler's divinity were proof against a foot of steel in his guts. . . . But any such happy moment was still in the future.

Down they went, into the stupendous depression. The air grew warmer; the vegetation, denser. By the end of the day they were slogging through a land of steaming jungle warmth and swampy forest, which overhung the road in dense masses of somber dark green, relieved by the brilliant blossoms of flowering trees. Bright-hued birds sang and screeched. Monkeys chattered in the trees. Insects buzzed and bit. Snakes and lizards slithered out of the path of the party.

It was Conan's first acquaintance with a tropical jungle, and he did not like it. The insects bothered him, and the sweat ran off him in streams. Juma, on the other hand, grinned as he stretched and filled his huge lungs.

"It is like my homeland," he said.

Conan was struck silent with awe at the fantastic landscape of verdant jungle and steamy swamp. He could almost believe that this vast valley of Meru was, in truth, the home of the gods, where they had dwelt since the dawn of time. Never had he seen such trees as those colossal cycads and redwoods, which towered into the misty heavens. He wondered how such a tropical jungle could be surrounded by mountains clad in eternal snows.

Once an enormous tiger stepped noiselessly into the path before them—a monster nine feet long, with fangs like daggers. Princess Zosara, watching from her litter, gave a little scream. There was a quick motion among the Azweri and a rattle of accouterments as they readied their weapons. The tiger, evidently thinking the party too strong for it, slipped into the jungle as silently as it had come.

Later, the earth shook to a heavy tread. With a loud snort, a huge beast burst from the rhododendron thickets and thundered across their path. As gray and rounded as a mountainous boulder, it somewhat resembled an enormous pig, with thick hide folded into bands. From its snout, a stout, blunt, recurved horn, a foot in length, arose. It halted, staring stupidly at the cavalcade from dim little pig's eyes; then, with another snort, it crashed off through the underbrush.

"Nose-horn," said Juma. "We have them in Kush."

The jungle gave way at length to the shores of the great

blue lake or inland sea that Conan had seen from the heights. For a time, they followed the curve of this unknown body of water, which the Azweri called *Sumeru Tso*. At last, across a bay of this sea, they sighted the walls, domes, and spires of a city of rose-red stone, standing amid fields and paddies between the jungle and the sea.

"Shamballah!" cried the commander of the Azweri. As one man, their captors dismounted, knelt, and touched their foreheads to the damp earth, while Conan and Juma exchanged a mystified glance.

"Here gods dwell!" said the chief. "You walk fast, now. If you make us late, they skin you alive. Hurry!"

3. *The City of Skulls*

The gates of the city were fashioned of bronze, green with age and cast in the likeness of a gigantic, horned human skull. Square, barred windows above the portal made the skulls's eye sockets, while below them the barred grill of the portcullis grinned at them like the teeth in fleshless jaws. The leader of the little warriors winded his twisted bronze trumpet, and the portcullis rose. They entered the unknown city.

Here, everything was hewn and carved from rose-pink stone. The architecture was ornate, cluttered with sculpture and friezes swarming with demons and monsters and many-armed gods. Gigantic faces of red stone glared down from the sides of towers, which dwindled tier upon tier into tapering spires.

Every where he looked, Conan saw carvings in the form of human skulls. They were set into the lintels over doorways. They hung on golden chains about the yellow-brown necks of the Meruvians, whose only other garment, both for men and for women, was a short skirt. They appeared on the bosses of the shields of the guards at the gate and were riveted to the fronts of their bronze helmets.

Through the broad, well-planned avenues of this fantastic city the troop pursued its course. The half-naked Meruvians stepped out of their way, casting brief, incurious glances at the two stalwart prisoners and at the horse litter containing the princess. Among the throngs of bare-breasted city-dwellers moved, like crimson shadows, the forms of shaven-headed priests, swathed from neck to ankle in voluminous robes of gauzy red stuff.

Amid groves of trees, covered with flowers of scarlet, azure, and gold, the palace of the god-king loomed up before them. It consisted of one gigantic cone or spire, tapering up from a squat, circular base. Made entirely of red stone, the round tower wall climbed upwards in a spiral, like that of some curious, conical sea-shell. On each stone of the spiral parapet was graved the likeness of a human skull. The palace gave the impression of a tremendous tower made of death's heads. Zosara could scarcely repress a shudder at this sinister ornamentation, and even Conan set his jaw grimly.

They entered through another skull-gate and thence through massive stone walls and huge rooms into the throne-room of the god-king. The Azweri, dirty and travel-stained, remained in the rear, while a pair of gilded guardsmen, each armed with an ornate halberd, took the arms of each of the three prisoners and led them to the throne.

The throne, which rested atop a dais of black marble, was all of one huge piece of pale jade, carven into the likeness of ropes and chains of skulls, fantastically looped and interwoven. Upon this greenish-white chair of death sat the half-divine monarch, who had summoned the prisoners into this unknown world.

For all the seriousness of his plight, Conan could not repress a grin. For the *rimpoche* Jalung Thongpa was very short and fat, with scrawny bow legs that scarcely reached the floor. His huge belly was swathed in a sash of cloth-of-gold, which blazed with gems. His naked arms, swollen with flabby fat, were clasped by a dozen golden armlets, and jeweled rings flashed and winked on his pudgy fingers.

The bald head that lolled on top of his misshapen body was notably ugly, with dangling dewlaps, pendulous lips, and crooked, discolored teeth. The head was topped by a spired helmet or crown of solid gold, blazing with rubies. Its weight seemed to bow its wearer beneath it.

As Conan looked more closely at the god-king, he saw that Jalung Thongpa was peculiarly deformed. One side of his face did not match the other. It hung slackly from the bone and bore a blank, filmed eye, while the other eye was bright with the glint of malicious intelligence.

The rimpoche's good eye was now fixed upon Zosara, ignoring the two gigantic warriors who accompanied her. Beside the throne stood a tall, gaunt man in the scarlet robes of a Meruvian priest. Beneath his shaven pate, cold green eyes looked out upon the scene with icy contempt. To him the god-king turned and spoke in a high, squeaky voice. From the few words of Meruvian that Conan had picked up from the Azweri, he pieced together enough to understand that the tall priest was the king's chief wizard, the Grand Shaman, Tanzong Tengri.

From scraps of the ensuing conversation, Conan further guessed that, by his magic, the shaman had seen the approach of the troop escorting the Princess Zosara to her Kuigar bridegroom and had shown this vision to the god-king. Filled with simple, human lust for the slim Turanian girl, Jalung Thongpa had dispatched the troop of his Azweri horsemen to seize her and fetch her to his seraglio.

That was all that Conan wanted to know. For seven days, ever since his capture, he had been pushed and prodded and bedeviled. He had walked his feet off, and his temper was at the breaking point.

The two guards that flanked him were facing the throne with respectfully downcast eyes, giving their full attention to the rimpoche, who might at any instant issue a command. Conan gently helfted the chains that bound his wrists. They were too stout for him to break by main force; he had tried in the first days of this captivity and failed.

Quietly, he brought his wrists together, so that the length of chain hung down in a loop for a foot. Then, pivoting, he suddenly snapped his arms up past the head of the left-hand guard. The slack of the chain, swung like a whip, caught the guard across the face and sent him staggering back, blood gushing from a broken nose.

At Conan's first violent movement, the other guard had whirled and brought down the head of his halberd to the guard position. As he did so, Conan caught the head of the halberd in the slack of the chain and jerked the pole arm out of the guard's grasp.

A slash with the slack of the chain sent another guard reeling back, clutching the bloody ruin of his mouth and spitting a broken tooth. Conan's feet were chained too closely together to permit a full stride. But from the floor in front of the dais he leaped with both feet together, like a frog. In two such grotesque bounds, Conan was up on the dais, and his hands were locked about the fat neck of the slobbering little god-king, squatting on his pile of skulls. The rimpoche's good eye goggled in terror, and his face blackened from the pressure of Conan's thumbs on his windpipe.

The guards and nobles fluttered about, squealing with panic, or stood frozen with shock and terror at this strange giant who dared to lay violent hands upon their divinity.

"One move toward me, and I crush the life from this fat toad!" Conan growled.

Alone of the Meruvians in the room, the Grand Shaman had shown no sign of panic or surprise when the ragged youth had exploded in a whirlwind of fury. In perfect Hyrkanian, he asked:

"What is your will, barbarian?"

"Set free the girl and the black! Give us horses, and we will quit your accursed valley forever. Refuse—or try to trick us—and I'll crush your little king to a pulp!"

The shaman nodded his skull-like head. His green eyes were as cold as ice in the masklike face of tight-stretched, saffron skin. With a commanding gesture, he raised his carven staff of ebony.

"Set free the princess Zosara and the black-skinned captive," he ordered calmly. Pale-faced servitors with frightened eyes scurried to do his bidding. Juma grunted, rubbing his wrists. Beside him, the princess shivered. Conan swung the limp form of the king in front of him and stepped from the dais.

"Conan!" bellowed Juma. "Beware!"

Conan whirled, but too late. As he had moved to the edge of the dais, the Grand Shaman acted. Nimble as a striking cobra, his ebony staff flicked out and lightly tapped Conan's shoulder, where his naked skin bulged through the rents in his ragged clothing. Conan's lunge toward his antagonist was never completed. Numbness spread through his body, like venom from a reptile's fang. His mind clouded; his head, too heavy to hold up, fell forward on his chest. Limply, he collapsed. The half-strangled little god-king tore free from his grasp.

The last sound Conan heard was the thunderous bellow of the black as he went down under the wriggling swarm of brown bodies.

4. *The Ship of Blood*

Above all, it was hot and it stank. The dead, vitiated air of the dungeon was stale. It reeked with the stench of close-packed, sweating bodies. A score of naked men were crammed into one filthy hole, surrounded on all sides by huge blocks of stone weighing many tons. Many were small, brown Meruvians, who sprawled about, listless and apathetic. There were a handful of the squat, slant-eyed little warriors who guarded the sacred valley, the Azweri. There were a couple of hawk-nosed Hyrkanians. And there were Conan the Cimmerian and his giant black comrade, Juma. When the Grand Shaman's staff had struck him into insensibility and the warriors had pulled down the mighty Juma by weight of numbers, the infuriated rimpoche had commanded that they pay the ultimate penalty for their crime.

In Shamballah, however, the ultimate penalty was not death, which in Meruvian belief merely released the soul for its next incarnation. Enslavement they considered worse, since it robbed a man of his humanity, his individuality. So to slavery they were summarily condemned.

Thinking of it, Conan growled deep in his throat, and his eyes blazed with smouldering fires out of his dark face, peering through the shaggy, matted tangle of his uncut black mane. Chained beside him, Juma, sensing Conan's frustration, chuckled. Conan glowered at his comrade; sometimes Juma's invincible good humor irritated him. For a free-born Cimmerian, slavery was indeed an intolerable punishment.

To the Kushite, however, slavery was nothing new. Slave raiders had torn Juma as a child from his mother's arms and dragged him out of the sweltering jungles of Kush to the slave marts of Shem. For a while he had worked as a field hand on a Shemite farm. Then, as his great thews began to swell, he had been sold as an apprentice gladiator to the arenas of Argos.

For his victory in the games held to celebrate the victory of King Milo of Argos over King Ferdrugo of Zingara, Juma was given his freedom. For a time he lived in various Hyborian nations by thieving and by odd jobs. Then he drifted east to Turan, where his mighty stature and skill in combat won him a place in the ranks of King Yildiz's mercenaries.

There he had come to know the youthful Conan. He and the Cimmerian had struck it off from the first. They were the two tallest men among the mercenary troops, and both came from far, outlandish countries; they were the only members of their respective races among the Turanians. Their comradeship had now led them to the slave pits of Shamballah and would shortly lead them to the ultimate indignity of the slave block. There they would stand naked in the blinding sun, poked and prodded by prospective buyers while the slave dealer bellowed praises of their strength.

The days dragged slowly past, as crippled snakes drag their tails painfully through the dust. Conan, Juma, and the others slept and woke to receive wooden bowls of rice, stingily shared out by their overseers. They spent the long days fitfully dozing or languidly quarreling.

Conan was curious to learn more about these Meruvians, for in all his wanderings he had never encountered their like. They dwelt here in this strange valley as their ancestors had done since time began. They had no contact with the outside world and wanted none.

Conan became friendly with a Meruvian named Tashudang, from whom he learned something of their singsong language. When he asked why they called their king a god, Tashudang replied that the king had lived for ten thousand years, his spirit being reborn in a different body after each sojourn in mortal flesh. Conan was skeptical of this, for he knew the sort of lies that kings of other lands spread about themselves. But he prudently kept his opinion to himself. When Tashudang complained mildly and resignedly of the oppression of the king and his shamans, Conan asked:

"Why don't you and your fellows get together and throw the whole lot into the Sumeru Tso, and rule yourselves? That's what we would do in my country if anybody tried to tyrannize over us."

Tashudang looked shocked. "You know not what you say, foreigner! Many centuries ago, the priests tell us, this land was much higher than it now is. It stretched from the tops of the Himelias to the tops of the Talakmas—one great, lofty plain, covered with snow and whipped by icy winds. The Roof of the World, it was called.

"Then Yama, the king of the demons, determined to create this valley for us, his chosen people, to dwell in. By a mighty spell, he caused the land to sink. The ground shook with the sound of ten thousand thunders, molten rock poured from cracks in the earth, mountains crumbled, and forests went up in flame. When it was over, the land between the mountain chains was as you now see it. Because it was now a lowland, the climate warmed, and the plants and beasts of the warm countries came to dwell in it. Then Yama created the first Meruvians and placed them in the valley, to inhabit forever. And he appointed the shamans as leaders and enlighteners of the people.

"Sometimes the shamans forget their duties and oppress us, as if they were but greedy common men. But Yama's command, for us to obey the shamans, still holds good. If we defy it, Yama's great spell will be nullified, and this land will rise to the height of the mountain tops and again become a cold waste. So, no matter how they abuse us, we dare not revolt against the shamans."

"Well," said Conan, "if that filthy little toad is your idea of a god—"

"Oh, no!" said Tashudang, his eyeballs glistening white in the dimness with fear. "Say it not! He is the only-begotten son of the great god, Yama himself. And when he calls his father, the god *comes*!" Tashudang buried his face in his hands, and Conan could get no more words out of him that day.

The Meruvians were an odd race. Theirs was a peculiar lassitude of spirit—a somnolent fatalism that bade them bow to everything that came upon them as a predestined visitation from their cruel, enigmatic gods. Any resistance to fate on their part, they believed, would be punished, if not immediately, then in their next incarnation.

It was not easy to drag information out of them, but the Cimmerian youth kept doggedly at it. For one thing, it helped to pass the unending days. For another, he did not intend to remain in slavery long, and every bit of information that he could gather about this hidden kingdom and its peculiar people would be of value when he and Juma came to try for freedom. And finally, he knew how important it was in traveling through a strange country, to command at least a smattering of the local language. Although not at all a scholar by temperament, Conan picked up languages easily. He had already mastered several and could even read and write some of them a little.

At last came the fateful day when the overseers in black leather strode amongst the slaves, wielding heavy whips and herding their charges out the door. "Now," sneered one, "we shall see what prices the princes of the Sacred Land will pay for your unwieldy carcasses, outland swine!" And his whip raised a long weal across Conan's back.

Hot sun beat down on Conan's back like whips of fire. After being so long in darkness, he was dazzled by the brightness of day. After the slave auction, they led him up the gangplank to the deck of a great galley, which lay moored to the long, stone quays of Shamballah. He squinted against the sun and cursed in a growling undertone. This, then, was the doom to which they had sentenced him—to drudge at the oars until death took him.

"Get down in the hold, you dogs!" spat the ship's overseer, cuffing Conan's jaw with the back of his hand. "Only the children of Yama may stride the deck!"

Without thinking, the Cimmerian youth exploded into action. He drove his balled fist into the burly overseer's bulging belly. As the breath hissed from the man's lungs, Conan followed the blow with a hammerlike right to the jaw, which stretched the shipman on the deck. Behind him, Juma howled with joy and struggled to get up the line to stand beside him.

The commander of the ship's guard rapped out an order. In a flash, the points of a dozen pikes, in the hands of wiry little Meruvian marines, were leveled at Conan. The Cimmerian stood in the circle of them, a menacing growl rising to his lips. But he belatedly controlled his rage, knowing that any move would bring instant death.

It took a bucket of water to revive the overseer. He laboriously climbed to his feet, blowing like a walrus, while water ran down his bruised face into his sparse black beard. His eyes glared into Conan's with insane rage, then cooled to icy venom.

The officer began to issue a command to the marines: "Slay the—" but the overseer interrupted:

"Nay, slay him not. Death were too easy for the dog. I'll make him whimper to be put out of his misery ere I've done with him."

"Well, Gorthangpo?" said the officer.

The overseer stared over the oar pit, meeting the cowed gaze of a hundred-odd naked brown men. They were starved and scrawny, and their bent backs were criss-crossed by a thousand whip scars. The ship carried a single bank of long oars on each side. Some oars were manned by two rowers, some by three, depending upon the size and strength of the slaves. The overseer pointed to an oar in the waist, to which three gray-haired, skeletal old men were chained.

"Chain him to yonder oar! Those walking corpses are played out; they are of no more use to us. Clear the oar of them. This foreign lad needs to stretch his arms a bit; we'll give him all the room he needs. And if he follow not the pace, I'll open his back to the spine!"

As Conan watched impassively, the sailors unlocked the manacles that connected the wrist chains of the three old men to rings on the oar itself. The old men screamed with terror as brawny arms heaved them over the rail. They hit the water with a great splash and sank without a trace, save for the bubbles that rose one by one to the surface and burst.

Conan was chained to the oar in their place. He was to do the work of all three. As they fastened him to the filth-slimed bench, the overseer eyed him grimly.

"We'll see how you like pulling an oar, boy. You'll pull and pull until you think your back is breaking—and then you'll pull some more. And every time you slack off or miss a boat, I'll remind you of your place, like this!"

His arm swung; the whip uncoiled against the sky and came whistling down across Conan's shoulders. The pain was like that of a white-hot iron rod against his flesh. But Conan did not scream or move a muscle. It was as if he had felt nothing, so strong was the iron of his will.

The overseer grunted, and the lash cracked again. This time a muscle at one corner of Conan's grimly set mouth twitched, but his eyes looked stonily ahead. A third lash, and a fourth. Sweat formed on the Cimmerian's brow; it trickled down into his eyes, stinging and smarting, even as the red blood ran down his back. But he gave no sign of feeling pain.

Behind him, he heard Juma's whisper: "Courage!"

Then came a call from the afterdeck; the captain wished to sail. Reluctantly, the overseer gave up his pleasure of lashing the Cimmerian's back to pulp.

The sailors cast off the ropes that moored the ship to the quay and shoved off with boathooks. Aft of the oar benches but on the same level, in the shade of the catwalk that ran the length of the ship over the heads of the rowers, sat a naked Meruvian behind a huge drum. When the ship had cleared the quay, the coxswain lifted a wooden maul and began to thump the drum. With each beat, the slaves bent to the oars, rising to their feet, raising the looms, and leaning back until their weight brought them down on the benches; then pushing the looms down and forward and repeating. Conan soon caught the rhythm, as did Juma, chained to the oar behind him.

Conan had never before been on a ship. As he heaved at his oar, his quick eyes peered around him at the listless, dull-eyes slaves with whip-scarred backs, who worked on the slimy benches in the frightful stench of their own waste. The galley was low through the waist, where the slaves labored; the rail was only a few feet above the water. It was higher in the bow, where the seamen berthed, and in the carved and gilded stern, where the officers had their quarters. A single mast arose amidships. The yard of the single triangular sail, and the furled sail itself, lay along the catwalk over the oar pit.

When the ship had left the harbor, the sailors untied the lashings that held the sail and its yard to the catwalk and raised it, heaving on the halyard and grunting a chantey. The yard went up by jerks, a few inches at a time. As it rose, the gold-and-purple striped sail unfurled and shook out with snapping, booming sounds. Since the wind was fair on the quarter, the oarsmen were given a rest while the sail took over.

Conan noted that the entire galley had been made from some wood that either by nature or by staining was of a dark red color. As he gazed about, eyes half shut against the glare, the ship looked as if it had been dipped in blood. Then the whip sang above him and the overseer, on the catwalk above, yelled down:

"Now lay to, you lazy swine!"

A lash laid another welt across his shoulders. It is indeed a ship of blood, he thought to himself; slaves' blood.

5. *Rogue's Moon*

For seven days, Conan and Juma sweated over the massive oars of the red galley as it plodded its way around the shores of the Sumeru Tso, stopping overnight at each of the seven sacred cities of Meru: Shondakor, Thogara, Auzakia, Issedon, Paliana, Throana, and then—having made the circuit of the sea—back to Shamballah. Strong men though they were, it was not long before the unremitting labor brought them to the edge of exhaustion, when their aching muscles seemed incapable of further effort. Yet still the tireless drum and the hissing whip drove them on.

Once a day, sailors drew buckets of cold, brackish water up over the side and drenched the exhausted slaves. Once a day, when the sun stood at the zenith, they were given a heaping bowl of rice and a long dipperful of water. At night they slept on their oars. The animal-like round of unvarying drudgery sapped the will and drained the mind, leaving the rowers soulless automata.

It would have broken the strength of any man—save for such as Conan. The young Cimmerian did not yield to the crushing burden of fate as did the apathetic Meruvians. The unending labor at the oars, the brutal treatment, the indignity of the slimy benches, instead of sapping his will, only fed the fires within him.

When the ship returned to Shamballah and dropped

anchor in the wide harbor, Conan had reached the limits of his patience. It was dark and still; the new moon—a slim, silver scimitar—hung low in the western sky, casting a wan, illusive light. It would soon set. Such a night was called a "rogue's moon" in the nations of the West, for such poorly-lit nights were wont to be chosen by highwaymen, thieves, and assassins to ply their trades. Bent over their oars, ostensibly asleep, Conan and Juma discussed escape with the Meruvian slaves.

On the galley, the feet of the slaves were not fettered. But each wore a pair of manacles joined by a chain, and this chain was strung through an iron ring loosely looped around the loom of the oar. Although this ring slid freely along the loom, its travel was stopped at the outer end by the oarlock and, at the inner, by a collar or ferrule of lead. This collar, securely fastened to the butt end of the oar by an iron spike, acted as a counterweight to the blade of the oar. Conan had tested the strength of his chain and of the manacles and the ring a hundred times; but even his terrific strength, hardened by seven days of rowing, could not strain any of them. Still, in a tense, growling whisper, he urged schemes of revolt upon his fellow slaves.

"If we could get Gorthangpo down on our level," he said, "we could tear him to pieces with our nails and teeth. And he carries the keys to all our bonds. While we were unlocking the manacles, the marines would kill some of us; but once we got loose, we should outnumber them five or six to one—"

"Do not speak of it!" hissed the nearest Meruvian. "Do not even think of it!"

"Aren't you interested?" asked Conan in astonishment.

"Nay! Even to talk of such violence turns my bones to water."

"Mine, too," said another. "The hardships we suffer have been inflicted upon us by the gods, as a just punishment for some misdeed in a former life. To struggle against it were not only useless but a wicked blasphemy as well. I pray you, barbarian, hush your unholy talk and submit with becoming humility to your fate."

Such an attitude went against Conan's grain, nor was Juma a man to bow without resistance to any threat of doom. But the Meruvians would not listen to their arguments. Even Tashudang, unusually loquacious and friendly for a Meruvian, begged Conan to do nothing that would enrage Gorthangpo, the overseer, or bring down upon them a worse punishment from the gods than that which their divinities had already inflicted upon them.

Conan's argument was cut short by the song of the whip. Aroused by the murmur, Gorthangpo had crept out on the catwalk in the darkness. From the few whispered words he overheard, he divined that mutiny was brewing. Now his whip hissed and cracked on Conan's shoulders.

Conan had had enough. In one surge of motion, he bounded to his feet, seized the lashing end of the whip, and tore it out of Gorthangpo's grip. The overseer yelled for the marines.

There was still no way for Conan to get the iron ring off the loom of his oar. In his desperation, an inspiration struck him. The construction of the oarlock limited the vertical motion of the loom to a height of less than five feet above the deck on which he stood. Now he pushed the butt end of the oar up as far as it would go, climbed to the bench, and crouching, placed his shoulders beneath the loom. Then, with a terrific heave of his long, powerful legs, he straightened up. The oar broke in its oarlock with a rending crash. Quickly, Conan slipped his ring off the broken end. Now he had a serviceable weapon: a club or quarterstaff nine feet long, with a ten-pound mass of lead on one end.

Conan's first terrific swing caught the goggling overseer on the side of the head. His skull shattered like a melon, spattering the benches with a bloody spray of pulped brains. Then Conan hauled himself to the catwalk to meet the charge of the marines. Below on the benches, the scrawny, brown Meruvians crouched, whimpering prayers to their devil-gods. Only Juma imitated Conan's act, breaking his oar at the oarlock and slipping his slave ring loose.

The marines were Meruvians themselves, lax and lazy and fatalistic. They had never had to fight a slave mutiny; they did not believe such a thing possible. Least of all had they expected to have to face a burly young giant armed with a nine-foot club. Still, they came on bravely enough, although the width of the catwalk allowed them to approach Conan only two abreast.

Conan waded in, swinging wildly. His first blow hurled the first marine off the catwalk and into the benches with a broken sword arm. The second dropped the next man with a shattered skull. A pike was thrust at his naked breast; Conan knocked the pike out of its wielder's hand, and his next blow hurled two men at once off the catwalk; the one whom he had struck with crushed-in ribs, and his companion jostled off the walk by the impact of the first victim's body.

Then Juma climbed up beside him. The Kushite's naked torso gleamed like oiled ebony in the dim moonlight, and his oar mowed down the advancing Meruvians like a scythe. The marines, unprepared to face two such monsters, broke and ran for the safety of the poop deck, whence their officer, just aroused from slumber, was screeching confused commands.

Conan bent to the corpse of Gorthangpo and searched his pouch for the key ring. Swiftly he found the key to all the manacles on the ship and unlocked his own, then did the same for Juma.

A bow twanged, and an arrow whistled over Conan's head and struck the mast. The two freed slaves did not wait to pursue the battle further. Dropping off the catwalk, they pushed through the cowering rowers to the rail, vaulted over the side, and vanished into the dark waters of Shamballah's harbor. A few arrows sped after them, but in the dim light of the setting crescent moon the archers could do little more than shoot at random.

6. *Tunnels of Doom*

Two naked men hauled their dripping bodies out of the sea and peered about them in the murk. They had swum for hours, it seemed, looking for a way to get into Shamballah unobserved. At last they had found the outlet to one of the storm sewers of the ancient stone city. Juma still trailed the length of broken oar with which he had fought the marines; Conan had abandoned his on the ship. Occasionally a faint gleam of light came into the sewer from a storm grating set into a gutter in the street overhead, but the light was so feeble—the thin moon having set—that the darkness below remained impenetrable. So, in almost total darkness, the twain waded through the slimy waters, seeking a way out of these tuunels.

Huge rats squeaked and fled as they went through the stone corridors beneath the streets. They could see the glimmer of eyes through the dark. One ot the larger scavengers nipped Conan's ankle, but he caught and crushed the beast in his hands and flung its corpse at its more cautious fellows. These quickly engaged in a squealing, rustling battle over the feast, while Conan and Juma hurried on through the upward-winding tunnels.

It was Juma who found the secret passage. Sliding one hand along the dank wall, he accidentally released a catch and snorted with surprise when a portion of the stone gave way beneath his questing fingers. Although neither he nor Conan knew where the passage led, they took it, as it seemed to slope upward toward the city streets above.

At last, after a long climb, they came to another door. They groped in utter darkness until Conan found a bolt, which he slid back. The door opened with a squeak of dry hinges to his push, and the two fugitives stepped through and froze.

They stood on an ornamental balcony crowded with statues of gods or demons in a huge, octagonal temple The walls of the eight-sided chamber soared upward, past the balcony, to curve inward and meet to form an eight-sided dome. Conan remembered seeing such a dome towering among the lesser buildings of the city, but he had never inquired as to what lay within it.

Below, at one side of the octagonal floor, a colossal statue stood on a plinth of black marble, facing an altar in the exact center of the chamber. The statue dwarfed everything else in the chamber. Rising thirty feet high, its loins were on a level with the balcony on which Conan and Juma stood. It was a gigantic idol of a green stone that looked like jade, although never had men found true jade in so large a mass. It had six arms, and the eyes in its scowling face were immense rubies.

Facing the statue across the altar stood a throne of skulls, like that which Conan had already seen in the throne room of the palace on his arrival in Shamballah, but smaller. The toadlike little god-king of Meru was seated on this throne. As Conan's glance strayed from the idol's head to that of the ruler, he thought he saw a hideous suggestion of similarity between the two. He shuddered and his nape prickled at the hint of unguessable cosmic secrets that lay behind this resemblance.

The rimpoche was engaged in a ritual. Shamans in scarlet robes knelt in ranks around the throne and the altar, chanting ancient prayers and spells. Beyond them, against the walls of the chamber, several rows of Meruvians sat cross-legged on the marble pavement. From the richness of their jewels and their ornate if scanty apparel, they appeared to be the officials and the nobility of the kingdom. Above their heads, set in wall brackets around the balcony, a hundred torches flickered and smoked. On the floor of the chamber, in a square about the central altar, stood four torchères, each crowned by the rich, golden flame of a butter lamp. The four flames wavered and sputtered.

On the altar between the throne and the colossus lay the naked, white, slender body of a young girl, held to the altar by slender golden chains. It was Zosara.

A low growl rumbled in Conan's throat. His smouldering eyes burned with blue fire as he watched the hated figures of King Jalung Thonpa and his Grand Shaman, the wizard-priest Tanzong Tengri.

"Shall we take them, Conan?" whispered Juma, his teeth showing white in the flickering dimness. The Cimmerian grunted.

It was the festival of the new moon, and the god-king was wedding the daughter of the king of Turan on the altar, before the many-armed statue of the Great Dog of Death and Terror, Yama the Demon King. The ceremony was proceeding according to the ancient rites prescribed in the holy texts of the Book of the Death God. Placidly anticipating the public consummation of his nuptials with the slim, long-legged Turanian girl, the divine monarch of Meru lolled on his throne of skulls as ranks of scarlet-clad shamans droned the ancient prayers.

Then came an interruption. Two naked giants dropped from nowhere to the floor of the temple—one a heroic figure of living bronze, the other a long-limbed menace whose mighty physique seemed to have been carved from ebony. The shamans froze in mid-chant as these two howling devils burst into their midst.

Conan seized one of the torchères and hurled it into the

midst of the scarlet-robed shamans. They broke, screaming with pain and panic, as the flaming liquid butter set fire to their gauzy robes and turned them into living torches. The other three lamps followed in rapid succession, spreading fire and confusion over the floor of the chamber.

Juma sprang toward the dais, where the king sat with his good eye staring in fear and astonishment. The gaunt Grand Shaman met Juma on the marble steps with his magical staff lifted to smite. But the black giant still had his broken oar, and he swung it with terrific force. The ebony staff flew into a hundred fragments. A second swing caught the wizard-priest in the body and hurled him, broken and dying, into the chaos of running, screaming, flaming shamans.

King Jalung Thongpa came next. Grinning, Juma charged up the steps toward the cowering little god-king. But Jalung Thongpa was no longer on his throne. Instead, he knelt in front of the statue, arms raised and chanting a prayer.

Conan reached the altar at the same time and bent over the nude, writhing form of the terrified girl. The light golden chains were strong enough to hold her, but not strong enough to withstand Conan's strength. With a grunt, he braced his feet and heaved on one; a link of the soft metal stretched, opened, and snapped. The other three chains followed, and Conan scooped up the sobbing princess in his arms. He turned—but then a shadow fell over him.

Startled, he looked up and remembered what Tashudang had told him: "When he calls his father, the god *comes!*"

Now he realized the full extent of the horror behind those words. For, looming above him in the flickering torchlight, the arms of the gigantic idol of green stone were moving. The scarlet rubies that served it for eyes were glaring down at him, bright with intelligence.

7. *When the Green God Wakes*

The hairs lifted on Conan's nape, and he felt as if the blood in his veins had congealed to ice. Whimpering, Zosara pressed her face into the hollow of his shoulder and clung to his neck. On the black dais that upheld the throne of skulls, Juma also froze, the whites of his eyes showing as the superstitious terrors of his jungle heritage rose within him. The statue was coming to life.

As they watched, powerless to move, the image of green stone shifted one of its huge feet slowly, creakingly. Thirty feet above their heads, its great face leered down at them. The six arms moved jerkily, flexing like the limbs of some gigantic spider. The thing tilted, shifting its monstrous weight. One vast foot came down on the altar on which Zosara had lain. The stone block cracked and crumbled beneath the tons of living green stone.

"Crom!" breathed Conan. "Even stone lives and walks in this mad place! Come, girl—" He picked Zosara up and leaped down from the dais to the floor of the temple. From behind him came an ominous scraping sound of stone on stone. The statue was moving.

"Juma!" yelled Conan, casting a wild eye about for the Kushite. The black still crouched motionless beside the throne. Upon the throne, the little god-king pointed an arm, thick with fat and bright with jewels, at Conan and the girl.

"Kill—Yama! Kill—kill—kill!" he screamed.

The many-armed thing paused and peered about with its ruby eyes until it sighted Conan. The Cimmerian was nearly mad with the primitive night-fears of his barbarian people. But, as with many barbarians, his very fear drove him into combat with that which he dreaded. He put down the girl and heaved up a marble bench. Sinews creaking with the effort, he strode forward towards the lumbering colossus.

Juma yelled: "No, Conan! Get away! It sees you!"

Now Conan stood near the monstrous foot of the walking idol. The stone legs towered above him like the pillars of some colossal temple. His face congested with the effort, Conan raised the heavy bench over his head and hurled it at the leg. It crashed into the carven ankle of the colussus with terrific impact. The marble of the bench clouded with a web of cracks, which shot through it from end to end. He stepped even closer, picked up the bench again, and again swung it against the ankle. This time the bench shattered into a score of pieces; but the leg, though slightly chipped, was not materially damaged. Conan reeled back as the statue took another ponderous step toward him.

"Conan! Look out!"

Juma's yell made him look up. The green giant was stooping. The ruby eyes glared into his. Strange, to stare into the living eyes of a god! They were bottomlessly deep—shadow-veiled depths wherein his gaze sank endlessly through red eons of time without thought. And deep within those crystalline depths, a cold, inhuman malignancy coiled. The god's gaze locked on his own, and the young Cimmerian felt an icy numbness spread through him. He could neither move nor think. . . .

Juma, howling with primal rage and fear, whirled. He saw the many mighty hands of stone swoop toward his comrade, who stood staring like one entranced. Another stride would bring Yama upon the paralyzed Cimmerian.

The black was too far from the tableau to interfere, but his frustrated rage demanded an outlet. Without conscious thought, he picked up the god-king, who shrieked and wriggled in vain, and hurled him toward his infernal parent.

Jalung Thongpa whirled through the air and thudded down on the tessalated pave before the tramping feet of the idol. Dazed by his fall, the little monarch stared wildly about with his good eye. Then he screamed hideously as one titanic foot descended upon him.

The crunch of snapping bones resounded in the ringing silence. The god's foot slid on the marble, leaving a broad, crimson smear on the tiles. Creaking at the waist, the titanic figure bent and reached for Conan, then stopped.

The groping, green stone hands, fingers outspread, halted in mid-air. The burning crimson light faded from the ruby eyes. The vast body with its many arms and devil's head, which a moment before had been flexible and informed with life, froze into motionless stone once more.

Perhaps the death of the king, who had summoned this infernal spirit from the nighted depths of nameless dimensions, cancelled the spell that bound Yama to the idol. Or perhaps the king's death released the devil-god's will from the domination of his earthly kinsman. Whatever the cause, the instant the Jalung Thongpa was crushed into bubbling gore, the statue reverted to lifeless, immobile stone.

The spell that had gripped Conan's mind also broke. Numbly, the youth shook his head to clear it. He stared about him. The first thing of which he was aware was the princess Zosara, who flung herself into his arms, weeping hysterically. As his bronzed arms closed about her softness and he felt the feathery touch of her black, silken hair against his throat, a new kind of fire flared up in his eyes, and he laughed deeply.

Juma came running across the floor of the temple. "Conan! Everybody either is dead or has run away! There should be horses in the paddock behind the temple. Now is our chance to quit this accursed place!"

"Aye! By Crom, I shall be glad to shake the dust of

this damned land from my heels," growled the Cimmerian, tearing the robe from the body of the Grand Shaman and draping it over the princess's nakedness. He snatched her up and carried her out, feeling the warmth and softness of her supple young body against his own.

An hour later, well beyond the reach of pursuit, they reined in their horses and examined the branching roads. Conan looked up at the stars, pondered, and pointed. "This way!"

Juma wrinkled his brow. "North?"

"Aye, to Hyrkania." Conan laughed. "Have you forgotten that we still have this girl to deliver to her bridegroom?"

Juma's brow wrinkled with greater puzzlement than before, seeing how Zosara's slim, white arms were wound around his comrade's neck and how her small head was nestled contentedly against his mighty shoulder. To her bridegroom? He shook his head; never would he understand the ways of Cimmerians. But he followed Conan's lead and turned his steed toward the mighty Talakma Mountains, which rose like a wall to sunder the weird land of Meru from the windy steppes of Hyrkania.

A month later, they rode into the camp of Kujula, the Great Khan of the Kuigar nomads. Their appearance was entirely different from what it had been when they fled from Shamballah. In the villages on the southern slopes of the Talakmas, they had traded the links from the golden chains that still dangled from Zosara's wrists and ankles for clothing suitable to snowy mountain passes and gusty plains. They wore fur caps, sheepskin coats, baggy trousers of coarse wool, and stout boots.

When they presented Zosara to her black-bearded bridegroom, the khan feasted and praised and rewarded them. After a carousal that lasted for several days, he sent them back to Turan loaded with gifts of gold.

When they were well away from Khan Kujula's camp, Juma said to his friend: "That was a fine girl. I wonder you didn't keep her for yourself. She liked you, too."

Conan grinned. "Aye, she did. But I'm not ready to settle down yet. And Zosara will be happier with Kujula's jewels and soft cushions than she would be with me, galloping about the steppes and being roasted, frozen, and chased by wolves or hostile warriors." He chuckled. "Besides, though the Great Khan doesn't know it, his heir is already on the way."

"How do you know?"

"She told me, just before we parted."

Juma made clicking sounds from his native tongue. "Well, I will never, never underestimate a Cimmerian again!"